TO
LOVE A DARK
LORD

BOOKS BY KATHRYN ANN KINGSLEY

KATHRYN ANN KINGSLEY

TO LOVE A DARK LORD

SECOND SKY

Published by Second Sky in 2024

An imprint of Storyfire Ltd.
Carmelite House
50 Victoria Embankment
London EC4Y 0DZ
United Kingdom

www.secondskybooks.com

ISBN: 978-1-83525-044-0
eBook ISBN: 978-1-83525-043-3

FOREWORD

This foreword is going to be a bit different than the others.

Sometimes, people think that it's the role of the author to change the lives of their readers. That we're meant to inspire, to leave stories and characters that linger. And it's true. But it can also go both ways in very, very unexpected ways.

Let me tell you a story.

This one isn't about villains and heroes, though it is about love and loss.

It's about how you—all of you—changed my life.

I've spent the past decade of my life working in game design in one form or another. Either as a creative director for "immersive media" (think escape rooms on crack) or recently in the more formal world of video games.

I was the Chief of Staff, and one of the design Studio Managers, for a company called Volition, makers of games like *Saint's Row* and *Red Faction*. My job revolved around a combination of project management, staff management, and businessy-type stuff. I loved it. I *adored* it. While the work wasn't always engrossing, it was a role of service to those around me. And I loved the people I worked with. Many of them became lifelong friends of mine. The kind of connection you make with people that feels like magic, like something that could only work in a piece of fiction, until it happens to you.

Hopefully, you've experienced that magic for yourself.

Meanwhile, on the side, I wrote books. Romance novels, of all things. I spun the tales that lurked in the back of my mind, hoping to get them out of my head and onto the page. *Joke's on me, though—in the vacuum left by the previous book, more insane ideas just keep popping up.*

This is how you know me. As a writer of dark fantasy, romance, occult horror, and sexy villains. But you must understand that this part of my life was never really part of my day-to-day identity. I clocked in, had meetings, talked about how to manage the next set of projects, and clocked out.

That was until Volition was permanently closed.

And everything that I loved about that job was taken away from me because of the poor business decisions of some muckety-mucks in Sweden. We learned their lesson for them, and a thirty-year company was shuttered on August 30th, 2023.

I still grieve its loss, if you can't tell. I miss working with the people I loved. I thought that I would have to drift off into some other project management job and have to do the same grind that I was accustomed to.

Until something truly unexpected happened.

Out of the blue I was contacted by a prominent creative director for a very popular video game. She was curious if I would be interested in *writing for her full-time.*

As a day job.

Me.

Writing.

As a day job.

To pay the bills.

LMAO.

You have to understand how much of a paradigm shift that

caused in my head. I don't think of myself as a writer—I really don't—it's just a thing I do as a hobby. I'm a moron who works in game design. I don't *write for a living*, that's *ridiculous*.

But I said yes.

And here I am. Doing exactly that.

Do you know how she knew to contact me? Because she was a fan of my books. She has read twenty-five or so and wanted to bring me on because she... likes what I do. And believed I could do it.

Here was my hobby, become reality. Here was something I thought was a pipe dream, something I'd never be able to do to pay the bills, as my actual job.

I'm a writer.

It's what I do.

Officially.

Fuck.

And it's all because of you. Without readers, without people following along and enjoying my stories, I would've given up long ago. I would have abandoned this silly quest and gone on to some other pipe dream.

So whether this is the first series of mine you've ever picked up or you're a diehard fan who has followed every nutjob plot I've ever conceived, I can do this *because of you.*

If you weren't there, I'd never have wound up in the hands of someone who could change my life.

If it wasn't for you, these stories wouldn't exist.

You have changed my life.

You have altered its course and made a dream come true.

So this is for you, dear reader.

Thank you.

Thank you.

Thank you.

ONE

He wanted them dead.

He wanted them *all* dead.

Mordred knew that he was slowly going insane. Or perhaps he was not losing his mind—perhaps the voices that whispered to him from the dark abyss of his prison were truly there.

Though he could not make out their words, he knew they were mocking him.

It didn't matter whether the voices were real or figments of his fracturing sanity. The fact that he experienced them—the laughing, jeering yet understandable taunts—was very real.

He wanted them dead.

Yet no matter how hard he screamed into the darkness, at the nothingness, he could not make a single sound. He could not move. Was he even the owner of a body anymore, trapped inside the Iron Crystal as he was?

Did it matter?

Would any of it matter in the end?

It was too soon to surrender.

He had to steel himself. Had to brace himself for the agony that was to come. For he had something to return to. He had someone waiting for him. In the void, he could almost picture her.

Gwendolyn.

His Gwendolyn.

He could let himself dream of her. Of the touch of skin against his. Of her smile, of the sound of her laugh—of the warmth of her body next to his. He yearned for her. *Ached* for her. In his body, in his soul, and in his heart.

The love he had for her would sustain him.

For it was the only thing he had left.

* * *

Gwen needed to raise an army to free Mordred.

Turns out, that was a *lot* easier said than done.

"Bert." She put her head down on the surface of the large metal map table in Mordred's war room. "You're killin' me, smalls."

"I—first, I don't know what that means. Second, raising an army takes time." Bert sighed. "We're doing our best."

"It's been *weeks*." She shook her head.

"And some people have replied."

That was true. Everyone had left the keep after Mordred was put into the Crystal—even Galahad and Zoe. But in their place came a smattering of villagers in dribs and drabs in response to Bert's rallying call. "Fifty people isn't an army. I can't do anything against elementals with fifty villagers."

"But it's a start of an army." Bert put his mug down on the table with a thump. "We need to understand that people have lives they'll be giving up by answering. This will take time."

"I can't just... sit here and do nothing." She sat back up in the chair and ran her hands through her hair. "Who knows what Mordred's going through? Who knows how much time we have left?"

"He's at least in one place. He isn't about to die." Bert was clearly doing his best to sound reassuring. "We'll need the time to build the armor like you said—and weapons. Armaments. This isn't wasted time. And you'll need to figure out where they've hidden the Crystal."

Letting out a sigh, she pushed up from her chair. "Yeah, yeah... I'm going to go for a walk. See you in the morning."

"Sleep well, Gwen."

She waved at him as she left the room. She'd wish him the same, but he didn't sleep. "Have a good night."

As she walked, Gwen sighed again. She'd found herself in this terrible habit. She didn't know what to do with herself. There were plenty of villagers who had taken up semi-permanent residence in Mordred's keep since he had been imprisoned. They mostly kept to themselves, finding places in the giant keep to set up residence. A few of them had even started maintaining and using some of the outbuildings like the forge, the mill, or the stables.

Though nobody dared try to make use of the kitchen. That was Mae's domain, and she was not the kind to share.

Yet, somehow, the building had never felt more lifeless to Gwen.

And that was saying something.

Bert the scarecrow had become a sort of advisor to her, as she tried to chart her path forward. She knew these things took time, but it felt wrong to just sit around and wait. The elementals might come for her at any point. Or worse, they might just start murdering each other for fun, putting Bert's people at risk.

It was just so hard to *focus*. Gwen felt like something had been torn out of her chest. There was an ache in the pit of her stomach that just wouldn't go away, no matter how hard she tried to distract herself from it.

Mordred's absence might drive her to madness. Or at the very least, to alcoholism. She wished Galahad was still around;

he might have been able to give her advice on how to deal with the loneliness. But it felt wrong to pester Galahad about the loss of the man she loved, now that Galahad was allowed to be with the woman *he* loved.

Especially since Mordred was to blame for Galahad being away from Zoe for so long.

Gwen was pacing the keep late at night, suddenly understanding why Mordred had such a hard time sleeping. She just couldn't sit still. She was anxiously waiting for *something* without knowing what that *something* was. It was a restlessness that wouldn't leave her thoughts alone.

If she was waiting for Mordred, she was going to have to wait a really long-ass time if she didn't manage to free him. Nine hundred, ninety-nine years and forty-six weeks and three days. But who was counting?

Her late-night pacing had become a nightly occurrence the past four days. It was to the point now that Eod didn't even lift his head anymore when she climbed out of bed. He would just roll onto his back, grumble, and stretch out to take up the extra space.

Yeah. This sucked, and it was going to drive her up a wall. She wandered into Mordred's study and went to his bar, pouring herself a rather large glass of whatever burning amber liquid there was the most of. She wasn't going to be choosy; it wasn't about the flavor. It was about knocking her out cold.

As Gwen sipped her drink and stared at the dimly lit study, she couldn't help but feel a profound sense of emptiness. He was out there somewhere—Mordred. Suffering, trapped inside the Iron Crystal.

Was it justice? Did it even matter?

The fire in the hearth crackled and popped, casting dancing shadows on the walls, but it did little to dispel the loneliness that enveloped her.

She swirled the glass in her hand, lost in thought. Gwen

couldn't help but replay their last conversation in her mind, and her actions at the council that had decided Mordred's fate. She had chosen this for him over death.

With a heavy sigh, she walked over to his chair by the fire and sat down in it. It was huge, sized for him, not for her. The ornately carved arms were marred with scratches from his metal gauntlets. Slowly, she traced her fingertips along the gashes in the polished wooden surface.

Mordred was gone.

Pulling her legs up onto the chair with her, she snuggled into the upholstered back and shut her eyes. She could smell him—like metal, cedar, and a little woodsmoke.

How long would that scent linger? How long until it was gone? How long before all traces of him in the keep faded?

Gwen let herself be enveloped by the scent of Mordred that lingered in the chair, willing him to be there beside her. She could almost picture it. Could almost trick herself into thinking he was there and was just having one of his quiet brooding spells. But it was all just a ghost of the man she loved.

She knew that no matter how much she wanted to, she couldn't change the past. What was done, was done. Mordred was a prisoner, and war was inevitably going to return to Avalon. The only thing that remained to be seen... was what Gwen was going to do about it.

Leaving Mordred imprisoned meant war that would never end.

Freeing Mordred meant *worse* war, but maybe an eventual end to it.

And for some miserable reason, it was for her to decide which was better. Climbing out of the chair, she decided she needed a snack. Something to go with all the alcohol. Heading through the corridors, she couldn't help but reflect on how *normal* it was all starting to feel to her. She knew the twists and turns. Finding her way to the kitchen was no longer a task, and the sight of the iron guards was no longer strange and frightening.

"I'm starting to think the keep is cursed," Maewenn said as Gwen walked in.

"Oh?" Gwen smiled faintly. "How so?"

"First, Mordred couldn't sleep, now you? Pah." Maewenn went to the open fireplace to place a kettle on a hook over the low-burning fire. "And you need tea, not alcohol, to solve that problem."

"If you say so." Gwen sat down on a stool. "I was actually looking for a snack, if you have anything kicking around." She didn't like having the cook fuss over her, but it was how the metal woman showed she cared.

"Always! You know me. Can't be happy if I'm not busy." The cook headed over to a table to begin preparing some bread, meat, and cheese. Gwen's favorite. She had always been a grazer, and picking at things like that was both tasty *and* distracting.

She ran her hand over the wooden surface of the table in the center of the room. It was immensely thick, the kind of slab that you couldn't buy in modern America anymore. And the edges and surface had been worn smooth by touch and use over the centuries, giving it almost a wavy appearance. It had the kind of patina that only came with age.

Gwen frowned. "I don't know what to do. Bert says it'll take maybe *months* until we have an army together. It's already been weeks. I'm pulling my hair out."

"I know, dear. I know. But everyone's relying on you to make the careful choices."

"Which I hate." Gwen put her head in her hands. "I can't tell you how sick I am of having these stupid decisions to make. Why me? Why can't this place just take ten minutes to let me catch my breath? I'm not a leader. I have no business being in charge."

"Well, that scarecrow and his friends seem to disagree." Maewenn placed a platter of food in front of her. It was way more than a snack, but Gwen wasn't going to complain.

"They're desperate." Gwen popped a grape into her mouth. "It's not like they have a choice."

"Don't sell yourself so short. And let your heart guide you—do what you think is right." The cook went to fetch the softly whistling kettle. "Do you want me to put any of Mordred's sleeping powder in the tea?"

"Hell no," Gwen said through a chuckle. "I'd rather not mess with that stuff again."

"Fair enough." Maewenn let out a sad laugh. "I do miss him."

"Me too." She kept picking at the food. "I haven't even gone into his room."

"Why not, dear?"

"I guess I'm kind of afraid to?" She shrugged. "It doesn't make sense, I know. He's not dead, he's just—gone." She sighed. "And it is a bigger, nicer room with a better view." She tore off a piece of the bread and ate it.

Maewenn set down a clay mug half filled with tea in front of her. "I think he'd want you to be comfortable."

"I know, I know. It's just silly."

"Not silly at all. Maybe it'd be good for you. Help you sleep."

"Or I'll be up all night crying," Gwen added on dryly. "I'm not sure how that'll help."

"Crying is exhausting. But it's cathartic, isn't it?" Mae huffed out a breath, which was funny as she didn't need to breathe. Old habits, Gwen figured. "I'm sorry. It's a terrible idea."

"No, no. It isn't." Gwen sipped the tea. It was tasty, she had to admit. "I'm just in a lousy mood, I'm sorry."

"No reason to apologize, hon." Mae walked around to her

side and placed a metal hand on her shoulder. "But we'll all get through this. Somehow. And we'll do it together." The cook paused. "I don't know what good a rust bucket like me'll do, but I'll be here."

Gwen laughed and, reaching over, hugged the woman. It was like hugging a coat rack covered in pots and pans, but it didn't matter. "You're such a good friend. Thank you."

"Now, finish your tea on the walk. Go back to bed. Nothing gets solved tonight with you drinking yourself into a stupor." Mae patted her on the back. "Go on. Shoo."

"Fine, fine." Gwen smiled as she got up from the stool. "But I'm taking the cheese." She picked up the wedge of it and headed for the door. "Tea and cheese—a perfect combination."

"I could think of worse!" Mae called after her as she left.

Gwen supposed it could be worse. She had friends. She had a home. She had food. She was alive. That was a lot more than most people had in Avalon.

It wasn't long before she found herself standing at Mordred's door. The large wooden surface was carved with the same strange twisting, asymmetrical vines that he had favored. They reminded her of the metal door that had sealed off the Iron Crystal when it had been stored deep within the keep.

Bracing herself, she pushed the bedroom door open.

Part of her expected to find him sitting in his chair in front of the fire, or reclining at his desk, or lying in bed. None of those were true. He obviously wasn't there. But for that split second, she had wished *so hard* for there to be some kind of miracle.

She wasn't so lucky. This wasn't going to be that easy. Finishing the tea, she let out a wavering breath and closed the door behind her. Or rather, she was about to, before Eod popped his head into the room, sniffing at the piece of cheese in her hand.

Chuckling, she ruffled the dog's fur. "You have a knack for that. Here you go, buddy." She gave the dog the remaining piece. Eod gobbled it down happily before running and jumping up onto Mordred's bed, turning around a few times before flopping down on the fluffy down comforter.

"*Where Dad?*"

She cringed at the question. "He won't be back for a long while. I'm sorry."

Eod's ears drooped. "*Mom sad?*"

She was Mom now? That was sweet. Placing the empty mug down, she climbed onto the bed next to Eod and petted him. "Mom's just fine, especially with you here."

"*Dog protect.*" Eod licked her face, before rolling onto his back for a belly rub.

There was a frantic knock on the door.

Oh, great. More nonsense.

Climbing out of bed, she answered the door.

Tim was on the other side. The rusted and unfinished guard was shifting anxiously from foot to foot.

She frowned. "What is it, Tim?"

He pointed down the hallway. Whatever the issue was, it was that way.

Motioning for him to lead the way, she followed behind him, wondering what kind of stupid nonsense she'd have to deal with *now*.

The great hall had her answer. Standing there, looking entirely out of place... was Lady Thorn. And she wasn't alone— there were two other elementals with her who Gwen didn't recognize. The woman was glancing at everything around her a little nervously.

Gwen arched an eyebrow. "Afraid the walls will attack you?"

"This place was *his*. There's no way of knowing. All this metal—all this iron." Thorn gestured aimlessly at the room. "It's disgusting."

Gwen shrugged. "I like it, and you don't have to live here. I don't see a problem. Why're you here?" She had a suspicion, but she wanted to hear it plain.

Thorn huffed. "No offer of wine?"

Gwen stared at her flatly and didn't answer.

"I have come to tell you I plan to take the throne of Avalon. I want you either to pledge allegiance to me or to stay out of my way. Or else." Thorn sneered, her yellowed teeth making the expression even less welcoming.

"Mm-hm. So you've come to my home to threaten me, that's nice." Gwen rubbed a hand over her eyes. She was too tired to deal with this.

"This isn't your home. Not this castle, not this island—you don't belong here." Thorn took a step toward her.

The iron guards that lined the room all shifted, placing their gauntlets on their swords.

"It seems they beg to differ. And so does the island of Avalon itself. It gave me this power. It chose me to be here." Gwen smiled at the other woman faintly. "You came here to threaten *and* insult me. Tell me why I shouldn't just kill you now? You're surrounded."

"It would be against the laws of hospitality. Of Avalon," one of the other elementals said through a grunt. She couldn't tell what kind of power Thorn's two sidekicks had—they looked normal. Ish. Normal for Avalon, at any rate.

With a sigh, Gwen turned around to leave the room. "Fine. Go away."

"You're a fool not to stand down," Thorn called after her. "Stay out of my way, girl. You don't know what you're up against."

Stopping, Gwen turned back to face Thorn.

And she laughed.

That seemed to unsettle the three elementals. Whatever they'd been expecting from her—maybe for her to cower, to apologize for everything, who knew—it hadn't been laughter.

"Get out of my home. Oh! One last thing." Putting on as pleasant a tone and smile as she was capable of, Gwen added, "Go fuck yourself."

With that, she turned and left, heedless of Thorn calling after her to wait. No. She was going to bed. When she got to Mordred's room, where she'd taken up residence, she collapsed onto the bed next to where Eod was already snuggled up half asleep.

Bert had told her that she needed to wait for an army. That she needed to sit here and do *nothing* until she had a force to back her up. But at what cost? What was she losing with every second that ticked by with Mordred imprisoned in the Crystal?

She loved him. And he loved her. And how could she sit here with her thumb up her butt while he rotted and the elementals plotted her death?

She knew that a war was inevitable, that she would have to stand up for Bert and the villagers. But now?

How could she go on, pretending her soul wasn't shattered? No.

No, she couldn't stand this.

She couldn't just go about her business like nothing had happened. Like Mordred's absence wasn't going to haunt her every waking moment of every day. She didn't know how Galahad had put up with Zoe being trapped in the Crystal. He was stronger than Gwen was—because she wasn't going to make it two months.

Freeing Mordred would start *total* war. She would be firmly picking the side of the Prince in Iron—which would turn all the elementals against her. Bert and his folks might still stay by her side, but it was doubtful.

Shutting her eyes, she took a deep breath. This felt like a stupid decision. But fuck, if it didn't feel like the right decision. And one that she was making on her own, for a change. She was sick and tired of people pushing her around. Of people leading her by the nose, forcing her to go along with their plans. She was done. Just *done*. No more.

She was going to free Mordred. She was going to face off against all the elementals of Avalon if she had to. She didn't care anymore. And she was going to do all of it because *she* wanted to. Because it was *her* decision.

No one else's.

She was the witch of Avalon, after all.

Maybe it was time she started acting like it.

Rolling onto her back, she reached a hand up toward the ceiling. Shutting her eyes, she closed her fingers into a fist as if grasping a veil of fabric up above her. Mordred was out there. They had spoken in their dreams a dozen times. And even though the magic that bound them might be gone, their bond was not.

He was out there.

And she was going to find him.

Now.

TWO

The feeling of the sun against his face was something Galahad would never tire of. After missing it for so long, it felt like a blessing to have it returned to Avalon. He sat upon a rock in front of Zoe's home, leaning against the thatch and plaster wall of the ancient structure. The wooden strapping that the plaster was smoothed over showed here and there through the worn surface, revealing its structure to be little more than twigs mixed in with whatever the original builder could find—horsehair, hay, and the rest.

The holes for windows had no glass but only thick fabric drapes to hold out the weather and block the light when needed. The chimney had a faint cloud of white smoke that always seemed to be drifting from its top. The roof was thatched, and he often needed to patch holes that formed with time. Zoe often teased him for rarely needing a ladder to access it.

The building would look crude to some. But to him? It felt like home.

The surface was warm against his back—he was not

wearing his armor. He had no need of it and hopefully never would again.

If he never had to lift his sword once more, he would live out the rest of his years a happy man. Zoe was inside, humming as she made tea for them, the scent of the woodsmoke and the steeping leaves mixing with the crisp fall air.

Galahad was happy.

Or rather, he should have been.

Yet, like a single dark cloud blotting out the sun in an otherwise beautiful blue sky, something was wrong.

Galahad felt as though he was adrift amongst his dreams. For so long, this had only been a place he could visit again while sleeping. Only there had his love been with him, though she had been a figment of his mind.

This had been his wish for over three hundred years—to see her again. *And* to be free of the curse that Mordred had placed upon him? He never thought it would come to pass. But here he sat, free of the Prince in Iron. Free to be with Zoe. Free to do as he wished.

Free.

Then why was there such an ache in his heart?

He had served his dues. He had done all he could to stay true to his honor. It was not his fault that Mordred was trapped within the Crystal—it was justice. But the look on Gwendolyn's face as Zoe and Galahad departed the keep with the Crystal in tow... did not feel like justice.

Was it not fair, though? There was no question that it was—after all that Mordred had forced others to endure. Galahad had suffered for three hundred years without Zoe at his side.

So the question remained—was fairness enough?

It did not feel that way.

Perhaps he simply mourned for Gwendolyn. Perhaps it would pass in time, as all grief did. Shutting his eyes, he let himself bask in the warmth of the sun. In the chirping of the birds in the trees. In the life and the magic that surrounded him.

A gentle touch on his shoulder roused him. He must have dozed off. Smiling up at Zoe, he took the cup of tea she was offering. "I am growing old."

"You were old when I met you." Zoe chuckled as she sat down on the rock next to him, leaning against his arm as she sipped her own tea. "No, my love, you have simply been so tired for so very long and only now have been allowed to rest. Your vigil has ended."

"Perhaps you are right." He sipped the tea. It was more floral than the type he had grown accustomed to in the keep, but he was neither surprised nor disappointed. "Whatever will I do with myself?"

"Enjoy your life. Perhaps grow a garden." She leaned her cheek against him.

"That would be lovely."

They sat in silence for a long moment before Zoe, as she was always wont to do, prompted him to speak his mind. "What troubles you?"

"Is it so very obvious?"

"In short? Yes." He could hear the smile in her voice, though he was watching the leaves in the trees sway in the breeze.

"I cannot help but sympathize with what Gwendolyn is tasked with enduring." Galahad let out a long sigh. "It is not a fate I would wish on anyone."

"She is resilient. She will survive." Zoe straightened up so that she could drink her own tea. "Perhaps her heart will change—perhaps she will come to love another. She is young. And her closeness to Mordred was manufactured."

Galahad frowned down at his love. "You are suggesting that her love was not legitimate?"

"No—simply that the heart is flighty in its youth." Zoe

smiled sadly at him. "I was not your first love, nor were you mine."

He supposed that was fair. How tragic for Mordred, in the end—to be granted so precious a gift, only to have it taken from him by time. Or, perhaps, by madness. There was no telling what would emerge from the Crystal. Though many had seemed to come out the other side of their imprisonment intact, there was talk of those who... had not been so lucky.

Then there was the complication that the Iron Crystal was Mordred's own creation. Being trapped inside a cage of his own making might change the weight of its curse. Either for the better—or the worse.

There was no way to know. Not for another thousand years. And Galahad doubted he would live that long, by chance or by choice.

Bowing his head, he kissed the top of Zoe's. "Let us talk of cheerier topics."

"Agreed." Zoe's smile brightened. "How—" Unfortunately, her words were cut off as someone came from the woods. It was a familiar figure, and one Galahad was not keen to see. And judging by the frown quickly etched on her delicate features, neither was Zoe.

It was Lady Thorn.

Galahad stood, instinctually placing himself between Zoe and Thorn. He could summon his armor and his sword quickly if required, but he hoped it wouldn't be. "Greetings."

"At ease, soldier." Thorn grinned, her missing teeth making the expression more threatening than reassuring. "I come to talk, nothing else."

"Wonderful." Galahad could not keep the sarcasm out of his voice, though admittedly he did not try very hard. But he did relax his shoulders. "What do you want?"

Thorn approached, uncaring for the rocks under her bare feet. Her hair was as unkempt as ever. "It is time to choose a ruler for Avalon. The throne has been empty for too long. To keep the peace, someone must wear the crown."

Galahad felt a sinking sensation in the pit of his stomach. "And let me guess..."

"No need." Thorn's grin widened. "I come seeking your support. I am the obvious choice—well—so is your wife, but she lacks the conviction or the desire."

"You speak for me now, do you?" Zoe stepped beside him as she spoke.

"Am I wrong?" Thorn challenged, planting her hands on her hips. Zoe hesitated long enough to give the other woman her answer. "There we have it. I remain the obvious choice."

"I disagree with both your insistence that Avalon requires a monarch as well as your self-serving goal to become it." Galahad shook his head. "I shall not support you in this blatant grab for power in Mordred's absence."

"Would you doom this world to more infighting and chaos? To repeat itself, endlessly, as we have always done? No. Mordred was right in one thing—this world needs someone to guide it." Thorn squared her shoulders.

Galahad could not help but arch an eyebrow. "And you believe yourself to be that person. I cannot agree. No, Thorn—my answer remains as it was."

Thorn grimaced and spat on the ground at her feet. "And what of you, Gossamer Lady? Do you stand with your knight?"

"I..." Zoe sighed, her shoulders drooping. "Yes. I shall continue to be neutral—or shall strive to be."

"There is no such thing in this world as being *neutral*, Zoe," Thorn sneered. "Simply cowardice. If you attempt to stand against me, I will not hesitate to strike you down. And I will remember who my friends were when the time comes."

"Noted." Galahad disliked being threatened. "You have said your piece. Now, begone."

"As you wish. Fools. Fools, the both of you." Thorn turned

her back on them as she walked into the woods. "Perhaps your brothers will see sense."

Galahad doubted that Bors, Gawain, or Percival would throw their fates in with the elemental. But who was he to say? They were their own men—and now, after over a thousand years, finally allowed to make their own decisions. He would not interfere. It was not his place.

"Come, my love." Zoe took his hand gently in hers. It was so small and soft compared to his own. Like a work of art. "Think on it no longer."

Nodding, he followed her into her home. Oh, how he felt suddenly weary of it all. There was a tiredness that crept into his bones at the thought of what was to come. He had hoped, foolishly, that the elementals would value the freedom they had nearly lost forever. That perhaps they would learn.

Yet he knew Thorn was right. Chaos was inevitable. And from that chaos, an order would seek to impose itself.

He did not know who would win.

But he knew he wanted no part in it.

* * *

"You summoned me, my lady?"

Gwen snorted in laughter as Bert bowed dramatically, folding an arm in front of him with a flourish. "Knock that off," she said.

Bert chuckled as he sat down at the table next to her. "I had to. Just because it clearly makes you so uncomfortable."

"It's just weird. And I'm not a lady. I'm just some girl from Kansas." She shifted and folded a foot under herself before sitting back down. "So. Um." Better to just rip off the bandage, she figured. "Walk me through what happens if we successfully free Mordred." It wasn't swaying her from her goal—not at all.

But she wanted to know what was going to happen to her *when* she did.

Bert let out a rush of air. Which was entirely for show, seeing as he didn't really breathe. Funny how much behavior was really just buried in social cues. "Oh, boy. Well. I don't know for certain."

"I know. But you've been here forever. You've seen things from not just an elemental-versus-elemental standpoint. You're the source of the best advice I can get."

Wonderful. A talking, metal-pumpkin-headed *scarecrow* was her most reliable source of information.

Fuck her life right about now, seriously.

Bert looked off into the distance as he thought it through. "First, the elementals will come for you. All of them. Unified in their hatred—and fear—of Mordred." He paused as if afraid to say what was coming next.

"Go on."

"And they might not be wrong." Bert shook his head. "Mordred was ready to kill them all *before* being stuck in that Crystal. And who knows what his opinion will be when he comes out? Not to mention, a unified war against him will give him the excuse he needs to justify mass murder."

Gwen considered his words. "There's one difference, though. I can stop him. I *can't* stop the elementals. He'll listen to me—they won't."

Bert stared at her. He didn't need to be able to show expression for her to sense the doubt in him. If he had eyebrows, one of them would probably be arched.

"I know it's risky. You're right, there's no telling if he'll come out of the Iron Crystal in one piece. But I can't do this alone." Doc was gone. Mordred was gone. Galahad was gone.

"You *aren't* alone, Gwen. You have us."

"A bunch of—I'm sorry—squishy villagers. And like, what? Fifty of you, so far? You'll get destroyed. I don't want all your deaths on my hands. I know people will die, that's inevitable. But at least the elementals have a choice. They can stand down or they can attack us. If they stand down, we'll leave them alone." Gwen tried to sound confident. Mordred would have to listen to reason, she'd make sure of it. He was a rational man. He understood the cost of war and spending lives. He wouldn't needlessly slaughter everyone.

Right?

Right.

She had to go on that. She had to believe that. She had to trust the man she loved. The man who wanted to marry her. The man who was probably slowly going insane trapped inside a prison of his own making.

"And if he *doesn't* stand down?" The scarecrow leaned on his stuffed elbows. "What then? If we get him out of there, and he goes on a rampage and *doesn't* listen to you?"

"Then..." She chewed on her bottom lip. "Then I'll stop him." She shut her eyes and clenched her fists. "Before you say it—I know what I'm saying." Her voice wavered and almost cracked. The idea of having to kill him... the final betrayal. He wouldn't see it coming from her. He would never expect her to go that far. "If he's out of control, I'll put him down."

Bert was silent.

She opened her eyes and met his gaze. Or, at least, she assumed she did. "I'll stop him."

"I'd love to believe you, I really would. You're our savior— our only hope for peace. For how life in Avalon was meant to be. I'll stand beside you until the end. But freeing Mordred is an enormous risk."

"I know. But it's a risk I have to take. I'm sorry."

Bert sighed, his stuffed-hay shoulders slumping. "I don't honestly disagree with you, that's the worst part. I just wish I did."

The smile she gave him didn't last long. "Well, don't worry. I still have to figure out where he is and how to set him free."

Bert huffed. "Nothing's seemed to stand in your path before."

"I hope you're right." She wished she shared in his confidence. "I really hope you're right. Now, I just need to come up with a plan."

Because all her plans had gone so well for her in the past.

* * *

Mordred could feel the echo of his thoughts in the void around him. He could not hear it, but he could *sense* it. A never-ending reflection of a reflection that extended in all directions around him, fading into nothingness like all the rest.

Every memory.

Every emotion.

Every piece of himself, shown back to him, again and again and again...

Hope. Fear. Hatred. Boredom. Loneliness.

The faces of all those he had known. Of all those he had lost. Of all those he had forgotten, dredged up from the recesses of his mind.

All that he was, laid bare. Like a series of impossible corridors stretching from him in all directions, above, beneath, and all around. A maze in which he could see every corner and turn in unison.

It was impossible. A figment of his mind—or what was left of it.

An echo. Back and forth and back and forth, around and around again. He was reflecting against the Iron Crystal—sinking deeper into the magic that he had used to create his own prison. He wondered if this was an experience that was unique to him. He assumed so. Though he supposed it did not matter.

"*Mordred!*"

A voice, calling to him in the shadows. Her voice. Was it real? Or simply another ghost of a memory? He could not respond. He had no corporeal form. No way to even dream of one. He could simply wish her nearer, wish her there with him.

"*Where are you?*"

He willed himself to respond. Wanting her to find him, there. Somehow, despite the impossibility of it. No, not wanting —*needing.*

A memory found him, not his Gwendolyn. A memory of his mother.

* * *

"*Remember who you are, boy.*" *She glowered down at him, her dark eyes like onyx against her pale skin and raven-black hair. There was always a mystery about her, a sense that there was something lurking within that gaze. Something terrible. Something powerful. Something that schemed.*

Morgana was fae, after all. Or, at least, that was what she told those who questioned her power. Her magic was strong enough.

"*But you will not tell me who I am, Mother.*" *He frowned up at her. "You will not tell me who fathered me.*"

"*It does not matter. You are* my *son. And that is more than enough for you.*" *She knelt and took his face in her palms. Those onyx eyes bored into him, revealing everything. Seeing through him. "And it should be enough for you now, locked away in that damnable creation of yours.*"

Wait.

That was not the way the memory had gone.

He was but a child when this had taken place. "I..."

"*You are the son of Morgana. You are Mordred, the dread prince. The rightful ruler of Avalon. The throne was always meant to be yours. Avalon chose* you, *not that insipid brother of mine. For* you *are the one who had the strength to do what is needed." Morgana's expression was unwavering. Unflinching.*

Perhaps this was a product of his imagination.

Or perhaps it was real. A ghost of his mother, come to haunt him.

He supposed it did not matter.

"Find a way out of this cage. And take the throne, as you were meant to so long ago." Morgana stood, towering over his small frame. "Become the King in Iron. Fulfill your destiny. Destroy them all."

* * *

Dream or ghost, he did not know, but it all faded away, returning him to the echoes of his mind. He did not know which he preferred. But one thing was becoming very clear.

He was going insane.

It was maddening.

Heh.

Finally, they will all be right about me.

THREE

Gwen sipped her drink as she watched the field that surrounded Mordred's keep. She decided one more day to gather her thoughts and figure out her best plan of attack couldn't be a bad thing.

It was midafternoon, so at least she didn't feel *too* bad about hitting the whiskey already. The weight of it all was grueling—between not sleeping, and now deciding that she was going to raise an army to free Mordred.

Which would start total war.

But it seemed that was the direction Avalon was headed, no matter what she did. Maybe it was inevitable. Maybe it was fate. Maybe the people here just sucked at not killing each other. She supposed it didn't matter.

She was sitting on the stone base of one of the towers that sat to the side of the main gate. The keep had a yard around it, and then a defensive wall that circled it on all sides except for the cliff. She wanted to get some air—wanted to get away from the clatter and clanking of all of Mordred's guards and servants. It wasn't their fault, but her lack of sleep and worsening mood were giving her a short fuse. She didn't want to scream at a guard for making squeaky metal noises when he literally couldn't help it.

Leaning her head back against the stone wall behind her, she let out a long, weary sigh. "This sucks."

"Tell me about it."

She jolted, nearly falling off the stone base and spilling her drink. "What the f—" It was Doc. At some point, he had sat down next to her, also watching the field as the green strands blew idly in the wind.

"See why I drink so much?" He sipped his own bottle. "Shame you build a tolerance over time. At least I like the flavor."

"I really don't want to become an alcoholic."

"Eh, live long enough, and you'll try a little bit of everything." Doc sniffed. "Boredom'll do that."

"I suppose. I guess I can take up a bunch of hobbies." She smirked. "Maybe I'll take up painting. Or crochet."

They went silent for a long time as she watched the woods beyond the field. She wasn't sure why. She supposed part of her was expecting someone to come marching out on horseback, declaring war on her for some reason or another. "Doc?"

"Yeah?"

"Can I ask you something?"

"I probably can't tell you the answer, but sure. Hasn't stopped you before."

Gwen let out a half-laugh. That was fair. "Is Mordred... is he suffering?"

The wizard paused before he replied. "You already know the answer to that."

"I know, but—is he *okay*?"

"You don't need me to figure that out."

Gwen shut her eyes. "Doc. Please. Just this once, speak plainly. I'm really, really not in the mood."

"Fine, fine." He took a swig from his bottle. "You're a witch.

Use your magic to contact him. He's not the only one who can wiggle his fingers and invade dreams, y'know."

"I wish I knew more about how to use my power. Can't you teach me?" She looked down at her palm, half expecting to find something there.

"All magic is different. It's like handwriting. You're on your own, kid." Doc leaned back against the rock wall. "And I mean that in more ways than one."

She turned to face Doc. "What?"

"It's time for me to go. Avalon doesn't need me anymore—and neither do you." He smiled up at the sky, clearly watching the clouds drift by. "I'm ready to retire."

"You—you can't leave me alone, not right now." She shook her head. "I need your help figuring all this out, and if I'm going to free Mordred, I—"

"No. You don't need me. I can promise you that. You have plenty of other friends and resources." He pushed up with a grunt. "The future will play itself out on its own without my silly meddling. It's time for me to go home."

Something told her that he didn't mean his house by the mountain. "Where are you going to go?"

"I don't know." He chuckled. "I think I'll just step into the void. Wherever it takes me is where I'll stay. Maybe I'll find a new adventure. Or maybe I'll get blown to bits. Either way, I'm ready to move on." He took another swig of his bottle and placed it down on the stone next to her. "This has been fun, kid, but it's time for me to say goodbye."

"No. No, no, no." She stood and brushed off her dress. "I won't lose you—I can't lose another friend. Mordred's gone, and Galahad—and—" She winced. "I guess Grinn kind of counts, but—"

Doc chuckled and hugged her. He smelled like alcohol, and maybe weed. She couldn't say she was shocked. "I'll just be in the way annoying you with all my bad jokes and non-answers. You'll be too busy to miss me."

"No. I won't be." She held him tighter. "Please don't go."

"You'll say that a lot in your life, I'm afraid. That's the curse of living as long as we do. The time we have with the ones we care about is never long enough, no matter how many centuries we live." Doc kissed her temple. "But it's time for me to be done. I'm tired, Gwen. *Exhausted.* And Avalon has you now. It doesn't need me to be the wizard anymore."

She took his hands in hers and squeezed them. It was hard to believe she'd never see him again. Letting out a wavering breath, she finally let him go. "I am going to miss you, though. No matter what you say."

"I know. I'm just trying to make you feel better." He nudged her shoulder.

"You suck at it."

"I know that too." He chuckled. "All right, kid. Tell the dog I said he wins."

"What?"

"Oh, we had a bet running."

"Which was what?"

"Which one of us would die first." He snickered. "I said it would be him. He said it would be me. He wins."

She felt her eyes go wide. "That's a terrible bet."

"Meh." Doc shrugged and turned to walk away. "Animals think about death a lot differently than we do. They aren't hung up on it. It's just a thing that happens."

She watched Doc as he headed into the long grass. "Goodbye, Doc. And thanks for being a friend."

"You too, kid. You were fun." He waved over his shoulder without turning. And just like that, he disappeared. There was no shimmer of light—no cosmic whoosh or swirl of smoke. He was just gone.

Picking up his bottle of booze, she headed inside, her heart heavy. Doc wasn't a whole lot of help when it came to it, but he was someone to talk to. Someone to have around. Someone who *might* know *something* about what she should do next.

She was losing friends faster than she was making them.

Walking into Mordred's study, with the large iron table in the middle of it, she slumped into one of the chairs, staring at the map in front of her. *If I were Zoe and Galahad, where would I hide the Iron Crystal?* There were too many options. Maybe they buried it. Maybe they hid it deep in a forest. Or in the caves. There was no telling. Hell, they could've dropped it into the ocean.

Doc was gone—not like he'd tell her where the Iron Crystal was, anyway—and there was nobody else she could ask. Resting her forehead on her arms, she let out a long, dreary sigh.

"I was going to ask how you were doing, but I think I already know."

Glancing up, she watched Bert walk into the room. "Yeah." She put her head back down. "Having a real fucking great time right now." She heard him sit at the table next to her. She'd offer him some of her alcohol if he, y'know, had a face. Well, a face with a mouth that worked, anyway. "Doc is gone."

"He took off again?"

"No, I mean *gone*. Gone—gone. Forever gone."

"... Oh." The scarecrow sat there in silence for a long moment before reaching out and placing a hand on her back. "I'm sorry."

Straightening up, she did her best to force a smile. It probably looked as half-assed as it felt. "It is what it is. I couldn't stop him. Wasn't my decision to make, anyway." She picked up the bottle of alcohol, thought about it for a moment, then put it back down in front of her.

He paused. "I'm sorry to add more trouble to your day, but there's something you need to know immediately."

"Oh good, more problems. What's going on?" That's all she needed. More shit to worry about.

"Thorn's army is on the move. It's making its way south." He paused. "Toward us."

"Fuck." She reached for the bottle of booze and took a swig. "You know what? I really don't like her."

Bert snorted. "Nobody does. But she's dangerous. She's one of the strongest on the island. Second only to Mordred and maybe Galahad. But rumor is he's given up the sword and is going into retirement. Not like I blame the bastard."

"No, neither do I. After everything." Even if Galahad had betrayed Mordred. Kind of. Sort of. She still didn't know how she felt about both Zoe and Galahad voting to put Mordred into imprisonment. Zoe, she supposed she could understand. But Galahad? The Knight in Gold was supposed to be Mordred's friend.

Insomuch as Mordred had friends. He wasn't wrong not to trust people, but he was also very good at giving people reasons to dislike him. She wasn't sure she blamed either group for their beliefs or behavior.

"I just wish we could all get along for, like, five fucking minutes." She pinched the bridge of her nose. "It's all giving me a goddamn headache." She signed up for this mess when she made a deal with Avalon. Though she knew it wasn't going to be easy, she didn't think it'd be like this. That's what she got for underestimating Avalon's aptitude for screwing her over or putting her into gnarly situations.

But she supposed that wasn't entirely fair. It had given her everything she had wished for back on Earth. She mattered here —she was *somebody*. Her panic attacks had all but disappeared. She had a man she loved and who loved her in return. And she had friends.

Never mind the fact that the man she loved was the island's favorite villain and her friends were mostly made out of metal and straw. Beggars couldn't be choosers, she supposed. "Here's what I know, Bert. I can't let him stay in there for a thousand years. I can't. Even if I thought I could go that long without him, there wouldn't be much left of either of us by the end of it. I need to free him, come what may. I *need* to. Or I'm going to die trying."

She didn't like the idea of still waiting for an army to hunt Mordred down. But she didn't see any sensible way around it. Trying to go at it single-handedly was probably a great way to get killed. "No. I'm going to see if I can get in touch with him through magic, but odds are slim. I don't really have any other ideas. I guess I could just go *ask* Zoe and Galahad, but I highly doubt that'll work." She chuckled sadly. "I'm still new to all this."

"Well, that's what spies are for. I'll see if my people can find something. Between the two of us, we should be able to figure something out. Right?" The scarecrow shrugged.

She loved his optimism. It was something she could use a little of these days. She smiled. "A witch and a scarecrow. We make a great pair."

"Exactly!" Bert stood and headed out of the room, leaving her to her own devices. The silence in his absence was like a heavy weight pressing down on her.

She needed Mordred back.

He'll be fine. I won't have to kill him. He's the strongest person I've ever met. He's survived over a thousand years. We'll stand against the elementals, and we'll all live happily ever after.

She couldn't help but laugh.

"Yeah right," she muttered into the bottle as she took another swig.

Nothing had been that easy so far. And something told her that this wouldn't be either.

FOUR

Mordred was lost within himself. Wandering the hallways of his mind, the endless twisting nether of his memories. He could not decide which was worse—revisiting unwanted memories or the nothingness that filled the space in between.

He could not say how much time had passed.

A day? A century? A single breath? An eon?

It did not matter.

For he was still here.

And here, with his power echoing back at himself endlessly, it did not matter. It was destroying him. Chipping away at his mind—his soul.

There would be nothing left of him when he emerged. He mourned for Gwendolyn. He wished her to find happiness with another. For what would come out of the Crystal after he served his time would be a broken thing. A husk.

Let them all forget about me. Let me rot in this place. Let me unravel my mind and spend eternity in this place. Gwendolyn. Oh, Gwendolyn. How he loved her—how he would cling to the thought of her. The memory of her touch, of her presence, of her laughter. Of her kindness, of her humor. Of the way she smiled at him. The taste of her lips on his.

This, too, would be taken from him someday, like all the rest of his mind. Ripped apart in the storm of the Crystal. But he hoped it would go last. So that he could hold onto her, shelter in her, and remember her long after he had forgotten even his own self.

When a hand gently rested on his shoulder, he was certain it was another memory. He had willed her into being.

"Mordred?"

Her voice. He dared not turn around.

"Are you all right? That... that's a stupid question, I'm sorry. Of course you're not. Where are we?" She paused. "Another stupid question." Her arms wrapped around his waist from behind, and he felt the warmth of her cheek press against his back.

That was not a memory. This had never happened before. Turning, he could not believe what he saw. Yes—*saw*—he was corporeal. Standing in the middle of an emptiness that stretched out in all directions. The ground was discernible only by the slight shine of its surface, like obsidian or polished steel.

But none of it mattered. There, in front of him, was Gwendolyn. Hair like the colors of fire, her wings unfurled but relaxed behind her. Those eyes that flickered like embers—*his Gwendolyn.*

"H—how?" He reached up, hesitantly, almost afraid that his hand would pass straight through her, before placing his palm to her cheek. He had no iron gauntlets here. And he was fine without them—he preferred to feel her skin against his.

"What's the good in being a witch if I can't use it for shit?" She smiled up at him, but it was clear she was fighting through tears. "Oh, God—Mordred—are—"

"No. Do not ask again." He folded her into his embrace,

clutching her close as if a gust of wind might pull her away. "Tell me this is not a figment of my madness."

"I'm here. I'm really here." She wrapped her arms around him again and squeezed him as tightly as she could. "And I'm coming to save you."

Pulling his head back, he met her gaze. "You know what that will mean."

"Total war. I don't—I don't care. I don't want to be here without you. I don't want—I can't—" She looked around the emptiness. "Shit, Mordred, is this where you're stuck?"

"No. It is far worse than this." He smirked faintly. "You seem to have grounded my mind enough that I can take my own shape. It is... blissfully quiet, with you here."

"Quiet?"

"My mind is so very loud." He knew he was not speaking sense. He could tell it by the concerned look on her face. "The memories batter at me like hail upon a windowpane. It will only be so long before the window shatters and the cold takes me." Taking her hands in his, he lifted them to his lips and kissed her fingers. "Leave me here. Forget about me. If you release me—"

She cut him off. "I don't give a shit, Mordred. Let them come for us. The villagers—they're raising an army. They're on my side. I am *going* to save you."

He could not help but smile.

She narrowed her eyes. "What's that look for?"

"I was wondering when it would happen. And it is glorious to see."

"When what would happen?"

"When you reached your breaking point and decided this world was yours to burn." He crooked a finger under her chin and tilted her head up toward him. "And by the Ancients, you are beautiful."

"I—"

It was his turn to cut her off, this time with a kiss. It never quite felt the same in a dream. But he would take whatever he could get. She wrapped an arm behind his neck, pulling herself closer and deepening the embrace.

When they finally parted, he felt a peace he had not known since his imprisonment began. Though he was afraid to know the answer, he had to ask. "How long has it been?"

"Only a few weeks."

The laugh that left him was not a pleasant one. His mind was doomed.

"I'm going to save you. I am. I just don't know where you *are*." She let out a breath. "Do you have any clue?"

"None. But I... will try to discern what I can." Running his knuckles over her cheek, he studied her features. Tried to recommit everything about her to his memory in hopes that it might linger. "Galahad will know."

"I doubt he'll tell me, but it's a start."

"When in doubt, torture him." When she stared at him in shock, he chuckled, and kissed her forehead. "I am not that far gone. Yet. I am simply teasing."

"Right. Sure." She hugged him and rested her head on his chest. "I promise I'm going to save you."

There were no words he could summon that would do him any good. He simply let out a quiet grunt in reply.

"I love you, Mordred. And—and when you're free—"

"If."

"*When*," she insisted.

Yes, he truly did enjoy her with her newfound backbone. He had always suspected that she would be a force of nature when she came into herself. And she had only just begun.

"*When* you're free," she continued as if he hadn't interrupted her, "I—I'd like if we could talk about—I mean, you and I, maybe—more permanently—I mean, *officially*—"

"Shush." He chuckled, listening to her awkwardly and obviously dance around the subject of marriage. "Now is not the time, and this is certainly not the place." He stroked a hand through her hair, combing the strands. "I would rather I propose to you somewhere a bit more romantic than the depths of my own quickly burgeoning madness."

"That's fair."

Mordred was uncertain when she disappeared. Perhaps she simply faded away. Perhaps she woke up. Did their conversation end there? Or had it continued, and he simply could not recall? Madness was a troublesome thing—elusive like a gnat flitting in and out of his line of sight. Never quite fully somehow present but always distracting.

It was destroying his mind.

Piece by piece.

Bit by bit.

One memory at a time.

* * *

"There you are, boy." Morgana glowered at him from over her gathered herbs. "Useless thing you are, you were meant to be back by dark."

"There were lights in the woods." He walked forward, shyly placing his bundle of herbs on the table next to the others. "I tried to follow them, but—"

"Fool!" Morgana's rage was instant and unstoppable. His mother stormed over to him, and smacked him with the back of her hand, sending him reeling. He was only a child. "Never follow the lights. Not unless you wish to be taken to Tir n'Aill and fed to some Unseelie beast. You know better than that."

"But the lights looked like home—I—" He refused to cry. He knew that would only earn him more shouting and admonishment.

"The lights always look like home. That is how the darkness takes you. It shows you peace. It shows you what you want, what

you love—and it uses it to lure you in. Anything the darkness shows you is a lie, boy. Remember that. Take that to your grave."

"Y—yes, Mother."

* * *

Had Gwendolyn been a lie?

Or had she been real?

It was so difficult to tell...

Perhaps it did not matter.

The darkness already had him, after all.

FIVE

Gwen wasn't sure what drove her out to the stables the next morning. The staff were going about their early routines—and she smiled as she saw a few of Bert's people mixed in with the iron guards. They needed work, and she was happy enough to have more folks around in the keep. She was sure Mordred would roll his eyes, but she looked forward to having that debate in person. And hopefully soon.

One of the mares reached her head over the door of the stall, investigating her. Smiling, she reached out her hand and let the horse sniff her hand for treats. "Sorry, hon. Nothing for you this morning. But you'll get fed soon."

The mare pulled her head back, clearly uninterested since Gwen didn't have treats to bribe her with. That was fine by her —the mare wasn't who she'd come to see, anyway. She wasn't sure what had inspired her to come down here. She had woken up feeling restless and let her feet guide her to where they wanted to take her.

It was when she reached the end of the stable that she figured it out. The heavy *thud* of a metal hoof smashed into a thick wooden door, rattling it on its cast-iron hinges.

Ah.

Right.

She looked up at Mordred's iron stallion—with its eerie, opalescent glowing eyes. It snorted at her, frustrated, and shook its head in defiance. Its mane was made of tiny chains, and suddenly she realized she had never really paid too much attention to the animal. It was too aggressive for her to really try to get to know him at all.

"Hi."

The horse snorted again.

"I bet you're really sick of being cooped up." She tucked her hands into her pockets. She had created a long woolen overcoat for herself. She kept forgetting she was able to summon clothes out of thin air like Doc had done—but slowly, she was getting more and more used to it. Her mind still had a hard time defaulting to "just use magic."

But it was nice to have a coat. Cloaks were good and all, but coats had pockets. And pockets were fantastic. Gwen watched the horse, and the horse watched her. "I'm sorry about what's happened. About Mordred, about... all of it." Why exactly she was saying all this to a metal horse, she had no idea. But it felt right.

"Leaving you in here doesn't feel right." She sighed. "I know you're not—y'know—flesh and blood, but... you're still alive. And being stuck in here without anyone to walk you or any time in the field must be miserable all the same." Shaking her head, she glanced out the front of the stables. "I'd try to take you out for a ride, but I like having my spleen on the inside. Something tells me you wouldn't let me get close."

A heavy *thud* of a hoof against the door was her answer. Nope.

"I'd go talk to Tiny, but he's asleep. Always. I think he only woke up to deal with Mordred because he had to." She chuckled sadly. "Whatever." She leaned up against the wall next to the stable, watching the morning sun slowly spread over the courtyard outside the stables. "So. You won't let anybody near you. And we can't leave you in there." Shutting her eyes, she rested her head against the beam behind her. "And I don't know if I'll be successful. I have to go to war, horsie. I have to get people killed. All in the name of saving him."

An angry huff was all she got from the animal.

"And there's a real, real good chance I fail and wind up dead. The odds of me surviving any of this are... minimal. I'm not naive enough to think anything else. And if I'm dead, this place'll get overrun. The elementals will come and slaughter everyone who's left." Gwen cringed at the thought. Tim. Mae. Eod. They wouldn't spare anyone or anything.

Including Mordred's horse.

"So, here are the options—I go to war, I succeed, and Mordred is free. And you get to go back to normal life. Or, I die, and you get destroyed. Or, even worse, I die, and they leave you here—and you wait a thousand years for Mordred to come back. And who knows what'll be left of him if *that* happens. Or you, for that matter." She rubbed a hand over her face. "I guess it's not fair to make you gamble on my choices. Even if you are a *super*-mean horse."

Another heavy *thud* against the wood was so perfectly timed that she had to laugh. "Well, if the dog can understand English, who's to say you can't too?" That made it even worse, she supposed. "Whatever."

Turning to face the huge metal animal, she had to crane her neck to really look up at him. He was *enormous*. Easily the size of a Clydesdale. He was a tank. Almost literally.

"Just don't—y'know—trample me, or some shit, okay?" She pulled the huge pin out of the gate's door.

The horse didn't hesitate a moment. He slammed the door open, forcing Gwen to jump out of the way. It smashed into the other wall, cracking from the impact. And just like that, the sound of hooves was like thunder pounding on the dirt as the stallion ran from the stables and for freedom.

She jogged from the stables herself to watch as the enormous metal creature ran into the field outside the keep. The guards shouted, looking to her for orders to catch the horse. She shook her head. "Let him go."

The beast ran through the grass, looking like someone had drawn a spooky monster horse onto some bucolic nature painting. He looked out of place. But also, he looked beautiful—his gait quickly reaching a gallop as he ran through the field and toward the woods.

She didn't know what'd happen to him. But at least he wasn't rusting away in his stall. Letting out a long breath, Gwen turned and headed back into the keep. She needed coffee. A lot of coffee.

Because today was the day she went to war.

* * *

It was midday when Gwen and the others set out, this time on much more normal-looking horses. Eod was running ahead of her. Tim was walking, as he wasn't coordinated enough to sit on a horse and stay up there. He'd tried a few times before she decided they'd just hike. Lina and Mirkon, Bert's loyal companions, were in the back, chatting and bickering like the old married couple they were. Mae had stayed behind, saying that road life was *not* for her, and somebody had to look after the place while everyone went off to war. Gwen couldn't blame her.

Gwen preferred riding to the city this way, as opposed to in the back of Bert's cart. It was a lot less bouncy, at any rate. She had picked Sunshine, the mare that she had befriended when she had first arrived. It felt like forever since she had crash-landed in Avalon.

She'd been so afraid. And for good reason. The memory of

meeting Mordred for the first time—and how abjectly terrified she'd been of him—made her smile, if a bit morosely. The whole thing had seemed so impossible. And she supposed it still was. If this turned out to be some fever dream, and she woke up in a hospital bed learning that all her friends here were the staff, and Eod was the therapy dog that came to visit her, she still wouldn't be surprised.

There was even a part of her that missed Grinn. Missed that asshole cat who had caused so much turmoil in her life. She hoped he made it back to hell to his family, but she knew that things like that didn't just happen because she wished them. Life wasn't fair. Grinn certainly had taught her that.

You know what else didn't feel real? The fact that her panic attacks were gone. She still didn't know why, but she suspected she had Avalon's magic to thank for it. It was such a relief.

Her parents would be proud of her.

That brought a small pang to her heart. She hoped they were okay. Idly, she wondered if she could send them a letter somehow. Just something to tell them that she was alive and all right. *At least for now. Give it a week, that might change.* In fact, now that she thought about it, it was probably for the best they didn't know anything. It might just end up causing more pain than it was worth. When she never showed back up, they'd think she was probably dead from some mysterious abduction and eventually mourn her loss and move on with life. If they thought she was out there, somewhere, they might never stop searching. They might never let go.

It was always something she wondered about when she watched *Peter Pan* as a kid. What about the parents? Didn't they notice Wendy and the others were missing? Weren't they panicking? But they got their kids back eventually, after all. Plus, a bonus kid, if she wasn't mistaken.

Hi, Mom. Yeah, we went missing, sorry about that. But hey, meet Peter. You always wanted a third son, right? Maybe that's what she should've done with Mordred. *Hi, Mom, I'm home. Meet my boyfriend. Turns out I'm into older men. Older, stabbier men.* She snorted to herself.

"What? Everything okay?" Bert asked from the horse next to her. Sunshine kept trying to eat the hay out of Bert's pant leg, so Gwen had to make sure to leave some distance between them. His own horse was eyeing him like a midday snack.

"Oh, nothing. Just thinking about home. And how ridiculous all this is." She smiled at him, doing her best to be reassuring. "I'm all right."

"It's a big thing, what you're doing. It's all right to be reflective about it." Bert gestured out at the woods around them. "But you remember how this place was when you got here—muted and trapped in a state of decay. None of this color, none of this beauty. Don't forget what you've done for us already and how much you mean to Avalon."

"Mordred broke the Crystal, not me. I tried and failed."

"Yeah, but he did it *because* of you. My friends would still be trapped in there, and I'd still be on the shelf in that general store if you hadn't come along. This island picked you for a reason. And I have faith that you'll see us through." She could hear the smile in his voice, even if his rusted metal jack o'lantern of a head never moved.

"I hope you're right."

"It hasn't led you astray yet, has it?"

She snorted again and shot him a look. "Grinn is dead. Doc is gone. Mordred's imprisoned. Lancelot is dead."

"*One* of those things isn't a bad thing," Bert retorted. "And I'll let you pick which one."

"Fair." Her half-laugh ended in a sigh. "Is it weird that I miss all of them?"

"It's weird that you miss one of them, and I'll let you pick which one."

That got her to laugh for real this time. The more she got to know Bert, the more she liked him. He was still overly zealous about a so-called revolution, but if she'd spent three hundred years hiding in plain sight, she'd probably be a little twitchy about the subject too. "What was it like?"

"Hum?" He pulled his foot back out of the way of his horse's hungry mouth, grumbling something about vultures.

"Being stuck on that shelf for, like, three hundred years. What was it like?"

"Boring. Really, *really* boring." Bert finally convinced his horse to stop trying to eat him and put his foot back in the stirrup. "I wasn't there for all that time, though. I was in some lady's shed for a while. Then I was a garden decoration. Then I was in an attic, and then I wound up in that store."

"What did you... like... *do* for all that time?"

"Told myself stories. Like I said, I don't sleep—I don't dream, not really—but I can tune out. If it wasn't for that, I'd have gone insane, I expect." He chuckled. "And I told myself that my waiting would pay off. That if I just held on a little longer, we'd all be saved. Lo and behold, I was right."

"I'm not Joan of Arc."

"I don't know who that is."

Gwen slapped a hand over her face. Right. She forgot about that. "I'm not your savior. I'm not some holy blessed warrior of God."

"No, but you were chosen by Avalon. You can't deny that. You *talked* to the island itself."

"Sort of?" She scrunched her nose a little. "Insomuch as you can talk to a thing like that."

"You know who was the last person to talk to the island? Your wizard friend." Bert sounded so proud. So certain. "And he saved this world once before. Now, it's your turn, and they all know that."

"Wait, what?" She blinked. "Doc saved the world? When?"

"He didn't tell you?" Bert tilted his pumpkin head to the

side slightly. "Huh. I wonder why." He shrugged it off. "It was when the demons arrived. When hell collided with Avalon for that brief moment."

"I know about that part—that's when Grinn and the others got stranded here, and everyone but Grinn was killed."

"Yeah. But do you really think a bunch of scattered, warring, unprepared elementals could murder a legion of demons? Especially demons in service to Astaroth, the Great Duke of War?"

"I... didn't think about that." Gwen frowned. She really hadn't, and now she felt like a moron for not having put that together.

"The wizard warned everyone. Got everyone together to fight them. Without him, we all might have been overrun. But because he did, well..." Bert trailed off.

"Because he got involved, all those demons died. At least— at least they go back to hell, though, right?"

"Some do. But not all of them. Or, at least, that's what Grinn said during his trial. That the newer the soul, the less likely it was that they'd go back. And that they only get so many times, also. There was no telling how many of the demons died for good." Bert's shoulders slumped. "Which, I know it sounds weird to feel bad about *demons*, but..."

"They can love and have families. That means they're not all bad. It means they're worth caring about too." Gwen stared ahead at the dirt road that stretched into the woods in front of them. "And Doc must have blamed himself. Especially for what happened with Grinn afterwards."

Bert nodded. "He felt responsible for Grinn's rampage. He vowed that was the last time he'd ever get involved."

That made so much sense. She shut her eyes and let out a sigh. "Now, I feel like such an asshole for pestering him for answers all the time."

"But if he hadn't gotten involved that day and saved us, we'd all be dead instead. I don't know how many lives have to go on the scales before it evens out. But I know what feels like justice and what doesn't. That felt terrible but unavoidable. But this? This feels like justice."

"Fighting Thorn and the elementals?"

Bert nodded. "I don't want them to die. I just want them to stop. And if that means war? It means war. Sometimes, you have to fight for the people you care about. Sometimes, you have to fight for the things you believe in."

"Yeah. I suppose you do." She just hoped things went differently for her than they had for Doc. She couldn't say that she wouldn't have done the same thing he had so long ago. And even if the choice was maybe not the wrong one, the deaths still would have haunted her too. The not knowing how many souls went back to hell or were gone for good. Or if Grinn's family was alive or dead. "War is messy."

"Even when you're on the right side of it, it's always messy."

"Isn't that the thing, though? Everybody thinks they're on the right side of the war." She paused. "Except maybe Mordred. He knew he was being a jerk."

Bert laughed. "That's fair."

"I think we're doing the right thing, though. We have to stop Thorn from taking over. We have to stop the elementals from tearing this world apart. And we have to free Mordred."

"How selfish is that last bit?"

She took a moment to think about it. "Honestly? Probably more than it should be. But we're going to need him. I'm sorry, but a bunch of pitchfork-wielding villagers and one idiot witch who doesn't know what she's doing? We wouldn't stand a chance."

"Don't sell us short!" Bert tutted. "We have better weapons than pitchforks."

It was her turn to laugh. Despite the stress of what was to come, she was smiling. "Thanks for being a friend, Bert."

"Thanks for being our savior, Gwen."

"I wish you'd stop calling me that. I'm not your savior." But she had made a promise to Avalon to protect it. One way or another. "But, fine. On one condition—no speeches. I refuse."

Bert slapped his hand on his thigh. "Deal!"

Somehow, she suspected he was lying.

SIX

Mordred was still not certain whether or not his speaking dreams were ghosts or figments of his own shattered psyche.

He did not know which was worse. Nor did he particularly care, to be honest. The effect was the same. This memory was harsher than the others. He knew the field immediately. While he had fought in many battles with his fellow knights in the service of his uncle, this one in particular stuck in his memory. *This* one was the worst.

The Battle of Camlann. What the mythos would remember of this day, he did not know. While he listened to other legends and stories with a sort of half-hearted amusement later in his years, he tried to avoid all the tales of Camlann. Sometimes, however, it was inevitable. It seemed that most agreed that this was where he and Arthur fought to the death. That was painfully untrue. He had never once raised his blade to his uncle. But it seemed even the history of Earth wished to paint him the villain, and there was no point in fighting it. The better story would always win, regardless of the facts.

And the facts were crisp in his mind, even a thousand years later.

The mud was thick, as it often was when two armies fought to the bitter end. The dirt and rain mixed with the blood of the fallen. Mordred was bleeding, too, from a deep wound. A lancer had landed a lucky strike between two sections of his plate armor.

But in the end, the other army lay slain. Arthur was victorious... but at a terrible cost. Mordred remembered him standing there, ankle-deep in the mud, chest rising and falling with exertion as the King of the Britons gazed out over the carnage. It was not until Mordred drew closer that he saw that he was not the only one who had suffered a wound.

Blood oozed from under Arthur's own armor, dripping down his thigh and to the ground below, mixing with that of the others. Panic welled in Mordred—a sudden fear that tore at him in a way he had not known since he was a child.

He ripped his helm from his head, tossing it away without a thought as he ran toward his uncle. "My king!"

Arthur turned his head to him and smiled faintly. "I have not been your king for some time. When will you let me go?"

Mordred's steps hitched to a halt. That was not what Arthur had said to him on that fateful day. Arthur had instead told him that he believed he might have made a *bit of an error*, downplaying the fatal wound he had received. "I—" He did not know what to say.

Arthur fell to one knee, gripping his side. He leaned heavily upon Caliburn. "You know what comes next. We both do."

It was only then that Mordred realized he was not the man he had been so long ago. He was himself from *now*. With the terrible, morbid iron armor and the rusted, jagged claws. This was not another simple memory, playing out before him like a stage production. This was something else. "Am I speaking to myself?"

"Does it matter?" Arthur undid the fastenings of his gauntlet with his teeth, shaking the piece of armor loose. He wiped his brow, trying to clear some of the dirt, sweat, and blood that was obviously obscuring his vision.

"I suppose it does not." Mordred stepped forward and offered his king a hand to his feet.

Arthur took it, accepting the help without pause. He had never been an egotistical man. He had never been overly proud or righteous. Sometimes—no, most of the time—Mordred found it positively infuriating how effortlessly *noble* his uncle had been. Arthur let out a sigh, looking out at the devastation of the battle. "I knew that this battle would be where I fell. Merlin came to me the night before and told me what would come to pass."

"Then why did you fight?"

"Because I had to be the man I was meant to be. And do what I was meant to do. Fate comes for us all, and we can only resist it for so long. Even you, though you have put it off better than most." Arthur huffed a laugh. "You always were a stubborn bastard."

Mordred could not help but smile, just a little, at the insult. It was true. "What do you mean, about my fate?"

Arthur took one step forward, and the scene around them changed and shifted. No longer on the battlefield, they were back in their camp. Arthur was lying on his cot, his chest bandaged. But a fever had set in quickly, and the pallor of his cheeks and the darkness of his eyes told of what was coming.

Their king was going to die.

The other knights were gone. Even Merlin was nowhere to be seen. Only Mordred and Arthur remained.

"This was the worst of it, you know." Arthur shut his eyes tiredly. "Being *nursed* by a pack of grown men who were about as delicate as a wild boar. Do you know how terrible Lancelot was at tending to a wound? By God, it was like being stabbed all over again."

Mordred chuckled. "I cannot imagine." Although, apparently, he could. This was still a memory, after all—even if it was warped by this strange interaction. He sat on a stool next to Arthur's cot. He did not bother to give his dying uncle any aid, though the impulse was still there.

This was not real.

"A bunch of bucks in heat, you lot were. I often felt like a nanny, not a king, trying to keep you all from beating each other senseless over some game of cards or some lass from the nearest village. You were all damnably exhausting." Arthur smiled, belying his fondness for them, despite his teasing.

"And you deserved it. Saint that you were—living in your shadow was impossible." Mordred rolled his eyes. "Always willing to die for whatever cause crossed your path, without a care for what it would do to the rest of us."

"You were never meant to live in my shadow, Mordred." Arthur turned his gaze to him. As always, he seemed to look straight through Mordred—seeing to his soul. "You were meant to *be* my shadow."

"I... don't understand."

"You never did. And look where it has gotten you." Arthur grunted and shut his eyes again. "If only you had paid a little more attention, you might have avoided all of this nonsense. Imprisoned within your own magic—within your own *mind*. Your mother would be beside herself. And likely is, in whatever nether realm she found her way to." He hummed thoughtfully. "Though I suppose she may have returned to the ether from which she came. If she were still in existence, she would have never let death keep her away."

"That is true." Mordred shook his head. Death would not have stopped Morgana for long. Her soul had likely returned to the dust and stars. "And I do not need reminding of how disappointed you both would be with me."

"It can change. You still have a chance to become who, and

what, you were meant to be." Those blue eyes met his again, faded though they were with the fever.

"You say I was meant to be your shadow. Was I not always at your heel, eager to learn? Eager to follow in your footsteps?" Mordred clenched his fist. "Yet I was never good enough—not for you, not for *them*"—the hatred in his voice for the other knights was thick, and he saw no need to hide it—"and you see what they tried to do."

"I did not need an heir, you fool!" Arthur coughed. It took everything in Mordred not to reach for the pitcher of water. "I needed the darkness in you. I needed you to do what I could not."

Mordred furrowed his brow. He shook his head before muttering, "You are making little sense, which I suppose is not surprising, given that you are a figment of my failing mind."

"There are times, as king, when decisions must be made. When lives must be spent. When the path of darkness must be followed. There are times when the sacrifice of the few protects the peace of the many. This cruelty—this unkindness—is necessary." Arthur sighed. "I needed you to be the enforcer of such deeds, where I could not."

"To what end? To protect your conscience, so you could sleep at night?" Mordred sneered.

"You are what you are meant to be, same as I. This was not to *protect* me, boy." Arthur shut his eyes, the sweat of the fever still beading upon his brow. "Your feeble attempt at nobility is what binds you. Weakens you. Holds you back from your potential. You are not meant to be the righteous king, son of Morgana—you are meant to be the knife in the shadows. The fear of the abyss that keeps others in the light."

Mordred ran a gauntleted hand over his face. This had to be the ramblings of his own mind. Arthur would never tell him to be the shark in the waters, waiting to maim any who strayed into deep waters.

Or would he?

It did not matter.

"You mean to tell me that my attempts to be *good* and *kind* are wrong. That is not the Arthur I knew."

"That is the Arthur you did not see. The one you could not accept. Why do you believe Avalon chose you over me? Why did it let me die, while you were given the gift to foil all the others in the land? No other soul was given the gift of iron."

"Save Gwendolyn."

"That girl..." Arthur chuckled. "She will be the death of you."

"I believe she already has been." Mordred gestured idly at the tent around them. "Or, at least, my downfall."

"Do not think my words are meant in derision." Arthur opened his eyes again to watch Mordred. "I would have adored her. And you two together are a perfect match. She reminds me of..." He coughed.

"I noticed the similarities, yes." Mordred smirked briefly. "I would think it a coincidence, if I did not know Avalon for what it was."

Arthur reached for the pitcher of water but was too weak to stretch his arm far enough to grasp it. With a heavy sigh, Mordred poured his phantom king a mug of water and helped the other man drink it. "This is foolish."

His uncle laid his head back into the pillow. "I will not argue with that."

Mordred studied the dying man. "What would you have me do?"

"Be true to yourself. Be true to your *nature*. All these centuries you have lingered within a purgatory of your own making as you strove to be what you cannot. You are right—God needs his devil. And Avalon needs you to fulfill your destiny, whether you like it or not."

"You wish me to become the monster that others believed me to be."

"Mordred, have you looked at yourself?" Arthur smiled. "You are hardly doing yourself any favors."

"Now, you sound like Gwendolyn." Mordred stood from the stool to pace the room. This was the work of his own mind, his own psyche. But the words hit him no less hard than if they had been uttered by the man himself.

It would be freeing, he supposed, to give in. To be that which others saw—that which they seemed to wish for. He wondered how Gwendolyn would react, should he surrender to his instincts to destroy all those who would stand in opposition to him, regardless of the cruelty it would require.

Would she still love him?

Would she still desire him?

But I cannot lie to myself to keep her. I cannot deny who I was meant to become any longer. If she truly loves me, she will see the truth in it.

"I miss you, Uncle." Mordred shut his eyes. And some part of him that had held the line for all those centuries finally put down the shield. "And I loved you like a father."

"I know. And I looked upon you like my son. But let me rest. Let the memory of me finally die. You were never meant to become King Arthur, or King of Avalon. You were meant to become Mordred, the King in Iron."

The King in Iron.

Yes.

He supposed that would be suitable.

Now, all that remained was to see how long he would remain trapped within his own psyche, or if Gwendolyn succeeded in freeing him.

And after that?

How many dead he would leave in his wake.

If this is what Avalon needs of me... so be it.

And may the Ancients have mercy on all those who stand in my way.

SEVEN

Gwen wondered what the point of having wings was if she was always going to be stuck on a horse traveling with people who couldn't fly. But it wasn't like she really knew how to use them. Her one real attempt at flight had ended in a crash landing, and she hadn't really worked up the nerve to jump off a cliff or the wall of the keep to force herself to learn.

But they made great extra insulation when it got chilly, though. She had to give them that. Their little motley band of Bert, Lina, Mirkon, Tim, and Eod were sitting around a campfire, while she was carefully cutting slits up the back of her coat so she could have her wings *and* be extra warm at the same time. She had tried to summon herself a coat to do the same thing, but she kept screwing it up. Probably couldn't visualize it well enough.

So, the good, old-fashioned, manual approach would have to do. Avalon was slipping into the depths of autumn quickly, and while the days were warm, the nights were getting almost frosty. The change in temperature didn't seem to bother Tim or Bert, though Tim's joints were extra squeaky. Eod seemed unaffected as well, as he chewed blissfully on the deer antler that Mirkon had cut from the buck he had caught for them to eat.

Gwen felt bad for the deer. But it was nice to have something more than fish while on the road.

"How far away are we?" She was now stitching up the slits she had made with a needle and thread that Mae had packed her. Mae had packed her just about everything for the road she could possibly have wanted.

"Hm. One more day's ride to the city," Bert replied, thoughtfully looking off into the woods. "And there my people will already be waiting to meet you."

"Once we get there, I have to leave to find Galahad. I need to know where he and Zoe took the Crystal." Gwen frowned down at her coat as she kept stitching the edges of the cuts she had made. She wasn't looking forward to the conversation with Galahad. She knew it wouldn't go well.

"Are you so sure we need Mordred?" The wariness in Mirkon's voice was thick as he whispered to his wife. Gwen knew she wasn't supposed to hear him, so she ignored it as best she could. To them, Mordred was some big, scary, spooky villain. They didn't understand.

Lina sighed and whispered back, "She loves him. And he's suffering. And I'd do the same thing in that case. I'd burn down the world to free you, you fat bastard, if I needed to."

"Love you too, darling," he muttered dryly.

Gwen smiled. She hoped she lived long enough with Mordred to get to the point of aimless bickering. It was a weird life goal, but it was something. Maybe she would just be happy to talk to Mordred in person again at all.

At this point, they had spent more time apart than together. At least they had their weird and semi-constant dreams together. She hoped those would go away once they could actually both be free and not under constant threat of war and death. If that ever was the case.

But she had to have hope.

Avalon chose her to help it. Right? Right.

Eod looked up. "*Mom sad?*"

"No, baby. Mom not sad." She reached out and scratched him between the ears. "Okay, maybe a little. But I'll be all right."

"*What wrong?*"

"I just miss Dad, that's all."

"*Me too.*" Eod went back to chewing on his antler. "*But is okay. Find Dad soon.*"

She smiled. *Find Dad soon.* That was the plan.

"You can talk to the dog?" Mirkon blinked. "You magic users. Weird folk."

"You're right. It is weird." She chuckled and went back to stitching. "But I don't mind it. I'm slowly getting used to it." She paused. "I hope I live long enough to really get used to it."

"You will," Bert chimed in cheerfully. "I'm sure of it."

At least Bert would always believe in her, even if she didn't always believe in herself. That was nice to have. They sat and finished their dinner—those of them who ate—before tucking themselves in for the night. Bert stayed up to keep watch since he didn't need to sleep. She was tempted to make a crack about him being a scarecrow and that being his job, but she figured it was too easy.

Yawning, she snuggled up next to Eod, draped an arm over him, and let sleep take her.

She wasn't surprised when she found herself in a dream that wasn't her own. For a moment, she wasn't sure she was anywhere at all, as a thick, impenetrable white fog stretched everywhere she looked. If it weren't for the grass beneath her feet, she might have thought she was in another weird void. She shivered as the chill of the air and the mist of the fog settled over her.

Furrowing her brow, she turned around slowly in a circle,

searching for any sign of where she was supposed to go. It wasn't until she heard soldiers with their clanking armor that she had any hints at all. She headed off in that direction, careful not to trip over a rock or fall into a hole. Soon, dark shapes were visible in the mist—a line of knights, two of them carrying a stretcher between them.

As she drew closer, she recognized them. Bors, Gawain, Percival, Lancelot, and the rest. The man on the stretcher was Arthur, his crown still resting on his head, his hands folded over Caliburn atop him as though he were already dead. But the creased expression of pain on his features told her otherwise. None of the knights seemed to register that she was there, simply trudging along in the memory. They were all clearly still human—well, except Galahad, who never was. This must be England before it was really England, before they took King Arthur to Avalon.

She turned to face the end of the line as a veritable nightmare stepped from the fog. She jolted, startled at first, as Mordred approached. He was as she knew him, with his jagged, rusted armor, and molten eyes. She'd hoped by this point she wouldn't feel awe at the sight of him. But she did. Awe, and just a little fear.

And fuck, did he look *angry*.

When he glanced at her, his expression softened slightly. "Gwendolyn." He did not stop walking, though, following the line of knights through the fog.

She fell in step beside him, reaching her hand out to weave her fingers into his, not caring how strange the metal gauntlet felt. "Watching reruns?" She shook her head, catching herself before he had the chance to remind her she was an idiot and he was from the past. "Never mind, sorry."

"I believe I gather your meaning. Yes. I am. It seems my psyche has taken shelter in these memories to protect me from

the storm. Though, I wish it would choose happier moments."
His expression darkened again.

"Do you have happier moments?" She nudged him, smiling,
trying to tease him into sparring with her.

"No."

So much for that plan. She sighed and looked ahead at the
marching knights. "This is when you took him to Avalon."

"I used to wonder if it would have not been better if I had
died at Camlann instead." His hand in hers tightened just
slightly. "If all of Avalon would not have been better for it. It
would have chosen him."

"You don't know that. He could have died, anyway, and the
island could have chosen nobody—then they'd all be dead." She
gestured at the line ahead with her other hand. "And you too."

"Some might argue that would still have been a favorable
outcome."

"Not me."

Gwen might have kicked him in the gut for the flash of pain
that crossed his features. Those rust-colored eyes met hers, and
there was grief in them. "Forgive me, my love. I have had far too
much time left alone with my thoughts."

"I'm working on it. I need to stop at a city to meet Bert's
people, and then I'm going to find Galahad and make him tell
me where you are." She frowned. "But I need you to hold on."

"Who is Bert?" He arched an eyebrow at her.

Right. They'd never met. "A friend. He's in charge of a
resistance movement of villagers who—"

Mordred laughed. "Oh, by the Ancients—you've fallen in
with *them?*" It made sense Mordred would know about their so-
called underground resistance. "Adorable fools. I let them carry
on with their... secrets and their plans. They are harmless."

"They have an army."

"An army of chaff—of foam thrown about by the sea. If you

fight the elementals with them, you are doomed." He shook his head.

"Which is precisely why I've convinced them we need you." She paused. "It's the only reason I think they're going to help me free you."

"All I did to contain the wrath of the elementals was for *them*, and you see how they still fear and loathe me?" He grimaced. His hand tightened around hers, but it didn't feel affectionate. "Three hundred years of peace I gave this world. Three hundred. And it has earned me nothing but suffering. I should have let them all burn."

Fear twisted in her stomach as she remembered her promise to Bert and the others about putting down Mordred if she had to. "Hey—" She pulled him to a stop, turning him to face her. "You don't mean that."

His gaze bored through her like liquid metal. "Perhaps I do. Perhaps I finally understand."

"They're just—look. When you put the elementals away, you put a lot of other magical people in there too. Villagers and the like. They were scared." She picked his hands up in hers and held them, heavy as they were, close to her. "Bert was in hiding all that time because he had enough magic that you'd probably have chucked him in there too. I don't blame them for being afraid of you. They don't know you. Not like I do."

"You believe I am somehow different than the monster they see in me?" He lifted a hand to cup her cheek, gently tracing the metal point of his thumb along her skin.

"No." She met his gaze. "I know who you are. I know what you are. I just know that isn't the whole story. There's so much more to you than what they see. You may be a monster, but for fuck's sake, you're *my* monster, and I'm not going to let—"

Mordred cut her off as he tipped her head to his. He leaned down to kiss her, capturing her lips in a searing embrace that seemed to search for something—anything—to hold onto. And she gave him all that she could. Every ounce of hope, every ounce of love, every ounce of need for him that she owned.

When he broke the kiss, he leaned his forehead against hers. "I will be as strong as I can be, my love. I will try to hold against this storm until you find me."

"I promise I'm going to find you. I'm going to free you. But if—if Galahad doesn't help me..."

"I will do everything to try to discern anything about my location from within here."

"I mean, the Crystal is still yours, right?" She looked up at him. "Can't you just, I don't know, *feel* where it is?"

He furrowed his brow slightly. "Yes? What do you—" He paused. "Ah. Yes. I suppose that makes perfect sense." He chuckled quietly. "I do not know why I did not think of that."

"You've been a little busy." She looked into the fog after the line of knights that were now long gone. "I'm sorry you have to go through this."

"As am I. But perhaps it will provide me some deeper understanding." He straightened his shoulders, cracking his neck from one side to the other. "For better or worse." He turned his attention toward the direction the knights had gone. "You should not linger here long. I cannot imagine it is doing you any kindness. You will need your rest for what is to come. Return to me tomorrow night, and I will tell you what I have discerned, if anything."

"I love you, Mordred. Please, be strong."

He rested his palm to her cheek again. "My sweet Gwendolyn, who took pity on a monster. How could I leave you now? You will have need of the darkness soon enough."

She blinked. "Wh—"

She never got to ask him what he meant.

Everything faded into the fog.

EIGHT

Gwen didn't need proof of what the elementals were capable of.

But she found herself staring at it all the same.

The city was in ruins.

And all those who lived there were slaughtered.

There was no way around it. No other words to describe the horrors in front of her. They'd known something was wrong the moment they crested a hill and saw the smoke pouring up from the buildings, black and thick. Bert had frantically kicked at his horse, sending it into a gallop down the hill toward the carnage. She had screamed at him to stop, but it was too late.

By the time they had all caught up with him, he was standing in the middle of the town square, staring at the desolation. His leather gloves covered in black soot. He must have gone searching for survivors.

A huge trench of volcanic rock sliced through several of the stone buildings. Others looked like they had been smashed through by a wrecking ball.

She recognized an elemental lying dead in the center of one of the volcanic pools. She hadn't known their name, but they were present at Mordred's sentencing. Their eyes gazed sightlessly up at the sky, which was a beautiful blue to mock the carnage around them. The sun was desperately trying to shine through the haze of the smoke.

Scattered about the ruins, or blocking off alleys, was another clue to what might have happened—thorns. Thick branches of twisting bramble, covered in vicious barbs the size of her hand. Where they hadn't been burned away, they covered the sides of buildings, of carts, and even the remains of a horse that lay crumpled where it fell.

"Is—is there anyone?" Lina asked Bert. "Anyone at all?"

The scarecrow shook his head. After a long pause, he broke his silence. "Any survivors have run, I'm sure."

"What do you think happened?" Mirkon hugged Lina to his side by draping an arm around her shoulders. The simple gesture made Gwen miss Mordred dearly. He'd know what to do in this situation. He'd have something to say to make it better.

"What always happens. Some elementals fought it out. And *we* paid the price." Bert's shoulders fell. He reached down and picked up a piece of wooden shrapnel from one of the nearby homes. She watched as tension built in him before, with a shout of rage, he hurled the piece of wood away from him. "This has to be stopped. *They* must be stopped. And it's clear that bitch Thorn had something to do with this."

Mirkon pointed to a corpse by one of the buildings. "I think that's Erreth, a fire elemental there."

"I'm betting someone didn't want to join her army." Gwen sighed. "What about your friends?" She was afraid to ask, but it was why they had come, after all.

Bert sat on the edge of the ruined fountain in the middle of town. It had once depicted a man in armor, but the upper half was now strewn about like a broken toy. "Likely dead. It wouldn't be like them to stand down. But if we're lucky, some ran for the woods and survived."

It felt dirty, using this as an opportunity. But there was one. She had always loved studying history, and nothing rallied the villagers of Boston together better than the perceived massacre of civilians. Running her hands through her hair, she shut her eyes. "We can use this to get more support. More people might be willing to join us if they know what happened here. We'll split up. Bert, Mirkon, Lina—travel wide and spread the word of this slaughter. I'll find Mordred on my own. We're going to lose too much time otherwise, and—and it's clear we don't have much, to begin with."

"You sure you can handle finding him?" Bert sounded wary. "Galahad and Zoe may be your friends for now, but when they learn what you're up to... they can be dangerous."

"I know. I'd like to think I can trust them, but I know you're right." It was hard to picture Zoe turning on anyone. "I'll fly there, so I can reach them faster." *If I can figure out how to fly without crashing and burning. Literally.* "We'll meet back at the keep. Mae will love having a whole army to feed." The thought would have made Gwen laugh if it hadn't been for the scene around her. Mae would have a fit. But she'd love the challenge.

"Or what's left of who we can rustle up. But, yes, ma'am." Bert stood. "I'll gather as many as I can. See? I knew you were a natural leader."

She shook her head. She didn't feel like one.

Eod barked.

"Sorry, puppo—I can't take you with me on this one." She knelt and scratched his ears. "You have to go with Bert."

"*Straw man smells funny.*"

"I know." She smiled and kept petting him. "But I have to go alone. I'll be back soon, I promise. And I'll have Dad with me." *Or neither of us will come back.* The thought of that broke her heart. Of Eod waiting for them. No, she had to make sure that didn't happen.

"*Okay.*" He licked her face, half-heartedly wagging his tail.

She didn't know what it said about her that she was going to fight to the death to make sure her dog wasn't sad, but there it was. "It'll only be for a few days, tops. I promise." She kissed his head. She unfurled her wings, glancing at them. "Now, I have to figure out how to use these things."

"I can't wait to see this." Bert brushed his gloves off on his overalls. "We'll meet back at the keep in two days. If you don't come back by then, we're coming to find you."

She didn't need to tell him how dangerous that would be. Nodding, she patted Eod on the head one last time before she realized she had forgotten one really important thing. "Do you have any idea where Zoe and Galahad *are*?"

Bert laughed at that, despite the tragedy. "There is a lake just south of the mountain, next to the glade that seems to always be blossoming with flowers. Look for a small house to the side of the lake."

"Lady of the Lake. Naturally." She rolled her eyes. "Thanks. I—I'll do what I can. Be safe."

"You as well."

Gwen stared at her wings for a moment again. Maybe a running start? She tried to remember how Tiny flew. He generally just... pushed off with his legs, flapped his wings, and off he went.

Running start it was.

Don't overthink it, Gwen. Don't overthink. Just let instinct take over. You have wings—they'll know what to do. Taking a deep breath, she figured it was now or never. She took off running away from her friends, and spreading her wings, beat them as hard as she could.

She jumped as she flapped her wings.

It wasn't a graceful takeoff.

Not by any stretch.

She could hear her friends laughing, but she didn't blame them. She probably looked like a baby seagull. A drunken baby seagull. But she was flying! It was a lot easier to stay aloft once she had some distance between her and the ground. The heat from the fires beneath her created an updraft that sent her circling higher.

She could hear Eod barking joyfully, and she resisted the urge to flip off her friends who were all clapping for her. It was well-meaning teasing.

I'm going to see them again. I'm going to. There's no option in the world where I don't. I will find Mordred and free him. And I will pet that dog again.

Priorities.

Whatever.

She circled higher and higher until she could no longer see her friends, and taking stock of where the sun was, she started off in that direction.

The sensation of it was unlike anything she'd ever experienced. She had flown that one time, but she'd been so terrified that she hadn't really had the chance to enjoy it.

Flying.

And it was glorious.

She could see dragons and gryphons circling around the mountain, specks against the blue sky. She wondered if they'd attack her—and she decided not to get close enough to find out.

This was freedom.

This was what she had wanted so desperately when she had been home on the farm. She laughed, the sound being pulled away by the wind as she soared.

It was amazing how much faster it was to travel by flying. The winding paths through the woods that snaked from village to city to town were like lines on a map as she looked down at them from overhead. A trip that'd take half a week through the thick woods might only take an hour or two now. She wondered how tiring it would be to go for that long. Right now, it felt effortless as she glided through the air, catching random updrafts or flapping her wings to gain more height.

The beauty of it all made her wish that Mordred was here to see her fly properly for the first time. She could almost imagine him on that enormous metal dragon, flying alongside her as she learned how to control her motion.

By the time she spotted the lake, she was certain at least a few hours had passed. She was getting tired, the ache in her wings reminiscent of how her feet felt after a long hike. Slowly, she started to circle lower.

A graceless takeoff was one thing.

A graceless landing was going to hurt.

She tried to remember everything she knew about planes. How they tilted up at the end to break their speed before touching down. Maybe she could just... flap really hard before she crashed into the earth. Land more like a helicopter than a plane.

It was around then that she realized she knew pretty much jack shit about planes and helicopters.

She saw the small hut, with its white plaster walls and thatched roof, as she descended from up above.

Don't fuck it up.

Don't fuck it up.

Don't fuck it up.

When her feet touched the ground, she staggered from the momentum. And promptly tripped over a rock. The taste of grass followed a second later, along with the accompanying pain.

"Owwww," she groaned.

Someone was laughing quietly. A deep laugh that sounded familiar. Lifting her head from the grass, she saw Galahad sitting atop a fallen log, watching her with a broad smile.

Pushing up to her knees, she brushed herself off. "Not funny."

"Very funny. You looked like a baby bird." He stood from the log and walked up to her, extending a hand down to her. He wasn't wearing his armor, only a plain linen shirt and dark brown trousers. He'd have looked normal if it weren't for his golden eyes.

She took his hand and let him help her up to her feet. She picked a piece of grass out of her hair. "I'm learning."

"And fast, by the looks of things. Was that your first flight?"

"More or less." She smiled faintly. "My first attempt at a landing, at any rate. The last time, a tree did all the work for me on that front."

"Well, I for one am proud of you." He patted her on the shoulder. "And I am grateful for your visit, though I worry about the reasons behind it." Turning, Galahad headed back to the log and sat on it, motioning to the spot next to him.

"Can't I be here to visit a friend?" She joined him on the log, glad to sit down.

"I am sure that is part of your motivation. But is it that, alone?"

"... No." She frowned, looking out at the lake. Dragonflies zipped along its blue-green surface, landing on cattails briefly, their wings like translucent gems. Fish shimmered beneath the water, their scales bright and silvery. "I'm sorry."

"You have much to contend with. I do not blame you. And the answer, I fear, is no. To your inevitable question." Galahad's voice grew firm at the end. He knew what she was coming for without her asking.

"I can't lose him, Galahad. I can't. Who knows what being in there will do to his mind? And if he's really your friend—" Her voice cracked.

"I spent well over a thousand years in Mordred's service, Gwendolyn. The feelings I hold for him are complicated. Please do not attempt to oversimplify them." He shut his eyes. "And do not assume that I am not grieving what will become of him."

"I'm sorry. But—but this doesn't have to happen." She twisted to face him. "Please, Galahad. I need to know where he is. I'm not asking you to do anything. Just tell me where the Crystal is. I'll take the blame. I'm not trying to get you involved."

"But you are. You are here, asking me to betray my people. To betray the laws of my kind. We sentenced him to this punishment, and you wish my aid to see that undone. Doing so puts us *all* at risk." He pulled his hands into fists in his lap.

"You're already at risk. Thorn is trying to take over. She's already torched one city—hundreds are dead, maybe more—because she's trying to browbeat them all into submission. I can't let this happen." Reaching out, she put her hand on his arm. "Please. I have to stop her. I have to protect the innocents here. And I need him to do it."

"And none of this is inspired by the fact that you love him?" Golden eyes met hers. There was sadness there—deep, fathomless sorrow. But also, a hardness that surprised her. "None of this is because you do not wish to endure another lonely night, wondering about the suffering of the one you love, trapped within such a terrible prison?"

Swallowing, she sat back, and pulled her hand from his arm. "What Mordred did to Zoe wasn't fair. What he did to everybody—but—this is a different situation."

"Is it?"

"He was *trying*—"

Galahad cut her off. "And so are we. This world is not his to rule. Squabbles amongst the elementals is... a fact of Avalon. That innocents suffer because of it is tragic. But what you ask for comes at a terrible cost." He stood, pacing away from her. She was struck again by how *long* he was. Long and tall. It was rare that somebody made Mordred seem short. "He will not rest until they are all dead this time. Others will take their place, and he will hunt them down all the same. It will be an endless slaughter."

"And that's different from what Thorn is doing *how* exactly?" Now, she was the one getting frustrated. "I can stop Mordred from going on a murder spree. You can help. He'll listen to us."

Galahad laughed, but it wasn't cruel. It was sad. Defeated. He ran a hand down his face slowly. "Oh, Gwendolyn. I am sorry. I cannot help you free him."

There was a finality to that, that took a second to sink in. Tears stung her eyes. She didn't bother begging. She didn't bother arguing. He wouldn't budge. "All right. I'll do it without you."

"Please, stay for dinner. Speak to Zoe and me about this. Let us explain why you must give up this quest of yours."

"No." She hated the idea of another long-ass flight right now. Her wings were already tired. But she couldn't stay here. "Thanks." Pushing up to her feet, she took a deep breath, and let it out. "Mordred loves you, you know. You're family to him."

"And he, to me." Galahad's shoulders fell. "It does not change my answer."

Nodding, she started running, and with a leap, took off into the air. She didn't want to talk to Zoe. She didn't want them to look at her with pity in their eyes, like she somehow was just a child and she didn't understand. Yeah, sure, that might be true —but she didn't want to deal with it.

The sun was setting, and it was getting late. She'd have to make camp in the woods for the night on her own. But she couldn't stay there with Galahad. She just couldn't.

It was all up to Mordred now. If he couldn't give her a hint of where the Iron Crystal had been hidden away... this plan to stop Thorn and save the villagers would be over before it began.

And the man she loved would be gone forever.

NINE

Mordred remembered the wonder he felt when he first set foot in Avalon. The magic that his mother had gifted him by her lineage sang within him in a way he had never heard before. It knew its own kind—it knew that Avalon was a place of power.

He wondered, now, so many centuries later, if that was why Avalon had chosen him over Arthur. Kin to kin, magic to magic, chaos to chaos. But it was only speculation.

The knights had trudged through the fog and mist for days before reaching the shore of a lake that he did not recognize, nor had he seen on any map. But Merlin had never led them astray in such matters. And there the wizard stood, waiting, leaning upon his gnarled wooden staff. A skiff sat in the water beside him, the still waters of the mirrorlike surface undisturbed by its presence. The figurehead was carved in the shape of a dragon, its eyes glowing a faint white that glimmered with shades of every color.

The silence in the air was deafening. There was no wind. No rustle of leaves or chirp of animals. Not even insects buzzed. It was as though this were a place somehow removed from reality, separate from all that they knew.

There would be no going back.

What waited for them on the other side, he had not known at the time. But in his heart, he was certain of the fact that this was, one way or another, a journey from which he would not return. The duty remained, however. The king lay dying, and only the magic of the isle of Avalon could save him.

What choice did he have?

He had sworn an oath.

They carefully lifted Arthur's stretcher into the skiff. It barely moved with their weight as they clambered in, as gracefully as they could in their armor. Merlin was the last to board, his face set in grim determination.

Mordred always wondered if he knew what was to follow. If he had a vision of the future and could see with certainty that Arthur was already doomed. If he could have but told Mordred to stay behind—to change his path forward.

If such things were even possible.

Wondering whether or not his fate could have been rewritten was pointless. Such backward gazing did no good to change the path ahead. He climbed aboard that skiff. It set away from the world as he knew it. And when the mist broke, the beauty before him had taken his breath away.

Such *color*. Such wonder. Creatures the likes of which he had never seen nor even dreamed of. Bizarre and wonderful, strange and fantastical. Only Galahad seemed unimpressed— but as he was Seelie, Mordred knew the fae knight was far more accustomed to such things than the others.

Their march had not yet ended.

Merlin led the way through the woods. None of them dared question the wizard as to where they were headed. Arthur's fever was slowly worsening. They did not whisper of the possibility of the king's demise. Such things were unheard of. Unthinkable. Impossible.

He was the King of the Britons. The rightful ruler of them

all. The world would be lost without him. It was as the sun turned the sky ambers and reds when it set toward the horizon that they finally stopped to make camp.

Mordred was the one on watch when the elementals arrived, though he had not known them by such a name at the time.

She drifted into camp like a wisp upon the wind, her butterfly wings shimmering in the firelight as she approached from the darkness, a bundle of gifts in her hands. Herbs. Food. Medicines.

When she approached Arthur, Mordred gripped the hilt of his sword. Galahad was the one who stopped him from drawing it, the fae placing his hand on Mordred's arm to give him pause. Mordred had not missed the expression of awe on the other knight's face, though at the time he had not been able to name it for what it was.

Wordlessly, the woman he would come to know as the Gossamer Lady placed the gifts on the ground next to King Arthur, bowing her head in reverence to the dying man.

Others came then. Beings made of fire. Of ice. Of water. Of the trees. Of the very air itself. Men and women and all else that seemed to be born of the very marrow of the world around them.

One by one, in a procession, bringing gifts of their own. It was not until the last visitor had placed their gifts that the Gossamer Lady spoke, her hands clutched over her heart.

"Long have we waited for the King of Avalon to come." Her soft words carried through the air like the caress of a spring breeze. "Long will he reign, and long will we serve." She bowed her head. "Noble King Arthur, we welcome you."

Each of the elementals bowed before retreating into the darkness. It was only as the last one disappeared into the shadows of the woods that Mordred allowed himself to exhale the breath he had been holding perhaps the entire time they had been present.

The sense of hope was palpable. If the denizens of Avalon knew of their coming, Arthur *must* be destined to live. There was laughter amongst the knights for the first time since the Battle of Camlann as they shared in the bounty of the gifts.

Only Mordred stayed at his post by the king's side, keeping guard while he watched the others banter and tease each other.

"You were always the outsider. Always different."

This conversation had not happened. "Yes," Mordred said. "You needn't remind me."

"You *knew* you were different. And they could sense it." Arthur's voice was thin and strained. "Sense in you the river of darkness that runs so deep in your soul."

"This conversation is merely a figment of my shattering mind. This is not *real*. Your opinions do not matter." Mordred rolled his eyes. "Please stop disgracing the memory of the man who would never have wished me to become a rampaging beast."

"When did I tell you to become the feral wolf?" The king sighed. "You are not listening to me."

"*You are not here!*" Mordred fought the urge to punch the vision of his uncle to death. His shout of rage did nothing to alert the other knights who still chattered and told each other stories the way they had on that fateful night.

The night that his life had taken such a terrible turn.

The night that Arthur had died.

"Perhaps. Perhaps you are talking to yourself. Or, perhaps you are not. Either way, there is wisdom in listening to one's heart, do you not agree?" Arthur turned his head to watch the other knights. "I gave you Caliburn and my crown in hopes you would do what they could not."

"Murder."

"No. What needed to be done. What *needs* to be done still to this day."

Mordred curled his knuckles and rubbed his temples with them; using his clawed fingertips would certainly add to his headache, not relieve it. "This is farcical. If I must relive these dreadful memories, must you provide commentary? Though, I suppose I only have myself to blame if you are a figment of my own soul."

"That is precisely what I am attempting to tell you—repeating the mistakes of the past will get you nowhere new, Mordred. If Gwendolyn frees you—*when* she frees you—what will you do? Act in self-defense alone as the elementals unite against you? Raise your head up high and pretend to be the noble king you were never meant to be?"

"I have given up on such foolhardy hopes."

"Then why do you still act as if you have not?" Arthur grunted in frustration. "You muzzle your wrath. They should *fear* you."

"They do."

"But not enough. You present to them a foe that can be challenged. A wall that can be breached. There is another way forward. A way that embraces your true nature. Your true self." Arthur reached out a hand and weakly placed it upon Mordred's wrist. "The wrath in the shadows. The fear of what will come when they disobey."

He grimaced. "You would have me become some fairytale boggart? The whispers that are told to children to ensure they eat their vegetables? Now, you insult me."

"If you had ever met a boggart, you would know they are far more than myth." Arthur let his hand fall back into his lap. "She needs you. And she needs you to be your true self. For she cannot walk the path you are meant to tread."

Mordred felt his jaw tick. To that, he had no answer. To that, he had no riposte.

For Gwendolyn, he would do anything.

Become anyone.

And destroy the world if he must.

For her.

He shut his eyes. "I am remiss in my duties. I promised her I would seek to find a hint to where they have hidden the Crystal. If I am to become this wrath in the darkness that you entreat me to become, I cannot do so languishing inside a prison of my own madness."

"Now you are finally speaking sense, boy." Arthur struggled to sit up but was too weak to do so. "Perhaps I can be of some assistance."

Mordred resisted the urge to help him. "Finally, you may prove to have an actual purpose."

"Now, now. I am not the truth you must face. I am not the one blocking the path to your freedom. There is another you must confront for such things."

Fantastic. "Who?"

Arthur laughed as the memory faded away. "*You know who.*"

Yes. He supposed he did.

* * *

Gwen decided that the ability to magically fashion herself *things* was really coming in handy. It made the idea of camping under the stars with no supplies more palatable than sleeping on the dirt in her clothes. She could at least create enough fabric to make a bedroll and some blankets. Starting a campfire was the easiest part, for obvious reasons.

She snuggled into the makeshift pillow and watched the fire dance. She missed having someone to talk to. Or Eod to snuggle with. It was... strange, being on her own. She hoped everyone was okay. She hoped all of Bert's friends survived, though she knew that was highly unlikely.

Rolling onto her back, she gazed up at the stars overhead. They weren't the stars from home, not that she was expecting them to be. Avalon was a world between worlds, after all—a junction between other realities. She wondered how many there were. Probably countless universes, filled with strange and fascinating people and monsters. She wondered if that's what Avalon's stars were—all those worlds.

It made her feel a little less alone, strangely. Watching them watching her, twinkling high above. Taking a deep breath, she let it out, and reached her hand up toward them. She didn't know why. She didn't even know what she was after.

Letting her hand fall back down after a moment, she rolled onto her side and snuggled into the pseudo-pillow again. When she dreamed, she would be with Mordred. Or what was left of him, at any rate. The thought of it encouraged her to take a deep breath and try her best to fall asleep. And not long after, she was.

For better or worse.

She didn't need to ask what memory she had popped into. She could guess, judging by the shouting. Judging by the knights standing off against Mordred.

"Traitor!"

"Murderer!"

"Usurper!"

Even Galahad stood with his sword raised, ready to attack.

Mordred was on one knee, tears streaking down his cheeks, staring down at his palms which were now covered in iron with those twisted, cruel, and jagged claws. King Arthur lay on the cot behind him, eyes open and sightlessly staring at the night sky. At the same stars she had just been contemplating.

He was dead.

Mordred had become an elemental.

And the knights sought to kill him for it.

"I did—I did nothing—this is not my fault!" he shouted at the other knights, his voice cracking in his grief. "I do not know what has transpired, my brothers, *please*—"

Lancelot stepped forward. "You killed him. This place was clearly meant to choose him, and would have, had you not murdered him first!"

"I did not—he died of the fever—" Mordred pushed himself up to his feet, grief and rage now mixing on his features in equal measure. "I am no usurper! He is my uncle, my family. He was going to leave his crown to me, why would I hurry to have him dead?"

"He left his crown to *you?*" Lancelot sneered. "Liar. Thief. Usurper. He would have *never* chosen you over any of us. Your blood is cursed, your mother saw to that when she seduced Arthur!"

Mordred snarled, his hands clenching into fists. "I will have your slanderous tongue."

"Come and take it. I have long awaited the chance to make you eat my blade, *bastard.*" Lancelot laughed.

"Enough." Galahad stepped in between Lancelot and Mordred. "Our king is dead. Our brother has become..." Galahad's jaw twitched. "Something else entirely. I recommend we rest and grieve, and deal with this in the morning when cooler heads might prevail."

"You mean to make camp with this—this—" Lancelot paced away, incensed. "I will not break bread with him."

"Then do not. I do not care." Galahad shook his head. "The truth of the matter is, we do not know what has happened." He turned his gaze mournfully to the dead king. "And I have no taste for bloodshed."

Lancelot spat on the ground and paced farther away, slumping down on a rock by the edge of the clearing. The others dispersed. All save Mordred and Galahad.

Galahad said nothing, simply stared at Mordred for a pregnant pause before shaking his head and turning away in clear disappointment.

"They will wait until I am asleep," Mordred said, addressing Gwen for the first time. His tears were dry, but it was clear his anger and sorrow remained. "They will plot to slit my throat. You know what happens next."

"Y... yeah, I do." She walked up to him, almost afraid to approach. But he wouldn't hurt her. That much she was certain of. Reaching out, she hugged him, pulling him close and letting him bury his head in the crook of her shoulder. He clutched her to him like she was a lifeline. Or a raft in a terrible ocean storm.

Maybe she was.

"I know what I must become to be free," he murmured, barely audible.

Furrowing her brow, she pulled back to meet his rusty-colored gaze. "What do you mean?"

The smile he wore was weary, but there was affection in his eyes. More than affection—love. He stroked her cheek with the back of his knuckle. "I will leave the decision to you, my lady. Would you still love me, come what may?"

"I—yeah, but—I—I don't know what you're asking me." Nervousness began to prick at her. "What are you saying, Mordred?"

"I know now what must be done. What I must do to save Avalon from itself." There was a look in his eyes then, a darkness she had only seen a few times. It sent a shiver of fear down her spine, and if she was being honest with herself, attraction. "Can you love me as a monster? For if you cannot, I would rather languish here in this cage until there is nothing of me left to rescue."

The idea of him surrendering twisted something in her gut. "I love you, Mordred. I love you for who you are—not in spite of it. You can't give up. I *need* you. I can't do this alone. I can't—I don't want to do this without you."

He smiled. And his expression was not altogether kind. "That is all I needed to hear. Come. Let us discover what we can together." He held his hand out to her, palm up. Those claws of his never ceased to be intimidating, even if she knew how gentle he could be with them when he wanted to.

This was a mistake.

This was a big fucking mistake.

Swallowing the rock in her throat, she put her hand in his.

But she loved him.

And in the end, that was all there was to it.

TEN

Galahad donned his armor and summoned his golden dragon. He had wished never to do so again in his remaining years. But fate had other designs for him, it seemed.

Zoe stood by the door to her home, leaning against the jamb, concern etched on her delicate features. "Why must you go?"

"She is searching for Mordred. I must ensure she does not free him." Letting out a breath, he turned back to the house and decided he wished for another kiss goodbye.

"You assume she will find him. And you assume she has the means of destroying the Crystal." Zoe shook her head. "You have proof of neither. Why are you so concerned?"

"If there is one thing I have learned about Lady Gwendolyn, it is that the impossible seems to follow her wherever she goes." He leaned down to kiss the Gossamer Lady.

She met his embrace, her hands resting upon the golden armor that covered his chest. "I hope you are wrong."

"As am I. But I cannot take that chance. None of us can. If he is set free... I loathe to imagine what will follow. None of us will be safe." Summoning his helmet, he turned back to his dragon. It glimmered in the setting sun, all shades of gold, amber, red, and yellow. The beast was restless, his claws digging into the dirt.

"In that, I fear I must agree with you." It was Zoe's turn to let out a weary sigh. "But she is a smart young woman. Empathetic to those around her. She will listen to reason."

"She is also fighting to save the man she loves." Galahad climbed atop his dragon, settling into the ridges on the animal's back. "Which is what worries me."

Zoe could not argue with him on that front. She simply nodded, and waved farewell as he kicked his dragon, spurring the animal into action. It was eager to go, leaping from the ground and taking off into the sky with a heavy beat of its metallic wings.

Galahad knew what it was like to be separated from his true love. How many times had he sat up at night, exhausted but unable to sleep, wishing for his Gossamer Lady?

How many times had his mind and his heart dueled for supremacy? One begging him to kill Mordred and free his lady love, the other half reminding him that he had sworn an oath to the Prince in Iron.

Never mind the curse that kept him obedient.

He had never reached a conclusion, so the matter had never been tested, unlike Lancelot.

But in his weaker moments, he had come close to attempting to kill Mordred, if it meant a chance to see his Zoe again. In the darkest moments of the night, the answer seemed so simple. But in the clear light of day, the certainty had always fallen away.

Gwendolyn was under no such oath. She was a woman of honor but had no code to guide her. She was also far younger and perhaps found it hard to believe the horrors and atrocities Mordred was capable of performing.

She was also a witch. The extent of her powers was likely unclear even to her, let alone the rest of them.

No.

She was dangerous.

She would have to be convinced.

And if he could not convince her? She would have to be stopped.

At all costs.

* * *

Gwen didn't know where Mordred was taking them. These were his dreams—and while before he hadn't seemed to have any control over them, something about that seemed to have changed. The world melted away from them as the scenery shifted. They were no longer in the woods, surrounded by trees and Arthur's knights. They were standing inside the ruins of Camelot.

"Somewhere familiar. Somewhere without distractions. We will both need to focus, for this to work." Mordred turned to her, and she watched as his armor melted away, his gauntlets dissipating. Palms up, he asked for her hands.

She didn't hesitate. It was so strange to feel his skin against hers. She was getting so used to the metal. "Mind clueing me in on what we're doing?"

"I am trapped within the Crystal. But you are in the waking world. You are my link—my tether. I can use your awareness of Avalon to see outside my prison." He grasped her hands and gently pulled her closer. "In theory."

"In theory." She arched an eyebrow.

"This is uncharted territory, my love." He smirked. "I am doing my best. If you have another suggestion, I would be glad to hear it."

No, she was out of ideas. Especially since Galahad had refused to tell her where the Iron Crystal was. Letting out a grunt, she shrugged. "Fine. Let's try it. Worst-case, we stand here like a pair of morons."

"Precisely." He rested his forehead against hers and shut his eyes. She did the same. "I want you to focus on remembering your surroundings, the place where you fell asleep. Picture yourself there. Wake up, just a little—just enough, so that you are in both places at once. I can—"

"Stop."

The unexpected voice cut Mordred off. Only, it was a voice that Gwen recognized.

She blinked in surprise, turning to face the newcomer.

It was Mordred.

Another Mordred. Not the one standing next to her, in his horrifying iron armor. This one was *human*. His hair wasn't iron, but blond. His eyes were green, not shades of molten rust. And his armor looked similar in style to King Arthur's. He held Caliburn in his hand, head held high. "You will stop here, fiend."

"What the *actual* fuck—" Gwen's eyes went wide.

Her Mordred chuckled darkly. "Yes, I had supposed this might be the final test." He took a step forward, summoning his own blade. It was in stark contrast to Caliburn's beauty and simple, clean lines. It was jagged and rusted like the rest of Mordred, the sections of the blade that were missing only making it look all the more dangerous. No, not dangerous— *fiendish*.

The human Mordred met the elemental's challenge and prepared for a fight. "You shall die here, monster. I will not allow you to spread your plague upon Avalon any longer."

"Hold the *fuck* up—" Gwen stormed in between the two men. "Will one of you explain what's going on?"

The human Mordred was the one who spoke first. "There is still goodness within him. Within *me*. There is honor and duty.

There is a part of my conscience that clings to the promises I made to Arthur so long ago."

The iron Mordred scoffed. "And if I am to be free—then I must kill the part of me that clings to the path that I mistakenly sought for so many centuries. If I am to set foot outside the Iron Crystal, I must surrender entirely the man I once was."

"But... why?" She furrowed her brow.

"Because only then will I be capable of doing what is required..." The iron Mordred shifted his gaze to her. "To protect you."

"No, no—this isn't about me. This isn't, this—"

The human Mordred interrupted her. It seemed he liked to do that. "You are correct, in part. No, this is not about you. This is about killing the corruption that has spread in me. If you free *him*, the bloodshed will be unlike anything Avalon has ever known. I deserve to die in here, in this prison."

His iron half laughed cruelly. "What a coward I have been. The answer has been in front of me for so long. I tried my best to find a middle ground, to negotiate a truce in my own heart. Imprisonment was better than death, surely. Yet when the seasons stopped and the clouds covered the sun, and the world lost its color, I still somehow believed my actions to be *just*. Please." He took a few steps to the side, circling his human self. The blond Mordred swiveled to watch him. Gwen had the option of jumping in the middle again and stopping the fight, but something told her it wouldn't matter. This fight was coming, one way or another. It had been coming for a very long time.

And everything depended on who won.

"If I am freed, they all must die. They will come for us. They will *never* let us rest. They will hound us until the end of time, or until we both lie dead." The elemental shifted his grip on his sword. "To be free, I must embrace the darkness in my heart."

"Which is precisely why I must stay here and perish. My soul depends upon it. That kind of slaughter is beyond cruel. Better I die." Human Mordred raised Caliburn, readying for the fight that was about to begin.

The sound of steel on steel followed. It was... so bizarre, watching Mordred fight with himself. Both figures moved identically. They had identical strengths, identical weaknesses. Good versus evil. Duty versus love. Soul versus heart.

Gwen didn't know who she wanted to win.

Both of them, honestly.

But that time was long gone. That wasn't an option. It was clear this was a fight to the death. The ringing of the metal was deafening as the swords clashed. Blade met armor. Fist met face. Neither side was winning. Neither side was losing.

She wanted to cry. She wanted to scream. She wanted to use her magic to stop the battle—but she had no power here. All she could do was watch and avoid getting crashed into.

A chair wasn't so lucky, as the human Mordred threw his iron self through the furniture, smashing it into tiny pieces as the weight of the enormous knight turned it to kindling and splinters. The Prince in Iron rolled onto his side, spitting blood onto the ground. He didn't get up.

The human Mordred wiped some blood from his split lip. "You can stop this, Gwen. You can make this choice for me."

"I—I can't—" She shook her head. "I can't tell you to... to go on a murderous rampage, and I can't tell you to stay in here and die. I love you. Both of you—all of you." She bit back tears again, her voice cracking from the effort of it.

"And you need me." The Prince in Iron watched her keenly from where he still lay on the floor. "Can you really watch as I dissolve in here, consumed by my own mind?"

She wavered. "No."

"Can you condemn all the elementals to a certain death?" his human half countered.

Shutting her eyes, she wanted to scream. "No."

"It's all right, Gwendolyn. I am going to win this fight." The knight walked up to her, the echo of his footsteps on the stone walls surrounding her. She couldn't look. But when he placed his fingertips to her jawline, gentle and sweet, he tilted her head up to him. There was such love in his eyes, such kindness. This was the man he had once been, long ago. "And you will be all right. You and I can dream together. It will be a slow, painless death. And after that, you may dream of me whenever you like."

"But—it wouldn't be real."

"I will always be with you. One way or another. Because I love you. And I will always be in your heart and in your mind, even after I am gone. You must let me go, Gwendolyn. Please."

When she went to protest, Mordred's human half kissed her. It was filled with so much love, so much kindness, she finally lost her fight with her tears.

Could she really say goodbye?

Could she really let Mordred die?

The human Mordred lurched in front of her. She blinked in confusion, and pulled her head back to see what was wrong.

Four tips of clawed fingers jutted from the knight's throat. The iron Mordred had snuck up on him from the back... and rammed his fingers straight through his human counterpart's neck.

Blood began to run from the gashes and disappeared underneath the knight's armor.

Gwen gasped and staggered backwards.

The elemental ripped his claws from the knight's throat. The blond Mordred collapsed to the ground in a heap. His green eyes glassy and empty. Dead.

"To think I was ever such a fool." Mordred flicked his hand, sending bits of gore to the stone beside him. He cracked his neck to one side and then to the other. "Well. Now that is concluded, shall we pick up where we left off?" He smiled at her, a devious flicker to his eyes. "There is nothing to stop us now, my love." He reached his hand out for her.

This was all her fault.

And she'd come too far to stop now. Mordred had done this because of her. He was becoming this monster *for* her. She couldn't turn her back on him. She couldn't reject her love for him. Squeezing her eyes shut for a moment, sending a new line of tears down her cheeks, she took a deep breath and steeled herself.

"I am as I ever was. Only now, I am no longer split by indecision. No part of me has died today, my lady."

"Tell that to the guy on the floor." She gestured aimlessly at the corpse.

"He was not real. Simply another figment of my tortured mind." Mordred stepped over his own fallen self to pull her into an embrace. "This was merely... a rather spectacular internal debate."

Maybe. Or, maybe it was something more. She didn't fight him, but rested her cheek against his chest, feeling the ridges of the twisting vine artwork that covered his jagged armor. He stroked her hair gently. "I need you to wake up, just enough to allow me to follow. Describe to me where you fell asleep."

"In a clearing by a fire. I made a bedroll out of some fabric I summoned using my magic. I don't know what I'm capable of yet." She shut her eyes again, trying to recall all the details.

"I look forward to helping you find out," he murmured, his voice a low rumble that she felt just as much as she heard.

"I fell asleep watching the stars. They're so different to the ones from home, but they're just as beautiful." She pictured them, flickering high above. She could feel the ground beneath her, the lumps in the grass and the one rock she'd managed to miss, which was digging into her thigh. The fire had died and was now just flickering embers.

Mordred was quiet for a long moment. "I am somewhere I

cannot see the stars. I am deep under the ground. I am... submerged." His voice sounded far away and dreamy. "I—" He stopped suddenly, and barked a laugh that jolted her out of her half-awake state and back into the dream.

He let go of her to turn toward the ruins of Camelot. "Of course!" He laughed hard as if someone had just played a brilliant prank on him. "Of *course!* How could I not see it before?"

"I—Mordred?" She swallowed a lump in her throat. Had the rest of his mind shattered?

"I have been trying to tell myself where I am this entire time. I have known it, somewhere, buried deep." He sighed and stared up at the broken beams overhead. "I truly am an idiot. Where else would they hide me? Where else would Galahad send me? To Camelot, of course." He turned toward her and closed the distance between them in a split second. He placed his palm to her cheek, the metal of his claws resting against her skin. His expression was so intense it scared her. "There is a lake, deep beneath the castle ruins. I am there. The entrance is in the tomb. Come find me. Come set me free. And then nothing and no one will ever stand between us again."

He kissed her, his mouth so insatiable and needy that it left her stunned. So wild that it shattered her dream entirely and she woke to find it was early morning, the sun just starting to peek through the trees, the birds around her singing their songs, blissfully unaware of what she'd been through.

She rolled onto her side once more in the clearing. Her head was swimming. She felt woozy, like she'd been drinking all night. Slowly but surely, the world stopped wheeling and she could breathe without fearing she was going to throw up.

Could she set the monster free?

Could she turn her back on the man she loved?

This time, she knew she'd have to make a choice.

And there would be no going back.

ELEVEN

Gwen decided she was going to take a long, long walk. Partly because she needed a clearing or stretch of road where she could take off from, partly because she was *freezing*, but also because she needed to think.

She had woken up shivering. It was the time of year in later fall where during the day, the sun kept everything wonderfully cozy and warm, but once the sun set, things became surprisingly cold.

It certainly didn't help her mood. She had known that Mordred was likely to kill anyone who came after them after she freed him from the Crystal—that had never been in question. But she didn't think he was going to go full killer psychopath on her either. She thought she could temper him. Convince him *not* to murder all the elementals for the sake of it.

Now, she wasn't so sure.

A tiny part of her said maybe murdering the elementals wasn't such a bad idea. They were dangerous, slaughtering villagers and innocent, defenseless people without a second thought. They treated the "normal" folk of Avalon like they were nothing more than insects.

But they're not all like that. Just a shitty few, stirring every-thing up. It doesn't mean they all deserve to die. Letting out a groan of frustration, she ran her hands through her hair, tugging on the strands.

Mordred was bent on revenge. Not just against Thorn but against *everyone*. If—when—Mordred went on a murderous rampage, she had promised to kill him before that'd happen.

Could she?

Sure, she'd promised to.

But if it came down to it... could she *really?*

Mordred would likely not bother the villagers at least. They weren't a threat to him, and he seemed as keen on protecting them as she was. But the ongoing slaughter of elementals, both the ones currently in Avalon and all the ones to follow—really, *really* didn't sit right with her. They weren't all bad. Galahad was an elemental. So was Zoe.

Thorn could fuck right off, but whatever.

There were other nice ones out there. She just hadn't had a chance to meet them. It didn't help that they were terrified of Mordred, and she was his... what was she, anyway? Girlfriend? Lover? De facto fiancée? It didn't matter.

She needed to talk to Bert. To get his advice. But there wasn't time. The longer she left Mordred in that Crystal, the more his sanity was going to crack, and the more damage Thorn was going to cause with her half-assed play for the throne.

Rounding a bend in the path, she saw a clearing up ahead, large enough that she could get a running start to take flight. But as she drew closer, she saw she wasn't alone.

"Hi, Zoe." Gwen slowed her steps. She didn't trust the Gossamer Lady. Especially with her appearing out of nowhere like this. "What's up?"

Zoe stood up from the rock she had been sitting on, twisting her hands in front of her nervously. "I came to speak with you."

Gwen didn't bother asking how the Gossamer Lady found

her. Letting out a heavy sigh, she rubbed her temple with her fingers. "You're here to talk me out of freeing Mordred."

"I am here to stop you, if I must."

Oh, good. Good. "I don't want to fight you, Zoe." She dropped her hand to her side. "Please, can we not do this?"

Zoe frowned as she stepped closer. "Neither do I wish to fight you, my friend. But I cannot allow you to free the Prince in Iron. The devastation he will bring... this cannot come to pass."

"Yeah. I know. But I can't leave him in there to slowly die either. Besides, you want to talk devastation? Have you seen what Thorn's already done? She and her goons destroyed a city. I don't even know how many villagers died." Gwen shrugged out of her coat. If she was going to get into a brawl, the last thing she wanted was to burn it to bits after she had spent so much time stitching the slits up the back. Sure, she could summon another one, but she was still getting the hang of it. And it tired her out, to boot.

"I mourn their loss. Truly I do. But there will be another chance to stop Thorn that does not involve freeing such a monster." Zoe sounded sincere. She clasped her hands in front of her heart. "Please, Gwendolyn—please break from this path you walk."

"You mourn the loss of those who died, but you won't do anything to stop it, will you? If I asked for your help in stopping Thorn instead of Mordred, would you get involved?" Gwen was getting really sick of everybody's games. And while she'd like to think of Zoe as a friend, after she cast Mordred into the Crystal... she wasn't so sure.

"I—I fear I must remain neutral in that matter." Zoe shook her head.

"But you'll interfere here by trying to stop me. You're fine with a bunch of villagers getting slaughtered while Thorn makes a play for power, but you don't want me to stop Mordred because *elementals* might die?"

"It is not 'might,' Gwendolyn. We will all die. Galahad. Myself. Many others." Zoe fluttered her wings, floating a few feet closer. "And you are at peace with this?"

"I don't want anybody to die!" Gwen felt the fire erupt around her, setting her ablaze. *See you later, clothing.* She'd make herself more before she flew off. The last thing she wanted to do was fly over Avalon butt-ass naked, although it'd make for a hysterical show. "I haven't wanted anybody to die since I got here, but nobody listens to me. Lancelot didn't have to die. Neither did Grinn. But here we are. I can't step over the bodies of hundreds of innocent souls because you want to protect the twenty or thirty elementals who *aren't* assholes, I'm sorry."

"And none of this has anything to do with the fact that you are in love with Mordred?" Zoe's lips turned into a small sneer, her first expression of derision. If Gwen wasn't mistaken, her normally magenta-pink eyes were slowly turning black.

Great.

Just great.

"Of course it has something to do with it. If Galahad were locked away, losing his mind, you'd try to free him too." Before Zoe could counter, Gwen cut her off again. "I know! I know. I know they're different men. I get it. But I'm going to go free him, Zoe. I'm sorry."

"It seems Thorn is not the only one with designs on the throne." There was a strange undercurrent to Zoe's voice. Like a rumble, almost, undercutting her normally sweet and wistful tone.

"I don't want the throne. I don't want anything except to live in peace in the keep with Mordred, and to know that people aren't dying in the streets because of a turf war between over-powered morons." Gwen clenched her hands into fists at her sides.

"You sweet, naive child. You are at the same crossroads that

Mordred found himself so long ago. When peace cannot be found, will you accept the blood on your hands?" The grass around Zoe began to shift and change, turning black and curling over as if from a blight. It circled her, slowly growing larger, spreading out like veins through the plant life.

"I can deal with Mordred."

"You do not sound so sure."

"That's *my* fucking problem, not yours." Gwen gestured her hand. For a moment, she didn't know why. But when she was suddenly holding a sword made of fire, she let out a small *huh* of surprise. Cool. She could summon fire weapons. Neat.

"Charming that you maintained some of your connection to the flame. It will not help you." Zoe sighed. "Standing against me is pointless. If you were to free Mordred, I would be forced to destroy him." Zoe picked up the end of the necklace she wore —the iron shard. The one that Mordred had made, with the power to hurt him. "History will merely repeat."

"Not if I take that thing off of you."

"I believe you will try. And I believe I will be forced to kill you if you do. You do not even know the extent of your own gifts. You are young, Gwendolyn. Put all this tragedy behind you. Think no more of Mordred and look toward the future. When Thorn falls, I will—" Zoe stopped.

Gwen took a step back, more out of surprise than anything else. "Oh. *Oooooh...* I get it. You plan on letting Thorn duke it out, probably die, and then *you* will take the throne of Avalon." Laughing, she shook her head. "Wow."

"It is mine by right. It was mine long ago. Before *he* came. Before the human Arthur arrived and I was forced to surrender it." Zoe bared her teeth in a grimace. "I am Avalon. I am its true ruler. I have been patient—I have waited—I have been graceful and kind. I will not go to war to seize it. But when all lies defeated, I will reclaim my crown."

There was no talking her way out of this one. "I fucking

hate politics," Gwen muttered under her breath. "Give me that necklace and I'll be on my way. We don't have to fight."

"You are going nowhere, Gwendolyn. Neither shall you have this necklace." Zoe lifted her chin in defiance. "Swear to me you will not seek to free him, and you will live. Give me your word."

"You aren't getting it."

"Then I fear there is no way around this."

Tilting her head to one side and then the other, Gwen cracked her neck. She was still sore from sleeping on the rough ground. "Awesome. Let's go."

Sparring with Mordred was nothing like fighting with Zoe. Fighting Mordred was like fighting a tank with legs. Unstoppable, but in *one* place at a time. Zoe, however, was like fighting a ghost. The woman blinked in and out of existence. Every time Gwen jumped forward with a slash of her sword or threw a fireball at her, the butterfly-winged woman disappeared.

But Zoe wasn't playing full defense either. Gwen yelped as something stung her arm. A thin black object, as skinny as a needle, had gone through her fire and dug into her bicep. Hissing in pain, she yanked it out, and watched it crack and burn like a wood splinter.

Snarling, Gwen gritted her teeth, and her fire changed colors—burning hotter. "Try that again, bitch."

Zoe did. This time, the vicious splinters of wood incinerated before they reached her. Zoe's now-black eyes went a little wider.

Gwen launched herself at Zoe, swinging her sword, but only met empty air. It was pointless trying to fight her like that. She had to try something else. But what?

Something struck her again, this time harder, knocking her forward and to the ground. It was a blast of some kind of energy. It didn't really matter what, she supposed. It shimmered as it disappeared into the air like smoke. But it had hit her hard enough to put stars in her vision.

Flapping her wings, Gwen dodged another strike right before it hit her. The force of the impact cracked into a tree next to the clearing, sending bark and a broken branch to the ground.

A third strike felt like a Mack Truck, sending her flying, impacting into another tree. She felt something pop in her spine as she impacted the surface. When she hit the dirt, she had to check to make sure she could still wiggle her toes and her fingers. Fuck, that had *hurt*. Another blow, and she'd be down for the count.

Zoe was hovering above the devastation, watching her with cold disdain. "I am as old as this island, Gwendolyn Wright. You cannot defeat me. You do not belong here. Stop this now, and I will let you live. Surrender."

"This island chose me, Zoe. I spoke to it. It told me this was home—it gave me this magic." Gwen struggled to get back to her feet, pain lancing up her legs. It felt like she had been run over. "I belong here. Same as you." She walked closer to Zoe, stalling for time while she caught her breath. "And I am not going to surrender. Not to you."

"A shame you think so." Zoe lifted her hands, and the circle of darkness around her grew. "I will make your death quick and painless." There was a surge of something that tasted acrid in the air. Like ozone. Gwen felt dizzy all of a sudden. "I am the elemental of life, Gwendolyn. And while I can gift it... I can also take it away."

Fuck.

That's what those blasts were.

Death. Or rather, the absence of life.

One more hit, and she was done. That was it. She'd have failed.

Mordred.

Her friends.

But it was, stupidly enough, the image of Eod sitting by the front steps of the keep, staring out at the field, waiting for her to come home, that did it. Tears stung her eyes. Not of grief. But of *rage*.

"*Enough!*" Gwen screamed.

And fire erupted around her. The air sparked and roared, and Zoe screamed as the wave of fire engulfed her without warning. The whole clearing was ablaze like a bomb had been dropped. And there, in the grass, was Zoe. Her wings were charred, and her skin was blackened in spots.

Falling to her knees, Gwendolyn let out a wavering breath. It took all her control to put the trees out—the last thing she needed was to start a forest fire. Black smoke rose into the air, and the sound of the explosion echoed around her.

Zoe coughed. She was alive. Injured, but alive.

Gwen could kill her. *Should* kill her.

Climbing back to her feet, she took a deep breath and let it out, extinguishing her fire. With a gesture of her hand, she summoned new clothes. Black slacks and a red halterneck top. She hadn't quite mastered the art of shoes yet. But it'd do for now. The embers underneath her bare feet didn't hurt at all as she walked up to the fallen butterfly. Her coat had been trashed in the explosion. Damn it. Whatever.

Reaching down, Gwen grasped the shard and twisted the chain of Zoe's necklace around her hand. One quick yank, and the thin links of gold snapped. "Yoink."

"Go ahead," Zoe murmured, her voice weak and broken. "Kill me."

"No." Gwen shook her head. "Go home, Zoe. We're done here." She looked off into the woods. The trees were still smoking, but the fire had stopped. "I kind of have to thank you, though." She smiled half-heartedly. "I was almost going to walk away from all this until you showed up. Thanks for helping me make up my mind."

"I will not stop." Zoe coughed.

"And neither will I." She sighed. "But I still won't kill you."

"Why...?"

"Two reasons. One? I'm sick of all the dying. And two?" She paused. "Galahad is my friend. I adore him. And I can't take you away from him. Even if you do deserve it." Before Zoe could respond, Gwen ran in the other direction, spreading her wings and taking off into the sky. She was getting the hang of it.

Killing Zoe would have been the smart move. But her heart told her it was wrong. Her heart was also telling her something else—

Galahad was going to be waiting for her at Camelot.

And that was a fight she *really* didn't know if she could win.

TWELVE

Galahad made his way to the gates of Camelot, certain that Gwendolyn would not be long. As he arrived, however, he already had an unexpected guest. Furrowing his brow, he found himself staring at Mordred's iron steed.

"What are *you* doing here?"

It snorted and stomped its hoof, as disagreeable as ever.

No matter. Shaking his head, Galahad took his post by the door. He did not have to wait long. Only a few hours at most. He watched the speck in the sky grow larger. It was smaller than a dragon, but bigger than a bird. And as the sunlight caught the red of dragon's wings, he knew who it was. He sighed. He would keep his sword sheathed for now. Gwendolyn was a sweet young woman, and their friendship was strong. Though he knew it was about to be tested.

Gwendolyn circled the ruins, lower and lower, before she landed. It was clear she was still new to the act of flight. She staggered a bit as she touched the ground but this time did not fall.

He smiled faintly. "You are learning quickly. He would be proud to watch you fly."

"He'd laugh his ass off at me, are you kidding?" Gwen swept her hair back from her face, clasping her wings to her shoulders and letting the leathery skin fall behind her like a cape. She was wearing what Galahad could only assume was modern clothing. It suited her well.

"Oh, he would tease. But his heart would soar beside you, to see you come into your own so well."

"Thanks." Gwen caught sight of Mordred's steed, her expression twisting to one of frustration and anger. "Oh *fuck you*, you stupid horse! You knew where he was this entire fucking time? God, I hate you."

Galahad chuckled at her outburst before he stepped forward, reaching out to embrace the young woman.

She took a step back.

He frowned. "Are we not friends?"

"We are—you know I love you like family, but—" She winced. "I just had a run-in with your wife."

Galahad paused. "What?"

"She tried to kill me. Said she was after the throne, and just wanted Thorn out of the way first." Gwen shook her head. "I—I hurt her, I'm sorry, but she's alive. She's just injured."

Fear churned in his stomach. Fear and dismay. He shook his head, pacing away from Gwendolyn. "If you love me as you say, promise me these are words of truth."

"I'm not lying to you. I give you my word—on my life. Fuck, on Eod's life, that's more important." Gwen sounded exhausted. He was certain it was not simply because of her flight.

"Oddly, yes, swearing upon the dog's life has meaning to me." He chuckled sadly. "You would never break such a vow." Shutting his eyes, he let the sadness wash over him. "I am sorry you came to blows. I did not know of her designs—on you or the island."

"I believe you." Gwen paused. "Are we going to have to

fight now? I—I really don't want to. And I think you'll win. I don't know if I have another explosion in me."

He blinked. He figured she meant that literally, but he did not bother to ask. "I do not wish to fight you either, Gwendolyn. But you must understand what will come of your actions."

"I do. I get it. Elementals will die. Mordred is... not okay. Going into that thing has changed him. I've been able to speak to him in my dreams and he's..." She hesitated again. "Pissed, to put it lightly."

Broken was more likely the word she had been searching for, he surmised. Perhaps insane. Bloodthirsty was a given. The matter was just how intractably so. "He is a brother to me. He is family. I have been at his side for over a thousand years. But I fear what he will do, should he be set free."

"I know. I am too. But... he's going to die in there. And soon if I don't let him out."

"How will you free him?" He arched an eyebrow. "Fire alone will not do it."

She shrugged, but from her expression, there was something she was not telling him. "I'll figure it out. Magic, or something. Right?" She wiggled her fingers in the air. "And if I can't, well, you win."

"This is not a victory." He turned his gaze toward the cavernous entryway of the ruins of Camelot. The wooden doors had long since rotted away, leaving only the metal hinges behind. The beams that had once held up the roof fared little better. "None of this is a victory."

"What would you do, in my place? Would you leave him there if you could save him?"

"I am the one who put him there." Galahad cringed, the guilt in his heart stabbing at him. "Though, now I wonder if exile had not been the better option."

"Probably. But the elementals would still be going nuts. Thorn would still be trying to steal the throne. Same with Zoe. I think we'd be in the same situation." Gwen walked up beside him and hugged his arm.

"Yes, but he would be sane." Galahad huffed a mirthless laugh. "Less insane, at any rate."

"Yeah." She went quiet for a moment. "He scares me, a little. But I just... I need him. I need his help. The villagers are being slaughtered."

It hurt him to know that innocents were already being put to the torch, though he could not say that he was surprised. It came down to the same debate, no matter the predicament. "Here we find ourselves again, my king."

"Huh?" Gwen looked up at him.

"This is the predicament all rulers find themselves in, one way or another. Though, if they are lucky, they will only have to register the math but once." He felt tired suddenly. Old. Weary. He walked to a rock by the entrance and sat. He had no intention of fighting Gwendolyn.

Frowning, the young woman joined him, sitting at his side. "What predicament?"

He shut his eyes, leaning his head back against the stone wall. He could almost hear the shouting of the armies that had once waged war over the stone structure, though it had been on Earth at the time. And it was a very long time ago. "How many innocents must die before the death of the elementals is justified? How many souls must be weighed before war is *righteous?*"

Gwen shook her head. "I wish I knew."

"There is never an answer. It is the cost of wearing the crown." The sky overhead was beautiful, the clouds lazily floating by. It looked like rain was amassing on the horizon, but it was hours away. "It is the weight you will carry upon your soul until the day it is taken from you. Do you understand?"

"I do. Everyone who dies at Mordred's hand will die

because of me. Because I set him free. But every innocent life that continues will be spared too. But that doesn't make the death less important. Less terrible." Letting out a ragged sigh, she put her head in her hands. "This fucking *sucks*."

Chuckling, Galahad rubbed her back. He could gather her meaning well enough. "Yes. In that, you are not wrong."

"Thank you for not treating me like a kid. Or a moron."

"You are neither. You are young in years but not in heart. And you are no fool."

Her smile was faint and faded quickly. "If I step in there, are you going to stop me?"

"No. I will not aid you, however. This, you must do alone." He stood, feeling his age once more. His body was not a day older since he had set foot on Avalon. But his soul felt every second. "I will go gather my injured wife."

"Tell her I'm sorry." Gwen headed for the entrance.

"Are you?" He arched an eyebrow.

She paused in her steps briefly. "I'm sorry it happened."

"Fair." He watched as she disappeared into the ruins. He would not tell her where to go, or how to access the lake beneath the tomb. That was her journey. And she achieved the impossible, everywhere she went. She would find her own way.

War would be coming.

And now it seemed he had to choose between the woman he loved and his brother-in-arms.

It would be a long flight home.

* * *

Gwen was glad to be spared a knock-out fight with Galahad. She'd have a real problem hurting him. Both emotionally and physically. The Knight in Gold had left with a troubled, weary expression on his face. Zoe's actions had shocked him, as had her motivations. He was going to have to go home and contend with all of that.

It would have been nice to have some company, and maybe some help, but she understood. Galahad was doing enough by letting her pass. The choice was hers to make, and so was the burden that would follow.

This was on her.

She was about to let out a rabid tiger. When it ate the countryside, it was her fault. Sure, Mordred was a grown man and could think for himself. But he'd made his intentions very clear.

Her jaw ticked as she walked into the ruins. A gust of wind rustled some of the dry leaves that had gathered in the corners of the rooms. She wished she could have seen it when it was in its prime—not just inside Mordred's dreams. It must have been a wonder. Now, it was mossy and overgrown, the stones stained with rain and worn smooth with time. She stepped over a fallen beam as she headed deeper into the structure. She didn't know where she was going. Not really.

Gwen turned the necklace over in her hand, running her thumb along the ridges of the iron shard. It reminded her of why she was there and that she wasn't truly alone. Mordred was here. Trapped and suffering.

She wound her way deeper into the old castle. All the tapestries that must have adorned the walls were gone, long since eaten away by critters and destroyed by the weather. But the wooden rods that had held them up were still there, at least some of them. They hung at odd angles, but a few held on against all odds, the ropes that perched them there somehow having survived.

It took her minutes of wandering to find a doorway that went down into the basement. Whatever had covered the door was long gone, leaving the gaping chasm of darkness that was more than a little foreboding. She was going to a tomb, after all.

And then after that, a lake.

"How the *fuck* did they get that giant spider to carry the Crystal down here?" She was asking nobody in particular and was glad no one responded. It was always a fifty–fifty shot in Avalon.

With only the sound of the wind and rustling leaves for company, the whole place felt vacant. Lonely. Dead. Holding her other hand over her head, she lit it on fire like a torch, before heading down the roughly hewn steps.

"If there are zombies down here, I swear, I'm gonna quit." She didn't spot any of those, but there were, however, spiders of the non-giant-and-iron variety. She cringed and ducked under a few of the gnarlier webs. She had a distaste for spiders, but that wasn't terribly uncommon. It wasn't a phobia. She just *really* hated walking through cobwebs or when one of the leggy bastards snuck up on her.

The stairs wound deeper into the darkness, spiraling down before reaching a landing. Taking a breath, she stepped out into the chamber beyond.

A large sarcophagus set on a dais dominated the center of the room, a stone tomb with the figure of a sleeping king lying atop it. There was no question who it was. A crown, ancient and golden, sat atop his chest, covered in dust and a stray cobweb.

The carving looked fresh, though—untouched by the weather down beneath the castle. It was remarkably detailed, showing every line of the dead king's face. He looked peaceful. Restful. Letting out a wavering breath, Gwen took a moment to appreciate the fact that she was at the tomb of King Arthur. A place that a hundred thousand historians would *murder* to be able to see.

Arthur's wasn't the only tomb in the room. Seven more sat around the center in a ring. Each of them made from a different metal, unlike the stone of Arthur's. Silver, copper, gold, tin, cobalt, nickel... and iron. One for each of the knights.

She winced as she saw the silver tomb. Walking up to it, she frowned down at the figure of Lancelot that lay there in repose. Tears stung her eyes. "I'm sorry, Lancelot. I really am." Slipping Zoe's necklace into her pocket, she placed her hand atop the tomb. She didn't know what was inside—elementals seemed to disappear into dust when they died. But it didn't really matter. "I'm sorry for the part I had to play in all of this."

She knew the beef between Lancelot and Mordred had started long, long before she arrived. But if she hadn't shown up and mucked everything up, he'd still be alive. Miserable, but alive. With another heavy sigh, she turned away, looking around the room for any sign an exit.

Mordred had said there was a lake deep beneath the castle, but he'd neglected to mention how she was supposed to get down there. The domed chamber was held up by enormous stone columns, each one carved with the figure of a knight or a soldier. Or, maybe they were gods. She had no idea.

But there, in the flickering shadows between two of the columns, she saw another doorway. Stairs led deeper into the darkness. She hoped this place wouldn't wind up being *her* tomb. She wasn't afraid of caves or dark places. Strangely, the whole place had a... peaceful vibe to it, down in the crypt and beneath.

She didn't feel in danger.

The air began to grow moist, and she could smell a damp mustiness the farther down she went. It wasn't too long before the stairs ended, dumping her on the shore of an underground lake. The firelight from her hand danced along the water's surface, which was as still and calm as glass. She couldn't see how far it stretched.

Shutting her eyes, she clutched the necklace in her palm again. If she focused, she could feel the power in it. The link to him—both iron and his magic. It was a little piece of Mordred, pulled from the rest. She tried to imagine using it like a key in an engine. That giant spider thing was down there below the surface—waiting. Waiting for her. Waiting for this.

She just had to call it.

Turning the proverbial key in her mind, she did just that. She willed it to come forward. For a moment, nothing happened, before a shudder at the surface of the water revealed something very large moving in the depths.

It looked like a nightmare.

A giant, seven-legged, twisted creature, its movements were bizarre and jerking as it lifted itself from the lake. The water must be immensely deep—even standing at its full height as it walked from the darkness, it was up to its first set of joints.

Gwen couldn't help but take a step back.

Its many eyes were glowing that same white and opal color as before, shining off the rough rock walls around her. And in its open chest cavity were chains like ribs, running to the suspended Iron Crystal within.

She shivered as a wave of cold traveled up her. This was the point of no return. If she did this, things would be set in motion that she could only hope to stop. The odds of her being successful were slim.

But she loved Mordred. And he loved her. And she had to hold onto that.

Tightening her grasp around the shard until she felt the edges digging into her skin, she shut her eyes. Holding her hand in front of her, brandishing the necklace, she reached out to the iron in the Crystal.

She felt it there, like she felt the fire still flickering from her hand.

Something to control. Something she could wield.

"Break," she commanded the Iron Crystal.

A loud *snap* echoed through the room, like the sound of a

steel cable going past its limit. There was a groan of metal, and then a wrenching, shearing noise. Cracks in the Crystal began to form, growing larger, until it detonated.

The last thing Gwen saw was a chunk of it flying straight for her.

THIRTEEN

Mordred knelt by Gwendolyn's unconscious body where she lay on the shore of the lake. She was alive, but a shard of the Crystal must have struck her when it broke apart. Poor thing. Poor, accident-prone thing. He vanished his gauntlet so he could run his fingers over her cheek, savoring the feeling of her skin against his. So soft.

So *his*.

Gwendolyn still clutched the necklace he had fashioned for Zoe in her hand. He gently took it from her before dissolving it, returning the iron and the magic back to himself. He would never make that mistake again.

It seemed so foolish in the first place, looking back at his decisions over the past few months since Gwendolyn's arrival in Avalon. How childish he had been. How weak. Never again. No, it was finally time for him to become the monster that Avalon believed him to be.

No one would ever think to oppose him again.

Carefully, he scooped Gwendolyn up into his arms. She would be fine. Witches and wizards of Avalon had the same unnatural healing capabilities as the elementals. The Ancients knew that Gwendolyn's irritating predecessor certainly would have been wiped from the face of the isle if not for it.

He kissed her forehead gently where it rested against his shoulder. "Let us go home, my love." His love, and soon to be his wife.

But first, he had a small matter to deal with.

The matter of exterminating all the elementals of Avalon. All those who lived today... and all those who would follow. One by one. Forever.

Until the end of time.

Or his life.

* * *

Gwen woke up slowly, groaning as she did. Her head hurt. She expected to wake up on a cold stone floor, or potentially half in a pool of water. But she wasn't. She was lying on soft grass. The sun was setting, and there was a crackle of fire from beside her. She blinked and rubbed her eyes. "What the..."

"Welcome back, firefly."

The voice startled her out of her grogginess. She sat up way too quickly, her head spinning. She groaned again, putting her hands to her temples.

Mordred chuckled. "You are mending quickly, but you should take it slow."

Taking a few slow, deep breaths, she focused on not throwing up or passing out again. When she could see straight, she looked up. There, sitting beside her on a fallen log, was Mordred. He was wearing black slacks and a black, loosely tied linen shirt. But he still wore his typical gauntlets, the iron armor running up his arms to his shoulders.

God, he was beautiful.

A rock lodged in her throat. She couldn't speak. She didn't

know what to say. She simply threw herself into his arms, clutching him close.

He scooped her up into his lap, holding her tight as she began to cry. He shushed her gently, kissing the top of her head. "I am here, my love. I am here. You were successful. I am free. *We* are free."

Wrapping her arms around behind his neck, she kissed him. She had been so terrified she'd never be able to do that again—never be able to hold him. Her heart was full of too many emotions all at once. Happiness. Joy at having him back with her. Love for him. Fear about what he was going to do. And a deep dread of what she'd be forced to do in return.

"I would soothe your worries another way, but I believe we are both too injured for such a foray." Mordred smiled at her before vanishing his gauntlets to stroke her tears away.

"Yeah." Though that wasn't to say she wasn't tempted. She watched him for a moment, studying his features and his rust-colored eyes. "Are you okay?"

"I am." He paused. "As for my convictions—they remain the same, if that is what you were asking."

It was.

"I will protect you. I will protect Avalon. This game I have played with the elementals must go on no longer. I am sorry for the grief the death will cause you." He rested his palm against her cheek. "But better that than to see your beloved villagers murdered en masse, no?"

She shut her eyes, not being able to help but sink into his touch. It felt so damn good. "I just wish it didn't have to be this way. There has to be some other option."

"I have spent a thousand years attempting to find just that. But perhaps you will see the way forward where I have been unable to discover it." He kissed her forehead tenderly. "And should you come up with such a scheme, I vow I will listen to it."

At least he hadn't gone full murderous despot and had a little bit of reason left in him. Well, hadn't gone full murderous despot *yet*. There was still time. She rested her head on his shoulder. It was strange to fear him and love him in equal measure. She was having a damn hard time wrapping her head around how both could be possible simultaneously.

She supposed it had to do with the fact that she trusted him not to hurt *her*. It was just everybody else who was fucked. "What about Galahad? And Zoe, I guess."

"Hm. From your tone, I take it she did not give you the necklace willingly?"

"No. She tried—" She stopped short of telling Mordred that Zoe had tried to kill her. That would be an instant death sentence for the Gossamer Lady. "—to stop me from setting you free." That was still the truth. Just not all of it.

Damn it, she was sick of doing that to him.

"You fought." He tilted her head to look at him, his eyes narrowing slightly. "And the Gossamer Lady does not fight without intending to end a life. Do not lie to me."

"I—I'm not, it's true." She looked away. Shit. "Just not all of it. Please, don't kill her."

"And why should I not?" His expression darkened. "It was she who declared war against us."

"It's—it's not her, really. I mean, I don't want anybody to die. I really don't. And I get why she's scared of what you'll do. She isn't wrong." She shook her head and tried another tactic. "It's Galahad. I don't want to hurt him like that."

Mordred shut his eyes as he took a moment to think. "If he kneels and swears fealty, I will let him live."

"You know he won't."

"Precisely."

"Mordred..."

"I do not wish to argue with you. Not tonight. Not here."

He opened his eyes to watch her again. "May we defer this discussion until we are home in my keep?"

"Fine. But I... um..." She paused. "About your keep."

He arched an eyebrow. "What did you do to it?"

"It's nothing, it's fine, it's just—we're going to have company." She smiled shyly. "The villagers are raising an army. I *might* have told them you'd help us defend them against the elementals."

The laugh that left him was genuine. As was the amusement and adoration in his eyes. "You seek to march a band of mortal villagers to fight creatures far more powerful than they are?"

"It's—I mean, they have a right to defend themselves. And I couldn't do it alone. With Thorn *and* Zoe trying to—" She broke off. Damn it. She just kept digging everyone deeper graves.

"Gwendolyn." His tone had that hardness to it that said she wasn't going to squeeze out of this one.

Her shoulders slumped. "They're both vying for the throne of Avalon. The moment you were gone, Thorn raised her own forces to try to take it. And Zoe is waiting for Thorn to get killed or wounded before she offs her and takes it for herself."

Mordred laughed again, but this time it was edged with a devious, almost sadistic joy. "How wonderful. So, if I understand correctly, we are looking at a fight between three forces. Ours, backed by my iron army and a motley crew of villagers. Thorn and her elementals. And the Gossamer Lady and whatever ploy she attempts to destroy us."

Gwen chewed her lip a little, thinking it through. "Yeah, I think that's all of it."

"You have been busy in my absence."

"Look, it isn't my fault! Zoe came after *me*, and Thorn is just a raging bitch already, so—"

Mordred broke her off with a kiss.

A kiss that slowly deepened, slowly grew in passion, until she was breathless as he broke away. His hand threaded into her hair as he feathered kisses along her jaw, working his way down her throat.

She shivered. "I thought..."

"I will go easy on us both," he murmured as he undid the tie of her halterneck top at the back of her neck.

It was probably a really stupid idea. But she couldn't bring herself to say no. Her eyes slipped shut as he finished untying the laces that held her shirt on, tossing the fabric aside. He shifted them, laying her down on the soft grass as his lips continued to wander over her skin. His breath was hot as it pooled against her in sharp contrast to the chill of the ground beneath her.

When he captured one of her nipples in his mouth, nipping it between his teeth, she couldn't hold back the quiet moan that left her. He was way, *way* too good at getting her engine running. He sat back on his heels briefly to pull his shirt off over his head and to finish stripping both of them off the rest of their clothes. His body was such a work of art, the muscles that seemed enhanced by his scars. It made him somehow real— somehow touchable.

She didn't try to stop herself from letting her hands roam over him, savoring it. Until this moment, she wasn't so sure she'd ever be with him again. Come what may, she loved him. And right now, she *needed* him.

He trailed his kisses downward again, picking up where he left off, wandering down to her navel. His goal was clear. She whimpered as he parted her legs—the sound turning into a quiet cry as his tongue ran along her core before delving inside.

It seemed he was in no rush. He was savoring this as well, taking his sweet time as he lavished her, his hands continuing to roam over her, squeezing and kneading whatever he could reach. It felt amazing—but it wasn't enough. She needed more. More of him.

"Mordred—" she said through a gasp. "Please..."

He kissed her thigh before working his way back up, pausing to lick and bite at her nipples again, hard enough to sting without hurting her. He didn't make her beg—he was obviously experiencing as much need as she was. Mordred hooked one of her legs over his arm, her knee in the crook of his elbow.

The kiss he gave her was searing but not harsh as he drove himself into her—slow and unstoppable, like a force of nature. Her cry of bliss was muffled against his lips, tangling with his own guttural growl of pleasure as he sank himself to the hilt.

This wasn't about sex. This wasn't like their rougher forays. This was about love. About them. The future might be uncertain, but this wasn't. This was known. And this would last for as long as they were both alive.

He rocked himself in her. Even when he was being gentle, she felt every inch of him stretch her, pressing in all the right places. It was just on the line of too much, and it was *perfect*. Neither of them could go for long, exhausted and injured as they both were.

Mordred took pity on her. He broke the kiss to pull in a deep and ragged breath as he picked up his pace, sending her to new heights as he drove them both to the crescendo that waited for them.

She could only gasp out his name as she clung to him.

The muscles in his back tensed as he rammed himself into her to the hilt. The sensation of him surging inside of her was enough to send her into her own peak of ecstasy. He buried his head into the crook of her elbow to muffle his roar before suddenly wrapping his arms around her, sitting back on his heels with her on his lap, straddling him, without breaking their union.

The extra pressure of her weight drove him farther, and she swore her eyes rolled back into her head at the sensation of it all. Mordred clutched her close, arms circling her, as he twitched and spasmed in his release as her own body tightened around him in waves.

When Gwen could think straight again, she was unsure of how much time had passed. Mordred was kissing her again tenderly, trying to pull her back down to reality.

"I thought... you were going to take it easy on me," she murmured.

"I did." His smile was just a bit fiendish. He gently placed her on the grass before lying down beside her, pulling his cloak up over them both. It'd do for a blanket. She was too exhausted to try to summon anything better. "Trust me. That was far sweeter than what I will do to you later."

"Don't threaten me with a good time." She snuggled into him, resting her head on his arm. He wasn't wearing his armor at least—talk about a shitty pillow if he had been.

"It is not a threat; it is a promise."

"It's a turn of phrase." She yawned, already feeling sleep coming for her. And this time, she wouldn't be invading anybody's mind. Maybe it'd actually be restful for once.

He kissed the back of her head. "Sleep, my firefly. We resume our travel at first light. There is much to contend with come the morrow..."

There was. And the darkness in his voice made it obvious what he was talking about. But at least for now, she could pretend that this was all that was waiting for them. That there wouldn't be a war. That there wouldn't be a slaughter.

That she wouldn't have to try to stop the man she loved.

Try being the operative word.

FOURTEEN

Mordred was happier than he could remember being for a very, very long time. Though to be truthful, it was hardly terribly difficult to achieve. But now—for this brief moment—he felt no crushing weight upon him. No grasp around his heart.

He was atop his stallion, with Gwendolyn sitting in front of him. She had clearly learned to apparate clothing, which would be very convenient for her. And her choice of style meant that, being taller than her, he had a rather wonderful downward view into her blouse.

It was a challenge not to stare. Instead, he distracted himself with the view of the landscape as they rode. He kept them to a brisk walk, neither wishing to hurry the journey back nor neglect those waiting for them at his keep.

Gwendolyn shivered, and Mordred pulled his cloak around them both. The fall was quickening toward winter, and the air smelled of an early winter storm. It had been three hundred years since he had seen snow—and he smiled at the thought of it.

His thoughts drifted back to those waiting at his keep. There would be an army—*her army*—camped outside his doors.

Or, worse, inside his halls. He cringed at the mental image of a hundred villagers ruining his home.

The floors would never be the same again.

And what of the ragtag army's commander? What of their Lady Gwendolyn? Mordred kissed the top of her head. She smiled up at him in return. His Lady Gwendolyn, leader of the common people. He did not bother asking her if she understood what it would mean for those who chose to fight. She had watched the ends of Lancelot and Grinn. She knew what death was. But one question remained. One that had been puzzling him all morning.

"Whose idea was it for you to lead an army?" He smiled again, amused at the thought of her standing on a chair giving some raucous speech to embolden her troops.

Gwen snorted. "Not mine. Bert the scarecrow." She paused, her mood falling. "I was on the fence about... about stopping the elementals. About doing anything at all. Bert took me to see some of his friends in that city just southwest of the keep."

When she didn't continue, he draped an arm around her, gently resting it in her lap. "And?"

"Thorn. She'd asked me to join her army. I refused, obviously. And when we got to the city, it... it was destroyed. So many people were just caught in the crossfire. So many bodies." She leaned her head back against his chest, her eyes shut. "And why? *Why?* Because Thorn had a spitting match with some other elemental. I keep thinking—maybe if I'd said yes to her. Maybe if I'd gone with her, I could have stopped her. And then all those people..."

"No." He tightened his arm around her slightly. "You would have been forced to stand between her and them. You were right to refuse her. Their deaths are not your doing."

"Well. I mean. It kinda is—" She gestured aimlessly in the air in front of her. "Because Thorn wouldn't be loose if I hadn't tried to blow up the Crystal, which pissed you off so badly you blew up the—"

"I get it. I get it." He rolled his eyes. But he could not hide his smile. "Yes. All the blame for every terrible turn of events that befalls Avalon from this point forward will be entirely yours."

"See? Exactly. Thanks for agreeing with me." A smile also graced her face. He knew she would be distraught at the deeds he was set upon performing. But in this moment, it seemed she shared in his happiness.

They were together.

And for this tiny respite, there was quiet.

A quiet that would be ruined the moment he set foot inside his home. He grimaced. "Why *villagers*? You do realize how poorly they will do in battle, do you not?"

Gwendolyn laughed. "You're a little elitist, aren't you, *prince*?"

"With good reason, *princess*." He teased her back. "Though now that you are a witch, I suppose you are no longer a princess."

"Lame." She huffed in false offense. "Do witches get cool titles?"

"Yes. Witch."

"I should get a black pointy hat and some green face paint," she murmured as she looked off into the woods. He did not bother to ask what she meant; he knew it would make little sense even after she attempted to explain it.

A thought occurred to him. "How did you manage to bring my stallion to Camelot?"

"He brought himself to Camelot," she snapped, glowering down at the iron horse. His steed snorted in response. The feeling was mutual. "I let the little shit out because I felt bad for him, all cooped up in his stable, and he took the fuck off. It wasn't until I got to Camelot that I saw him. He knew the whole damn time."

"Maybe if you were nicer to him," he teased. It had nothing to do with it. No one was kinder to animals than Gwendolyn Wright.

"He doesn't want nice. He likes assholes." She jabbed him in the thigh between the plates of his armor. "Some people like assholes."

"Hm. Careful." He kissed her temple. "There is a phrase about throwing stones..."

"Yeah, yeah." She turned her attention back to the road ahead of them. They went along in comfortable silence for quite some time. Nothing but wilderness surrounded them, the sun streaming through the branches of the trees. Autumn leaves drifted down about them. Birds sang, and the long grass rustled with creatures seeking to bury their winter stores.

This—this was bliss. This was happiness. This was *peace*.

This was what he would fight to keep.

"So," he began.

"Yes, I have an *army*, get over it." She laughed. "You're not the only one who can have one, y'know."

"That was not what I was going to clarify but thank you for reminding me of how ludicrous this situation is." He dug his claws into her thigh, just a little. Just enough. She squirmed in her seat. "What I was going to ask you, firefly, is what you intend to do with said army?"

Her silence spoke volumes. It took her nearly a minute to respond. She was getting better at predicting their verbal sparring matches and was clearly trying to find a way to navigate around this one. "I intend to stop the elementals."

"How?" He could not help but needle her playfully again. "Through petition?"

"Mordred." She sighed, shaking her head.

"Forgive me. I am in a good mood. I cannot help but tug on your hair like a young bully."

"At least you admit it." She leaned back against him. "No, I know what I'm trying to do. I know what's going to happen."

"Then what separates you and I?"

"The fact that you don't know is also part of the problem." Picking up the edge of his cloak, she drew it tighter around herself. "Not all the elementals are on the rampage. Some just want to live quietly on their own. There's a big difference between going to war against a few and declaring genocide against an entire group of people."

"You would wait for those to attack you before avenging yourself. I simply wish to cut the problem off before it has a chance to strike."

"You can't kill people for the crimes they *might* commit. That's not how this works!"

"I beg to differ."

"Can we—" She sighed and placed a hand over her eyes. "Can we not. Not here. There'll be a time to fight about this."

"I agree." The last thing he wished to do was ruin either of their enjoyment of the day. "I must admit, I wish that mutt of yours were here."

"He misses you, you know." She smiled. "Calls you Dad."

That did twist something in his gut, he had to admit. He had once let his dogs run amok in the same way that Gwendolyn preferred to do. But the loss of holding them as they passed became too much over the centuries. For he was destined not to die, and they fell within the same seasons of life as all of nature should follow.

But watching Gwendolyn cherish her friendship with the beast... made him miss those days deeply. "He is a good hound."

Perhaps those days were not gone for good.

"He's the best. Even though I really wish I couldn't understand him." She wrinkled her nose. "It's really weird to hear a dog comment to you when they're—"

"I do not need the details, thank you." He chuckled, and she joined him. "You will adjust to your magic in time. It will become more natural to you."

"I hope so. It's still so *weird*. And I keep forgetting about it. Like, the other day, I was walking along for about two hours, complaining to myself how thirsty I was, before I remembered I could just *make myself a drink*."

Grinning, he hugged her tighter for a moment. "Speaking of which, who knows that you command iron, the same as I?"

"No one." Her shoulders fell a little. "I figured if they really hated the fact that *one* person could void all their powers, they really wouldn't like it if there were *two*."

"You were wise to keep it a secret. Even Galahad does not know? What of your villager companions?"

"No one."

"Good. Very good. We can use that to our advantage." He was not certain how he would leverage such a reveal, but he knew it would come in handy.

"Seriously. Change of topic. No more discussing your impending murderous rampage."

"Yes, yes. Forgive me. I will only conclude the matter by saying this." He combed the claws of one hand through her hair. She hummed and leaned into his touch. "No matter what may follow, my firefly—I love you above all. Promise me that you will hold that close to your heart."

"I promise." She wound her fingers into his other hand. "And promise me the same thing in return."

"Of course." He kissed her cheek. And when she turned her head to him, he paid the same attention to her lips. He would do anything to protect her. To preserve this world of Avalon for her. Even if he had to turn the rivers and fields red, he would see her safe.

He would see her smile at him.

No matter the cost.

* * *

Galahad returned home, concern and anger clutching at him, sending his muscles tense with every step as he ducked under the jamb into the cottage he shared with Zoe.

The Gossamer Lady was sitting by the fire, wrapping a bandage around her arm. She was bruised, and a black spot marred her cheek by her ear. He hurried to her side, kneeling beside her, taking over the task of tending to her wounds.

Zoe watched him, her pink eyes searching his for information. "You let her pass."

"Yes." He made no attempt at excuses. He would not lie to his wife. "There was naught I could do to stop her, save... attempt to take her life."

She frowned, leaning back in her chair to gaze into the fire. "I did what I had to do. If Mordred is now free, we—we are all lost."

He paused for a long moment, not knowing in what order to best broach topics. "I am certain the Prince in Iron walks this land once more. We had best prepare as though he is free."

"If we wish to be spared his wrath, we best apologize, I suppose." Zoe cringed. "Though I loathe to do it."

"There is no bother. Gwendolyn understands and seems to hold you at no fault for attempting to stop her. Perhaps she is a bit embittered, but I would hardly say wrathful. She did spare your life, it seems." He moved on to another bandage. It was clear Gwendolyn could have ended his wife's life but instead chose to spare her.

The young woman would have made an excellent knight. Galahad was certain that Gwendolyn and Arthur would have gotten along famously. A little too well, perhaps. Pointless musings for another time. He broke the silence again. "She told me of your plans."

Zoe's hand tightened gently. "I—I should have spoken to you first, my love. Forgive me. But I fear I lacked conviction until the moment I fought her. I could not let her and Mordred or Thorn usurp that which is rightfully mine, as it was so long ago..."

Galahad rested his forehead against the part of her arm that was not wounded. He knew of her past as the Queen of Avalon. How the beautiful lady had appeared to them in the woods that night to present to Arthur not just the crown of the island, but *her* crown.

Because she knew she needed to. Because the isle had told her of the moment the true ruler of Avalon came to the shores from Earth.

It made the bitter twist of fate that followed all the worse, when Arthur was rejected and died a mortal man.

"Is it truly what you wish, my love?" He lifted his head again to watch her. "To become queen?"

Sadness creased her features as she shut her eyes. "No... I do not know." She sought his hand with hers, holding it tight. "I wish to cease all this pointless suffering in Avalon. I wish to stop them all from killing each other. Thorn will burn this world down to rule a pile of ashes, same as the demon. And Mordred... would be even worse than that."

"Gwendolyn is seeking to raise an army of the villagers."

"And they march to the slaughter—you know that as well as I." Zoe reached out, wrapping her arms around Galahad, pulling him into an embrace. "I simply wish for peace, my love."

"I know." He held her, gently stroking her back. "I know. But the only way to find it is through violence."

"Perhaps." She sat back. "Or perhaps there is another way. Yes, a few may need to die or be dealt with—but only those who rally the mobs. Would you not rather three souls meet their end in order to save three hundred?"

It was rare that his wife schemed. He watched her curiously. "I dislike weighing bargains with lives. I always have."

"As do I. But in times like these, it can sometimes not be avoided." Zoe stroked his cheek with her knuckles tenderly. "But I think there is a way to stop their war before it begins. I need your help."

The weight of his years fell over him with those words. He was tired of it all—of the constant battling and strife. He had wished to stay here with the woman he loved, in peace and quiet. But they were being taken from him now by the very woman he wished to share them with.

Which made it all the worse.

What was he to do?

Zoe would not stop her quest even if he asked it of her. She was steadfast when it came to her duties to Avalon. And the resolution in her eyes was clear. She would retake the throne and see peace finally reign for all.

It was a beautiful vision. And he had never seen his Gossamer Lady rule. It must have been a thing of rare beauty, like the fae courts of Tir n'Aill.

He bowed his head. "My sword is now and forever yours, my lady."

But there was nothing but dread in his heart.

FIFTEEN

"Ancients, spare me."

Gwen tried not to laugh at Mordred's dismayed mutter as they approached his keep, but she couldn't suppress the snicker that escaped. Through the open gates she could see tents set up inside the main outer wall, and several dozen more set up on the field outside his home. Smoke from fires drifted up into the air from the makeshift army that had set up camp.

"It'll be nice to have company. Maewenn is either *ecstatic* or *pissed*, and I can't guess which." Gwen smiled. "Come on, your home needed a little life in it."

"The life I could put up with. It is the odor I am more concerned about."

"Lighten up. It'll be fine." She smiled up at him, her expression turning into a grin at how dour he looked. "You're going to just hide in your tower like the spooky bastard you are, anyway."

"I am not going to hide." He paused. His lips twitched as he fought his own smile. "I am going to brood."

That got her to laugh again, and she faced forward toward the keep with a lingering smile. She knew this was going to get ugly, and soon. But for now, she had her friends and the man she loved. They rode in silence until they were a few hundred feet from the keep.

Distant barking told her they were about to have more company. The pack of hounds, eight in all, were tearing across the field toward them, with Eod in the lead.

"This, I do not mind."

"*Mom! Dad! Mom! Dad!*" Eod barked as he jumped around the horse. The stallion snorted angrily but knew better than to kick at the animals.

Gwen unceremoniously jump-slid off the horse to greet the dog, ruffling his ears and kneeling so the big creature could lick her face without jumping up and likely knocking her over. "Hey, you silly doofus. I told you I'd be back."

"*I protect! I good!*"

"You're the best pup." She smiled.

Mordred dismounted the horse a bit more gracefully than she did.

Eod jumped up to greet his master, tail wagging frantically. "*Dad! Dad-Dad-Dad-Dad-Dad—*"

"Yes, yes." Mordred petted the animal but allowed the ecstatic creature to get a few licks in before urging the animal back to all fours. "It is good to see you as well."

Eod sat, his tongue hanging out of the side of his mouth.

"Oh, tell the dog he's a good boy, will you? It won't kill you." Gwen stood, brushing the dirt from her knees.

Mordred rolled his eyes. "Good boy, Eod."

"*Yes!*" Eod shot back up to his feet and began running around gleefully. The other dogs were far more subdued in their excitement, but they all seemed thrilled they were home.

Mordred took the reins of his stallion as they headed through the encampment toward the keep. The villagers paused to stare at them as they passed. There were people of all shapes and sizes—there was even a damn *centaur*. Some people were normal-looking, but most had something unusual about them. Well, unusual to Gwen. They were probably perfectly average for Avalon.

They had armor and weapons, but most of their equipment looked like it had seen better days. Most of it didn't even look like it was made out of metal—it was wood, or leather, or even stone. *Right. Iron nullifies magic.* Sometimes, it was hard to remember that. She was usually around Mordred or his iron army. For everyone else, it was dangerous and unusual.

Mordred was quick to comment on the state of the army. "Look at their equipment. They will be lambs to the slaughter." He didn't bother lowering his voice. One woman nearby gasped.

Gwen shot him a look. "Well, it's too bad we don't know someone who can just summon armor and weapons. That'd be super useful right about now, wouldn't it? Where could we find one of those..."

"Yes, yes. I see your point." He sighed. "It will take time to create enough for everyone. But it will take less effort than it would to raise a larger iron army. The mortals will be faster and more agile in the field. There may be some sense to this mad scheme, after all."

She'd take that as a win. "I've been working at making armor for them the past few weeks. We've got a good start, but we're not there yet."

"But they will all still die," he added.

Slapping a hand over her eyes, she walked beside Mordred as they headed through the courtyard. He put his stallion back in the stable before they went inside, Eod happily leading the way.

It was Tim she saw first. The broken iron guard was standing by the wall, holding his lance with his better arm. His posture changed upon seeing them, shoulders relaxing.

Walking up to the soldier, Gwen hugged him. "Missed you. Glad to be back."

With a squeak, he turned his head to glance nervously at Mordred before returning the favor.

"You would befriend a candlestick if given the opportunity, I swear." Mordred kept walking without her.

"Maybe you could stand to befriend a few more candlesticks." She waved goodbye to Tim as she jogged after the Prince in Iron. "Or are you giving up on that, now that you've sworn to kill everyone who gets in your way?"

Mordred smirked. "You continue to say that as though it is a bad thing. I will convince you in time, when you see the inevitability of my actions."

"Whatever." There would be time for an argument. This still wasn't it. Her stomach grumbled, reminding her she hadn't eaten in a while.

When they entered Mordred's study, they weren't alone. Sitting at the table were Bert, Lina, and Mirkon. Maewenn was busy placing platters of food down on the table.

"How'd you know we were back already?" Gwen laughed as she walked up to the cook, hugging her.

"Pah. I haven't stopped feeding hungry mouths since this rabble arrived!" Mae hugged her back before quickly going back to fussing over the plates of food. "It's *wonderful*."

That answered that question. "I was worried you'd be pissed."

"Me? Angry? Hardly! I have scores of people to feed who are grateful for my talent. It is nice to finally be thanked for my work."

"Careful, Maewenn," Mordred warned as he reached forward to spear a roll with the end of one of his claws before taking a bite from it. "I am standing right here."

"Yes, and it is fantastic to see you, prince." Maewenn put her hands on her hips with a *clank*. "And I see your mood has been left intact after your stay in the Crystal." She paused. "I am glad that you are safe, my lord."

Mordred's smile was soft. "And I am happy to have returned. Now, shoo. Get back to your starving masses."

"Eagerly." She huffed in fake indignation and headed from the room.

Gwen shook her head at the exchange. Mordred was difficult, they all knew that. It was part of his *charm*. If she could call it that. "I see you were successful in raising an army," she said to Bert.

"More or less. This is half what we should have. But since Thorn has rallied her own forces and declared war on all those who've refused to join her... well." He leaned his elbows on the table, the weight of the deaths clearly burdening him. "This is all that's left."

Mordred sighed as he walked toward the window, gazing down on the field of villagers as he idly ate his roll. "It is best to leave them here to defend the keep, while I face Lady Thorn alone."

"We have a right to have a hand in saving ourselves." Lina glared at the back of Mordred's head. "We are here to fight for our own future."

"And die for it. Thorn and her minions will tear through you like wheat. Better that I dispose of her personally." Mordred rested his hands on the windowsill.

"What if you fail?" Bert sat back in his chair. "You had the chance to kill her a dozen times before, and you didn't."

Mordred laughed. It sent a chill down Gwen's spine. It wasn't a mirthful sound. Judging by the pallor that came over Lina and Mirkon, they understood what it meant.

"She lives purely by my own folly. This is an error I seek to rectify. Immediately."

Gwen's jaw twitched. She shut her eyes. "Let's back up and take a second."

"What is there to discuss?" Mordred turned from the window to face them. The setting sun cut him as a stark silhouette against the amber sky.

"I don't know, like, maybe there's another way to stop Thorn without killing her." Gwen threw up her hands in frustration. Her stomach grumbled, and she gave in to the temptation of the platter of food. She slumped down into a chair and began to gather a few slices of cheese and pieces of cured sausage.

"How many times must she work to end our lives before we return the favor? How many innocents must die?" The Prince in Iron paced back and forth near the wall, reminding her of a caged tiger.

A caged, rabid, bloodthirsty tiger.

"I don't know." She rubbed her eyes. She was exhausted, and this wasn't helping. "Can't we lock her up instead?"

"I have tried that," Mordred snapped.

"I mean in *jail*, not a torture chamber," she snapped back.

Mirkon did his best to try to calm the situation. "I—perhaps —we put it to a vote?"

Mordred laughed again, just as unkindly as the first time. "A *vote?* You sit in my home. I am the rightful King of Avalon—heir to Arthur's crown. I have not taken that which is mine by right out of *respect*. But that does not mean that I will entertain any notion that I am one of *you*."

"Great, is everybody fucking going after the throne now?" Gwen wanted to rip her hair out. "First Thorn. Then Zoe. Now you. Maybe I'll throw my goddamn hat in the ring! Why not? Queen Gwen. Fuck it."

"I'd vote for y—" Mirkon kept his voice quiet. But it didn't matter.

"There shall be no *vote!*" Mordred roared. He clenched his fists at his sides, positively shaking from rage. He took a deep breath, held it for a moment before slowly letting it out. "I leave at midnight. Alone. Thorn's head will be on a spike adorning my walls by dawn. There is nothing any of you can do to persuade me toward another course of action. No one shall stop me." His gaze met Gwen's, and she shrank back at the intensity there. "Not even you."

He stormed from the room then, slamming the large wooden door behind him. The echo of the impact made them all jolt in their seats. With a wavering breath, Gwen folded her arms on the table in front of her and put her forehead on them, wishing to crawl into a dark hole. "Fuck."

"That sums it up nicely." Bert pushed up from the chair. "I don't drink, but it seems like you need to." He headed over to Mordred's bar and fished around for a bottle of wine. Gwen wouldn't argue.

"What do we do now?" Lina frowned. "I mean, I don't—for the record, I don't think he's wrong. Thorn needs to be stopped."

"And what about Zoe? What about everyone who'll come next?" Gwen accepted a glass of wine from Bert as he passed the bottle to his friends.

Everyone was silent as they considered what was coming.

"You said you'd stop him, if he tried to go too far." Bert's tone was quiet, obviously not wanting to rub salt in a wound, but needing to say it all the same.

"I know. I know. And I'll try." She wanted a long, hot bath. And another whole bottle of wine to herself. "And if it comes to it, I'll..." She gritted her teeth. "I'll do what I promised to do. I'll drop him."

"How?" Lina furrowed her brow.

"I have a way. I just... I can't talk about it." She'd kept her powers over iron a secret until now. She wasn't about to blow her cover just yet. Standing, she went and fetched another bottle of wine and uncorked it. "We'll talk about this in the morning. If we agree Thorn has to die, I say we let him do what he has to do. Then... then I'll see if I can talk him down. And if I can't, so be it."

She wanted to be sick at the idea. But she knew this was the mess she was getting herself into.

"Sounds like a plan." Bert paused. "I'm going to go see if Maewenn needs any help."

There was something in the way he said it. "Wait." Gwen stopped and turned to face the scarecrow. "Wait. Are you crushing on the cook?"

"I—I'm—no." It was clear the answer was yes, yes, he was.

Gwen grinned. "I'm not sure how it'd work between you two—"

"It'd sound like throwing armor downhill in a barrel," Mirkon interjected with a grin. Lina smacked him in the chest. "Ow!"

Gwen ignored the comment. "But I say, go for it. Fingers crossed for you."

Bert muttered as Lina and Mirkon kept teasing him. With a half-hearted wave, she said goodnight and headed into the keep. She wanted to find that hot spring down in the basement. She'd had a long, chilly few days. And she was relishing the idea of getting drunk and having a nice soak. Eod was contentedly chewing on a piece of stew bone by the fireplace, and seemed fine where he was.

So, off she went. The halls were definitely more lively than she'd ever seen them before. Villagers had taken up portions of the keep—respectfully so. They weren't crammed in there anywhere that could fit, and none of the furniture looked moved or messed with. In fact, they seemed to be doing a perfectly fine job picking up after themselves.

And nobody stank, as far as she could tell.

Though it was obvious the iron soldiers didn't quite know what to do with themselves. One of them was standing perfectly still, clearly nervous as hell, as a pack of children tried to climb him like a tree. She laughed to herself as she passed them.

It was nice.

The place felt decidedly less spooky with a few more people in it. Galahad would have loved it. Even Lancelot would have enjoyed the chance to show off a bit and teach the villagers how to properly use a sword. The thought of Lancelot ruined her mood instantly.

She found the hot spring a little while later and, placing the bottle of wine down at the edge of the pool, stripped off her clothes and vanished her wings before climbing into the water. They were fun, and it took more of her focus to keep them gone than it did to have them, but they tended to get in the way sometimes.

Taking a sip from the bottle, she leaned back against the stone edge and stretched out. Letting out a long, beleaguered sigh, she let the heat of the water sink into her. She shut her eyes. Peace and quiet. For just a moment.

"Mind if I join you?"

So much for that.

Looking up, she watched as Mordred entered the room.

"Depends." She couldn't help but stare as he began to strip off his clothes.

"Just... let me get drunk, will you?" She took another sip of the bottle. "I need to dull the edges."

"You misunderstand me." He climbed into the water beside her before leaning over her to grasp the bottle, caging her in. "I intend to join you in that as well." He took a mouthful of the liquid before putting the bottle back. He trailed his lips close to her ear before whispering to her, "Unless you protest..."

Maybe it was the hot water. Or the glass of wine. But her head swam, and excitement and anticipation twisted in her stomach like two angry snakes.

"I guess you can stay." She felt her cheeks grow warm. She blamed the hot water. Totally the water.

No, she was not going to protest.

Which made her a certifiable idiot.

Studying him for a moment, she decided she needed to put a little space between them. She turned from him to scoot away.

He was having none of that. His hand twisted in her hair and pulled her back to his chest.

It earned him her most vicious glare. "Are you here to fight or to fuck?"

"Oh, my dear, sweet firefly. You know the answer to that already." He chuckled darkly before his next word sent shivers up her spine again for a very different reason than before.

"*Both.*"

SIXTEEN

Mordred delighted in these sparring matches of theirs. He could easily overpower Gwendolyn if he wished—he was three times her size and had centuries of practice. But it was more fun to let her gain a few inches of ground only to take it away. Especially because he knew he was not alone in his love of the game.

Gwendolyn put on a good show of being frustrated with him as she wrestled out of his grasp. But the flush to her cheeks and the desire in her eyes told him another story. That, and she never once said *stop* or *no*. She knew she could end their dance in the blink of an eye if she wished it.

But she wanted the struggle, the same as he did. When he captured her throat in his grasp and pulled her against him, her back flush to his chest, she went slack for a moment, her breath leaving her in a wavering rush.

When he dug his claws into her skin, just hard enough for her to feel it without breaking the surface, she shivered in his grasp. Vanishing the armor from his other hand, he slid it between her legs beneath the water, wasting no time in teasing her with his touch.

"Thorn will be dead within the week," he murmured into

her ear, deeply enjoying the juxtaposition of their situation. "I will find her camp and lay waste to her and her insipid minions. She has made too many attempts on *both* our lives."

"And—and then what?" Her voice was husky as she writhed, her back arching as he continued his ministrations. "What about—" Her words broke off as he sank a finger into her.

Chuckling at her reaction, he kissed her cheek. "The Gossamer Lady? Well... you told me of her designs upon the throne, and worse still her attempt to kill you. She is an enemy and must be treated as such."

"But—" She didn't get out her words again. He was being cruel, sinking a finger into her each time she went to argue with him. She moaned, her body clenching down around the invading digits as pleasure lanced through her. "—Galahad."

"He will make his own choices." Mordred was not thrilled at the idea of putting the Knight in Gold to the blade. His oldest companion was the only elemental he would let live, should he give his word never to interfere. But the noblest of all of Arthur's knights would not stand idly by. Not after Mordred ended his lover.

Gwendolyn went to protest again. He released her, if only briefly, to turn her around to face him. He yanked her up onto his lap, so she was straddling his thighs. When she went to strike him, he caught her wrists in his hands and pulled her arms behind her back.

The glare she was giving him was doing anything but dissuading him.

"You're an asshole."

"And you love it." He kissed her, searing and rough. He wanted her to feel him. Feel everything that he was. Feel the creature she had given her heart to, and whose heart she had stolen. Summoning a chain around her wrists, he cradled the back of her head in his clawed gauntlet, deepening the embrace.

She moaned against his lips. Taking that as encouragement, he grasped her by the hip, perhaps a little tighter than he had intended, and ground her body against his own desire that was trapped between them.

When he broke the kiss, her eyes were shut. "The chain is cheating." Her protest was half-hearted as he won her over.

"You can remove it. You know how. It is by that same means you intend to stop me, after all." He pulled her against him again, giving them both a hint of the wonderful friction they would soon share.

Her eyes fluttered open as she watched him, startled. "I—"

"Do not deny it. You will use your power over iron to hurt me, should I go too far in your eyes. But I ask you... are you capable of killing me, my firefly? Will you end my life to save those who despise you?" He kept up the tortuous dance. The mix of warring emotions on her features was breathtaking.

"I—" Her eyes searched his, flicking back and forth, as she sought to try to find an answer. "I don't know—" she finally admitted in an exhale.

"Honesty at last." He shifted both his hands to her hips, scooping her up. He was done with their teasing game. "How refreshing."

Gwendolyn opened her mouth, likely to levy more insults at him. But the words never escaped, as he pulled her back down to him in the water, burying his length into her to the hilt in one brutal stroke. It was enough to bring her to a peak of ecstasy, her body spasming around him, threatening to end him too soon.

Growling in his throat, he struggled to maintain control. She was so perfect, the way she fit him. Her plaintive, quiet wail of pleasure was just as damning as the sensation of her. But he would not end their dance so soon. He refused.

When she came down from her high, he began the dance, lifting her in the water and pulling her back to him. The movements were painfully slow and as forceful as he could make them without causing her real harm. The noise she made each time he impacted her was like music to his ears.

All words had left her. That was for the best. He was done arguing. The elementals would die—the choice was hers as to which side to take. His, or theirs.

Could his firefly take his life?

He knew he would not stop her if she did.

His life was hers—and in service to hers—even if she did not wish to see it that way. The King in Iron would reign to keep his Queen of Flames alight. And if she deemed him worthy of death, he would accept his fate.

Life without her would be far worse.

She sought his lips, kissing him even as she desperately tried to catch her breath between impacts. He greedily accepted the embrace. But it was not long before he could tell she was at the limit of how much abuse she could take. How many times her pleasure crashed over her and receded like the tide, he did not know. He had lost count.

When she breathed his name, begging, pleading, he took pity on her. On them both. He pulled her close, and drove into her one last time, burying his cry of release into the crook of her shoulder.

By the Ancients, he loved her.

He loved her and he would kill the world for her.

* * *

"*Ow.*" Gwen hissed through her teeth, wincing in pain. This was her fault. It really was. She was the idiot who had asked someone who could bend steel rebar in his bare hands to give her a neck massage.

First, she had to explain what a massage *was.* She had given him a neck rub first, trying to show him how it was done.

Then it was his turn. And to say that he was approaching it

like he was trying to open walnuts in his hands was putting it mildly.

"Easy on the leverage, crusher." She leaned into his touch, trying to ease off the pressure. "You're trying to rub the tendons, not rip them out."

Mordred wasn't exactly skilled, but he was a fast learner. He eased off, and Gwen could breathe again. After their rather bruising "fight," she demanded he make it up to her. And since she had already brought the wine, this was how she decided he'd pay it back to her.

It was also a great distraction from what he was planning to do. Killing Thorn was one thing. The "prickly" elemental was a problem and was going to continue to be a problem. Gwen could... reluctantly agree that her death was probably inevitable.

The only way Gwen could save her would be to kill Mordred. And there were some trades she wasn't willing to make. The question was—where was the line? How far could he go before she had to stop him?

He'd asked her if she had it in her to kill him. And, confronted with that? She realized she didn't really know. It was like being asked if she'd jump on a grenade to protect others. Nobody really knew how they'd react until the crisis was on them. And she wasn't looking forward to finding out.

Leaning back against Mordred's chest, she reached for the second bottle of wine that they'd fetched and refilled her mug. She wasn't drunk enough yet. She didn't want to get blasted, but she wanted to be just a little fluffier. "Can we come up with some kind of deal?"

"Like what?" He kissed the top of her head before refilling his own clay mug from the bottle. "I would entertain a bargain."

Her heavy sigh made him chuckle.

"When you come up with one, I will listen." He took a sip from his mug. "But that will require you to invent one, first."

"Yeah, yeah. I *know*." She drank from her mug. "I need time for that. Can we... delay your genocidal murder spree? Just a little?"

Mordred hummed. "Let it never be said that I am unreasonable. Very well. Thorn will die tomorrow. Then I will give you one month until I strike at the others—time enough for you to convince me to spare them."

She turned around to face him. "Really?" A month was more time than she'd been afforded by anybody lately.

"If we are attacked, those who transgressed will be dealt with." His tone left no question about how he planned to do the dealing. "Understood?"

"Yeah." She sighed. "One month. Gives us time to train the villagers—and by us, I mean you." She grinned, teasing him. "And... a month for me to figure out how I'm going to talk you out of this." *Or decide to kill you instead.*

God, that hurt her. It felt like a punch to the gut every single time she even thought the words. No, she wasn't ready to do that yet. Maybe not ever.

And the future of Avalon hung on her decision.

* * *

Galahad followed his wife as she led him deep through the wilds of Avalon. She had opened a portal for them, taking them somewhere he did not recognize. It was not because the area was unusual—it was the opposite. This seemed like any other glade on the isle. A clearing, separated from a field by a sparse set of shrubs.

A large boulder was the only defining element that made this area of the woods remarkable enough that he might recognize it a second time. That being said, it was nothing more than a normal rock. He could not for the life of him say why Zoe had brought them there. But he knew better than to ask. All would become clear in time.

Zoe fluttered her wings. They shimmered in the moonlight, reminding him of the stars themselves, as she settled down to the grass in front of the stone. She smiled at it. "The heart of Avalon's magic."

"It is... a rock."

Zoe glanced at him over her shoulder. "Yes. I am aware." She smiled. "It is not the first time a stone has come into focus in our lore." She placed her hand on the surface of the stone. "It was from this place that I drew Caliburn, so long ago. A piece of Avalon itself—a shard of the bleeding heart of this island. And it was to this place that its magic returned when Mordred sundered the blade." She turned to face him. "And from here I shall call forth that power again."

Galahad felt a coldness settle over him. "You plan to wield the blade?"

"Yes." She lifted her chin. "For I am the rightful Queen of Avalon. The blade and the crown are mine to claim. It is time that this world has the ruler it deserves. I had hoped that Mordred would become that which Arthur wished him to be. But now I see it shall never come to pass."

This was a terrible idea. Even wielding the ancient blade of Avalon, it was dangerous. Zoe was powerful, but she was not invincible. Gwendolyn had proven that well enough. Could his love stand against Mordred and the new witch and their respective armies?

And would he join her at her side?

Or, could he stop her if he wished—could he drive a dagger into her heart?

By all the old ones and all the Ba'na'ir of his people, he knew he could not. To kill her would be to destroy himself. He had sworn himself to her, and he could not fail her now.

A gentle hand rested against his cheek. He opened his eyes

and met the magenta-pink orbs of hers, so full of love. So full of compassion. She would rule Avalon with kindness. It meant destroying Mordred and Gwendolyn—and that was a tragedy he would bear until the end of his days.

But his choice had been made.

Now, he must play his part.

He dropped to one knee in front of the Gossamer Lady and bowed his head.

"Mordred must not be given time to rally any forces." Zoe drifted away, back to the stone. "Let us begin now."

SEVENTEEN

"I'm coming with you."

Mordred let out a breath, shutting his eyes. He had believed he had escaped without waking Gwendolyn, but he was mistaken. It was the middle of the night, and the moon was high, casting pale shadows as though the sun itself were caught in a dream. He had been about to climb onto the saddle of his stallion.

Dragons were not precisely the right method of approach for an assassination, after all.

Thorn was camped about a night's ride away from them with her forces. And he planned to end her before she attacked his keep for a second time. Once, he would have thought it cowardly—ignoble—to strike an enemy in the dead of night like a thief.

Now, he could not care less. No—that was not true.

He was rather looking forward to it.

Turning, he watched Gwendolyn pull on a thick coat that had two slits up the back to allow her wings to trail behind her like a cape. Her breath turned to fog in the chill, nearly winter air. Clouds were still moving in—there would be snow, soon.

"You should stay. You will not like what you witness."

Shrugging, she looked off into the field. "My dad used to say, 'You can't eat your steak and pretend you don't know what happened to the cow.' I'm coming."

"A wise man. A shame I will never have the chance to meet him." He mounted his stallion, turning the horse toward the open gate.

"You're not going to argue with me?"

"I know better than to attempt to turn your mind from something it is set upon. I recommend you saddle a horse quickly, however—I will not wait long for you." Was he annoyed? Yes. Was he looking forward to Gwendolyn's reaction to watching him murder Thorn and whatever elementals were foolish enough not to run from him? No.

But she was correct. If she was to stand at his side, and be his queen, she should know. She should witness it firsthand, what it meant to rule. What it meant to keep Avalon *peaceful*.

He expected her to go into the stables and fetch her favorite mare. Instead, she held out her hand in front of her and, with a twist, summoned a horse from the ground. He watched and had to admire how far she had come since her arrival. She had been so terrified of everything, even her own powers.

Although, he did not miss the gleeful smile on her face as she looked at her handiwork as though it was a piece of art. Made of onyx, its eyes glowed a smoldering, fiery red. When it snorted, sparks flew from its nostrils. It was a mare, and smaller than his stallion, but no less frightening. The horse's mane and tail were like Gwendolyn's hair when she was ablaze—more fire than not.

She climbed onto its back, and patted it on the neck, not caring for the fire that touched her. "We're supposed to be scary, right?" She wiggled her fingers at him. "Spoooooky horses."

It took every ounce of self-control not to slap his hand over his face. "Come. We have a long night of travel ahead of us."

"Do you know where we're going?"

"Thorn is not... subtle." He kicked the sides of his stallion and headed off into the field, urging the animal to a gallop as soon as they were clear of the keep. He did not look over his shoulder to see if Gwendolyn was following. He was certain she was.

He also did not wish to mention that it was the scarecrow's scouts who'd told him of Thorn's location. He had already given the villagers enough credit. He did not need to give them more, lest Gwendolyn get ideas in her head about them being welcome to stay long term.

Which he would not allow.

Under any circumstances.

Build a town nearby? Very well. But he would have his home back, and he would not hear any arguments otherwise. Even if it did make Maewenn happy, and he had caught one of his guards playing with a pack of children. *I am a miserable old bastard, after all.*

They rode in silence, with the sound of nothing but the pounding of hooves on the compacted dirt of the road beneath them. Gwendolyn kept pace, following close behind and never falling back. She was an impressive rider. He glanced back at her now and then, simply wishing to catch another sight of the woman he loved, his firefly, so very much having come into her own.

She would be a force of nature in a hundred years, perhaps fewer.

He could only pray to the Ancients that he would be around when that happened.

Hours passed like that, before they reached their destination. He slowed his stallion before stopping at the edge of the wood where it met a field. "Please extinguish your horse, Gwendolyn. I do not wish to give away our position."

Gwendolyn stopped beside him and leaned over to rest

against the neck of her onyx horse. The fire of its mane and tail went out as she did, leaving only gray-black hair in its wake. "*Ow.*"

The chuckle that left him was one of amused sympathy. "We will ride back slower. Or perhaps we will fly home."

"My ass is going to be bruised for a month." She sat back up with a sigh. "Did we really have to do that?"

"Thorn may yet believe I am still a captive of the Iron Crystal. The more time passes, the less likely that becomes." He kept his gaze ahead of them. Snow was falling now, drifting in thick flakes to the frosted grass. But it did not obscure the faint lights of an encampment. He estimated a dozen elementals and hangers-on, or thereabouts.

Summoning his sword to his hand, he glanced at Gwendolyn. "Do you wish to remain here, or join me in the fray?"

She frowned, pulling her coat tighter around her. Snowflakes were landing on her but melting quickly. "I... I'll come."

"Very well. Then stay out of the way if you do not wish to fight. I will not reject your assistance, should you choose to give it." Manifesting the rest of his armor, feeling its familiar weight settle on him, he turned his attention back to the camp. The restriction of his vision by his helm had bothered him once. Now, it was easy to ignore.

Kicking his stallion, he drove toward the camp at a trot. The quickly falling snow was dampening the sound of his approach —perfect. He did not want to alarm his enemy until it was too late.

They would be easy kills. He would seek out Thorn first— cut the head off the proverbial snake. The others would likely scatter once their leader was dead. He might not be able to catch them all, but those who fled would serve to spread the news.

Mordred the Prince in Iron had returned.

And the elementals were safe from his wrath no longer.

* * *

Gwen followed Mordred, staying about fifty feet behind him. He was a nightmare against the darkness and the snow. Her eyes had adjusted, but it was still *proper dark*. With no moonlight or starlight, the only way she knew where to go was the fact that Mordred was somehow an inkier blackness against the drifting white snow and distant firelight.

Honestly, she heard him more than she could see him.

This was going to be a massacre.

She wanted to shout. To warn the elementals to run. But while Mordred had begrudgingly put up with her antics before, anything close to betrayal now wasn't going to go well for her. At all.

And she knew, deep down inside, that this was the right call. That Thorn was going to be, well, a thorn in her side for the rest of her life. There was no jail, no Crystal, that was going to keep that from happening.

Lady Thorn had to die.

Gwen just really wished it was otherwise.

But if wishes were horses, and all that jazz.

Speaking of, her ass *hurt* from riding all night. Next time, she was going to create a horse out of cotton or something softer than goddamn onyx. She just wanted to look half as badass as Mordred. Not that it really mattered, she supposed. But damn it if she wasn't sick of looking like a derpy sidekick.

Mordred slowed his approach to a walk as they drew closer to the camp. When they were a good thirty feet away, he dismounted. Against the brighter glow of the firelight, he cut a terrifying figure, all sharp and jagged edges, and his cape made the faintest whisper against the snow. She dismounted as well, patting her horse before following, chewing her lower lip.

Mordred disappeared into a tent.

It wasn't long before the screaming began. Ducking close to another haphazard shelter, Gwen watched as Thorn ran from within her tent. Thick ropes of briars burst from the ground around her, trying to shield her from the demon who had come to collect his due.

Mordred slashed through the vines, unstoppable as a force of nature. They barely slowed him down. When a nearby elemental formed spears of ice to hurl his way, he flicked his wrist, his cape coming up and hardening to iron. The ice shattered against his shield, no more harmful than snowballs.

The elementals clearly knew better than to fight Mordred when they were surprised. Gwen watched as each one emerged from their tent, took one look at what was happening, and ran for the woods. She knew it wouldn't be the last she saw or heard from them.

"You *bastard!* How—" Thorn jumped back as Mordred swiped at her with his sword once more. "You should be—" That was when Thorn caught sight of Gwen. Her missing, yellowed and misaligned teeth were bared in a hateful snarl. "*You!*"

Suddenly, Gwen was the center of attention. Thorn was coming after her, forgetting the oncoming Prince in Iron in favor of trying to kill her. Gwen burst into flames and spread a circle of fire around her. But the vines were growing back faster than she could destroy them.

Thorn's attention was split, however. She couldn't keep attacking Gwen and defend against Mordred at the same time. When Mordred closed the distance between them, making to lop off Thorn's head, she turned and ran.

"Coward!" Mordred hollered. He lifted his hand, palm up, before clenching a fist.

Spikes of iron, twisted and jagged, sharpened like blades, shot up from the ground. They were curved, rusted, and vicious. Gwen watched as they snapped around Thorn like a cage. The elemental had nowhere to go. Her powers were useless against the metal that warded against all magic.

Mordred gestured again, sending a spike of iron shooting from the air near him, impaling another elemental who was running at him. The weapon passed through his body, leaving a gaping hole in his chest where it shouldn't have been. Gwen recoiled at the sight. The elemental fell to his knees before collapsing to the ground in a growing pool of blood that stained the fallen snow.

The rest of the elementals were running for their lives. At least they weren't total idiots.

Mordred, seeing that the rest of his quarry had fled, turned his focus back to Thorn. "I would have given you an honorable death."

Thorn was cussing in languages that Gwen didn't under-stand, but the meaning was crystal clear. She spat on the ground outside the cage of iron. "What do you think you will gain from this? This is murder! You will unite all of us against you. Is that what you want?"

"Yes." Mordred stopped at the edge of the cage.

That was not the answer Thorn was expecting. Her anger sputtered for a moment before she resumed swearing at the prince.

Mordred ignored her. "The solution was always so simple... yet I resisted the temptation to end you all." He sheathed his sword. However he was planning on ending Thorn, it wasn't with the blade. "I am, shall we say, no longer compelled to spare your lives."

Thorn looked to Gwen, fear in her eyes. "And you are allowing this?"

"On a mass scale? No." Gwen sighed. "But for you? Yeah. Yeah, I am."

Thorn roared in rage, cussing out them both.

"I would ask for your last words. But I believe I already have them." Mordred lifted his hand again, palm up, fingers open.

"Wait!" Thorn screamed, throwing herself at the blades that made up the bars of her cage.

But it was too late.

Mordred tightened his fist.

Gwen had to turn her back to the scene as the blades mirrored the motion of his fingers. Thorn's scream was cut short as they sliced through her. Covering her mouth, Gwen tried not to be sick from the wet sound of the blades pulling back out of Thorn's flesh.

"It had to be done." She heard Mordred's boots crunch through the snow behind her.

"I know. I don't—I just—" She took a deep breath, trying to keep her dinner down where it belonged.

"Gwendolyn."

"No. No. I need a minute." She waved her hand. "I don't want to puke, sorry."

"*Gwendolyn.*" Something in Mordred's tone had shifted. He sounded... pained.

Blinking, she turned around to face him. And all at once, everything changed. She barely noticed the corpse of Thorn lying in the snow behind Mordred. Because there was something else far more important directly in front of her.

Mordred.

And the sword that was jutting from his stomach. It had pierced through his armor. He was holding onto it with his gauntlet, but she could see the blood pouring from between his fingers.

"Wh—"

"I am sorry it came to this."

The sword wrenched out of Mordred. He collapsed to his knees, his hand pressing to the wound. Panicked, Gwen stepped between him and the person who had spoken.

Zoe.

The Gossamer Lady was floating there, wings flickering amber in the light of the fire. And hovering in the air beside her was a sword that looked *very* familiar. The last time Gwen had seen it, it was rusted and broken, but still no less formidable.

Caliburn.

"H-how—" Gwen stammered. Caliburn had been destroyed.

Standing beside her was Galahad, his own sword at the ready, resplendent in his golden armor. He was wearing his helm, and she couldn't see his face—or if he approved of what was happening. "Stand aside, Gwendolyn. Let us do this," he urged. "You do not have to die here with him."

"*Fuck you.*" Gwen was shaking. Mordred might die, even if they didn't finish him off. She had survived an arrow wound, but a *sword* was something else entirely. How was she going to get him home? How was she going to get him to safety? She couldn't carry him. She couldn't fly them both there.

"I warned you," Zoe said to her husband. "She will not abandon him."

"I know." Galahad sighed heavily. "Gwendolyn, I am so very sorry."

"I don't—I was going to try to get him to spare you both. I—I had a plan." She cringed. That was partially a lie. She had time to come up with a plan, which was close enough. "Please, don't. Don't. You've made your point."

Mordred grunted from behind her as he fought his way to standing. He stuck his sword into the snow and leaned on it for support. "They will not listen to you, Gwendolyn. Our last stand is here and now."

If that was true, they were doomed. She couldn't take on Zoe *and* Galahad—and Zoe had Caliburn. Somehow.

She clenched her hands at her sides. It was up to her. She had to get them out of here. But *how?*

If only they could fly home.

Then it hit her.

If she could create a horse...

Spreading her wings, she focused her power. Her flames burned brighter, shifting colors as the temperature rose. Shutting her eyes, she manifested the creature she saw in her mind. If Zoe and Galahad were going to play dirty? So could she. She opened her eyes.

Galahad took a step toward her, ready to fight.

"Hey." Gwen smiled. "Look up, assholes."

Galahad paused before both he and Zoe obeyed.

And it was right then that an enormous dragon landed in the center of the camp. It was made of onyx, like her horse—but its wings were ablaze, like hers. It set the nearby tents on fire as it bellowed out a screech that shook the ground beneath her, sending a jet of fire shooting from its maw as it did.

If it landed on her former friends, great.

But that wasn't her focus. She turned to Mordred and took his arm. It would be like trying to move a tank. "C'mon—we need to go."

He didn't respond, but nodded, walking toward the dragon on unsteady legs. The dragon was meanwhile amusing itself by setting more of the camp on fire, screeching and roaring as it blasted wave after wave of fire after Zoe and Galahad. The two were retreating, but she didn't know for how long. And she didn't know if her dragon could stand up against Caliburn.

She tried her best to help Mordred up onto the back of her dragon, but it really was all his doing. He weighed easily three times what she did, and that was without his armor. But he made it, slumping forward on the back of the beast as she clambered up with him.

"Go!" she shouted.

The dragon didn't hesitate to obey, jumping into the air and taking them off into the snowy night sky with a fiery *whoomf* of giant wings. It knew where to go because she did. It was strange, having herself linked to a creature. She had sensed her connection to the horse, but it was smaller—muted. A dragon was entirely something else. If she paid too much attention, she could feel its wings like she could feel her own.

She extinguished her flames, quickly summoning herself some clothing so she didn't have to fly back in the nude. She really didn't feel like freezing to death a few hundred feet up.

She placed her hand on Mordred's back. She could see the gash in the armor where the sword had pierced through him. He was bleeding. Badly.

"Stay with me, Mordred—you can't die. Not now. Not like this."

"I do not... intend to."

"And if you're going to faint, faint forward—if you fall off, I —" She winced. "Don't fall off."

"Noted." He lowered his head, still hidden beneath his helm.

Undoing the buckle of his chest armor, she slipped her hand underneath and put pressure on the wound. At least from one side, anyway.

Shutting her eyes, she rested her forehead against him.

He couldn't die.

He just couldn't.

Ancients, if you're here—if you're listening to me—if you care... please. I love him. I love him, and I can't let him go.

Save him.

EIGHTEEN

Gwen was so glad that Mordred at least made it back to the keep, and to the ground, before he passed out. He kept his word. He did not fall off her dragon.

He did, however, make it four steps toward his home before he collapsed. Luckily, his iron guards were more than strong enough to heft him to his feet and drag him inside. She followed close behind, mind reeling through different options, interspersed with sheer and total terror. The kind of cold, seeping fear that transcended panic.

Tim was standing by the door and took one look at them before running off into the keep. For what, she had no clue. She had other things to focus on. They brought Mordred to his room, where servants were already prepping the bed to deal with the amount of blood that was going to be coming from him.

Gwen stood at the foot of his bed and watched as the servants stripped off Mordred's armor, then his shirt, peeling the muslin fabric out of the wound. At least he was already unconscious, he couldn't feel it. It didn't stop Gwen's stomach from churning in sympathy with how badly it must have hurt.

They started to press thick pads of cheesecloth to the

wounds, rolling him on his side to treat where the sword both entered and exited his body.

He was sweating, his forehead creased in agony, even in his unconscious state.

Mordred was dying. Mordred was dying, and she had no clue what to do.

Desperately, she wished Doc was there.

Or Galahad, before he went and helped cause this mess.

Or fuck, even Grinn.

Someone. Anyone who would know how to fix this. Or, at least, shit, she could *try*.

"Out of my way!"

Maewenn shoved herself into the room, checking the guards aside with her shoulders as she came in like a hurricane, barking orders at the servants and waving her hand about. In the other, she was carrying a basket of supplies. "You—we have to stitch those wounds shut before we dress them—you're not stringing up a roast, we're trying to *save* him!"

Tim was standing in the door, shifting his weight from one side to the other. He must have gone to fetch her the moment they arrived.

"Mae?" Gwen blinked. Then she remembered something from history class—that ships' cooks were often their surgeons. Maybe it was true in this case.

"Best with a needle." Mae didn't waste much time on pleasantries, and immediately went to work. "I don't suppose you can heal him, can you? With your magic?"

"I—I don't know. I can try." It was worth a shot. "Zoe is the... is the healer, with her being the elemental of life, and all."

"Oh, is that what she does?" Mae let out a distracted *huh* as she began stitching Mordred's back up. Gwen had to keep from looking. "I never could quite figure it out. Never cared enough to ask either, I suppose. But that woman is an arse, if you ask me."

"Yeah. I'm coming around to that way of thinking." Gwen knelt beside the bed, facing Mordred, and stroked some hair out of his face. She had to try. Placing her hand on his bare chest, she felt his heart racing. It was struggling to keep his blood pressure up—she remembered that from one of her mom's favorite medical drama shows.

She dug deep. As deep as she could. Shutting her eyes, she took a breath, held it, and slowly let it out. *Please, Ancients. Save him. Help me save him. Give me the strength to heal him—to save his life. I need him. I can't do this without him.*

I want to save Avalon from all the death that's coming. I'll stop the monster who is nipping at its heels. I'll find a way.

But I need the monster.

I need him.

Please.

She felt something.

A presence.

Hope filled her heart.

And then the world fell out from beneath her.

Screaming, she fell into darkness.

* * *

When Gwen finally stopped falling, she... honestly didn't know what was happening or where she was. Or, when, exactly, she *had* stopped falling.

She was somewhere pitch black. Nothing was around her, no speck of light. It smelled vaguely like a cave, but not moist—it smelled like dust and rock and dirt. She had been falling, screaming her head off, and then she... just wasn't.

She was lying, face down, on something smooth and hard and cold. She assumed it was a stone floor. So, she was *somewhere*. The question was *where*. And *why*.

"Note to self," she muttered. "Don't pray to the Ancients. They're dicks."

Man, she hoped they took that as a jab, and not a real insult. Or else she'd probably wind up going back to falling, and that was way worse. Pushing herself up to her knees, she was distinctly glad to find that she *had* knees. And limbs. And fingers.

Lifting up her hand, she set it ablaze like a makeshift torch.

"Are you *fucking kidding me?*"

It was Arthur's tomb. She was on the floor next to the dais that held the sarcophagus of the dead king. Sighing, she rubbed her other hand down her face. She didn't really want to set her shirt on fire, she had just made it. The Ancients had brought her here. Why?

Or, maybe she brought herself here. She had been trying to use her magic. Maybe she misfired. But... why? Why the tomb? Why now?

Then it hit her. It didn't matter. She was hours away from the keep—hours that Mordred didn't have. By the time she flew there, it'd be the early morning, and he'd be dead. She wouldn't even be there when it happened. Tears stung her eyes. She didn't fight them. Sitting on the edge of the steps that led to the dais, she leaned back against the marble sarcophagus, and let herself cry.

Mordred was dying. And she had failed. She sat there and wept until she didn't have tears anymore. Until she was just too tired to cry. It had been a long, *long* day. Now, it had gotten worse. Why?

Because now she was alone.

Staring at the far wall, surrounded by the tombs, she choked up at the idea of bringing Mordred's body—or whatever would remain of him—to rest down here. How was she supposed to go on without him?

The question of whether or not she could kill him was

pretty clear to her now. And it was a resounding *no*. It didn't feel real. In the absence of tears came numbness, and that was somehow worse. "What do I do now?"

"Risky thing, praying to them."

Gwen shot up to her feet so quickly she almost tripped, screaming as someone appeared *right next to her* out of thin air.

"Let's have some real light in here." The stranger snapped his fingers. The torches around the room that she hadn't seen in the shadows ignited into flame. She extinguished her hand as she studied the man, trying to figure out who he was. Or, what was happening.

He was old. Long, gray hair that maybe had once been curly, but was now just frizzy, was pulled back in a ponytail at the back of his neck. He was balding at the temples. He was dressed in a well-worn dark gray robe.

He pushed himself up to his feet with a pained grunt, the years clearly weighing on him. He was taller than her, which wasn't too hard, but definitely lacked the stature of Mordred or Galahad. He brushed off his robe.

At least he didn't seem dangerous.

An elemental, maybe?

But there was something about him. Something about the air around him. "I'm... gonna ask a really stupid question." She tapped her fingers on her leg. "Are you—" Every time she'd asked this question, she was wrong. "Are you Merlin?"

He chuckled, leaning his hip against the tomb of Arthur like it was nothing more spectacular than his dining room table. "You were bound to be right *eventually*."

Merlin.

The Merlin.

Maybe there was hope, after all.

NINETEEN

"Really? Wait—no shit—" Gwen half-laughed and paced away for a moment before coming back. "Please tell me you're not making this up."

"No, I assure you. You are finally right." He smiled. With a gesture of his hand, he summoned a glowing ball of light, then vanished it a second later. That wasn't elemental magic. That was magic-magic. "Here I am."

But something still felt off. There was a quality to his voice. Something very familiar. Something in his eyes too. She blinked. "Wait. *Wait.*"

Merlin folded his arms across his chest and waited.

It was impossible. But Avalon was full of impossibilities. "Doc? Is that *you?*"

He smiled. Just enough to give her the answer. A dozen emotions hit her at once. Frustration that he had lied to her. Anger that he'd left her alone. Confusion over why he was now an old man, when he'd been gone only two weeks tops. Grief that Mordred was dying, or dead. Fear at her uncertain future.

The frustration and anger won. Stomping up to him, she

shoved him. Not too hard, he was an old man, after all—somehow—but still. "You *asshole!*"

Merlin—Doc—took a step back with the shove, clearly having expected it, and laughed. "I deserve that."

"I—but—what—*how*—" She couldn't wrap her head around what she was seeing. "And—and you bastard, you told me you weren't Merlin!"

"At the time, that was not a lie." The smile on his face turned a little melancholic. "It's so good to see you after so long."

"So long? It's only been a few weeks." Which meant his rapid aging made no sense.

"For you." With a grunt, he hopped to sit on the edge of Arthur's tomb. She was tempted to scold him about being disrespectful, but she figured neither Arthur nor *Merlin* probably cared.

"What do you mean, for me?" She put her hands over her face. "Please, just explain how this is possible. And how this helps Mordred."

"I'm not here to help Mordred. I'm here, at the behest of our mutual benefactors, to aid you." Merlin shrugged. Doc. Whoever. Whatever. Gwen was sick of people changing their names. "He is just part of the bargain."

It definitely sounded like he'd "grown up." If that was possible. Taking a breath, she held it, and slowly let it out. "I'd ask you to explain from the top, but we don't have much time, if any at all. He's dying."

"Hm. Yes. He is. But he has an hour." He shrugged. "Maybe an hour and five minutes. Hard to tell with him. That is neither here nor there." He waved his hand dismissively. "Yes, well. As for my grizzled appearance, it may have only been a few weeks for you since we last met, but it has been several thousand years for me."

She blinked. "Excuse me?"

"I wanted to retire." He huffed, clearly indignant about the subject. "But *no*. Our dear overlords wouldn't hear of it. I figured that since you were here now, they would not mind terribly if I wandered off. But instead of flitting between worlds, I fear I passed through *time* as well." He sighed. "I did not even get a short reprieve from the nonsense."

"So... you went... back in time?" Time travel was real. Why not. Sure. That tracked.

"I went forwards, and backwards, and forwards, and sideways, and rightways, and back again." His smile was tired. "Then I found myself on the isle of Britain long, long before it had a name. After centuries passed, who did I find, but my good friend Arthur and his knights." He patted the top of the tomb. "I recognized Mordred and the rest, but they did not recognize me. I realized why I'd been sent there—to be Merlin. So, I donned the name, and the rest is history."

She let the gears turn in her head for a second. "Wait. That makes no sense. You knew about the name Merlin because of the myths *about* Merlin. So, you couldn't have gotten that from yourself. You knew the name in the future, so you used it in the past, which then gave it to you in the future again." She shook her head. "That's the 'going back in time and killing your own grandfather' paradox."

"See, that's where humans get it all wrong, thinking about time travel. Everyone thinks the universe cares about paradoxes. That the physics of the universe will make it all make logical sense." He huffed a laugh. "The universe could not care less, trust me. It has *no* problems letting paradoxes exist. So. Yes. I got the name from myself."

"So, you weren't Merlin before. But you're Merlin now. Which is thousands of years in your future for you, and two weeks of time for me."

"Correct." He reached over and picked up the dusty golden crown from the top of the marble carving of the dead king. He started using the sleeve of his robe to clean and polish it. "Just don't think about it too hard, you are apt to give yourself a headache."

"Too late." She began to pace in front of him, trying to line everything up in her head. "The Ancients sent you with a bargain? To save Mordred?"

"Yes." He blew on the crown, trying to get some detritus out from where it was stuck next to a gem.

It was a beautiful crown, now that she really got a chance to take a look at it. It was clear that an elemental must have been part of making it—it was too delicate and intricate to have been made by human hands. It was a series of twisting, winding vines that grasped precious stones in a ring. It almost looked feminine.

"It used to belong to Zoe," he answered her unspoken thought. "She made it, long before the knights and Arthur arrived. She was once Queen of Avalon."

"She gave it to Arthur."

"Mm-hm. At the instruction of the Ancients. We're all just... their little playthings, really. But I suppose that's the right of gods. I cannot say I would be any different." He laughed. "I would make a terrible god."

"The worst." She joined him with a chuckle.

"She had a vision of the new King of Avalon. But they lied and chose Mordred instead. That got everything off on the wrong foot, I fear."

"Why'd they lie?"

"Why do they do anything? Damned if I know." He kept polishing the crown. "And trust me, do not bother asking. The last time I did that, they showed me, for a split second, the whole of all creation. I could not stop vomiting for three days."

"Noted." She cringed. "But what do they want from me? I've already promised to stay on the island and never go home. I'm a witch now. I don't have anything left to give them."

"Not true." He held up the crown, inspecting it, before deciding his work was done well enough. "There is one more burden they wish you to bear. And if you choose to do so, they will save Mordred's life."

She watched him for a second, putting everything together. "They... no. No, that makes no sense. I'd be the *worst* queen."

"I beg to differ. You desire peace. You want everyone to live, but you know that isn't possible. You understand the cost of war. You understand loss and betrayal. And you want more than anything else to protect those who can't protect themselves." He held the crown out to her. "That sounds like a queen to me."

She hesitated. "But... no. No. I'm just a *kid*."

"You're as old as Arthur was when he set out on his quest. Older, even." Merlin—Doc—smiled at the memory.

Shaking her head, she hesitated. "Taking that doesn't just magically make me queen, does it? I'll have to fight for it."

"You really think it will be that easy? No, you are right. You'll need to convince Zoe to stand down or kill her."

"And the same with Mordred." She chewed her lip. Mordred wanted the throne. And if she took this, she'd rob him of that. It would probably feel like yet another betrayal. Yet another stab in the back. She shut her eyes.

Become the Queen of Avalon or lose Mordred.

And she'd done so much to get this far already.

With a heavy sigh, she hung her head. "He's going to hate me for this."

"He will be livid, yes. Perhaps, he might try to capture you or make you his enemy. But he cannot hate you. It is not possible." It was clear he was trying to sound reassuring. He wasn't.

"Thanks for the optimism."

"I am simply being realistic." Merlin shifted with a grunt. "I recommend against aging. It is quite painful."

"I'll do my best. I don't think this place will let me live that long." Gwen rolled her eyes. "It keeps trying its damndest to kill me."

"And yet you are stronger than ever. The island has been preparing you for what is to come. Training you." He grinned.

"So that's where Merlin learned his tutoring technique." She paced for a moment again, scratching the back of her neck. "If I take the crown. If I agree to fight to become queen. They save Mordred?"

"Kind of."

She stopped in her tracks. "What do you mean, *kind of?*"

With a dismissive sniff, he looked off into the shadows of the chamber. "You know how gods can be. Always have to have clauses and gotchas."

When he didn't say anything more than that, she glared at him. "*Merlin.*"

"They have agreed to heal Mordred. But if you surrender your goal of taking the throne, or if you become queen and then relinquish it? Mordred will die."

A feeling like cold water ran down her spine. She stared at Merlin and searched his eyes for any hint that he was lying. Or, any hint that there might be something more, something else to the bargain. But he simply met her gaze and said nothing. Nothing at all.

If she didn't become queen, Mordred would die.

Either now or later.

If she ever gave up the crown, he would die.

But if she became queen, it was betraying Mordred and ensuring that she would be at odds with everyone on the island, possibly for eternity. She rubbed her hands over her face. Taking a deep breath, she let it out slowly.

She had to choose. And choose fast. Because Mordred didn't have much time.

Let Mordred die.

Save Mordred and make him her enemy. *And* declare war on all those who would seek to keep her from the throne.

Shutting her eyes again, she shook her head. "Fuck this place sometimes, seriously."

"You can say that again."

* * *

Galahad sat atop his golden steed as he watched his lady converse with a group of frightened elementals. They were from Thorn's pack and were terrified that the Gossamer Lady had come as an emissary of Mordred.

But such was not the case.

This was their third conversation like this. And he knew how it would go, for each time was the same. With Caliburn floating by her side, Zoe would smile and soothe their fears, telling those elementals who remembered her rule all those centuries ago that she would reclaim her throne. And telling those who had never known her as queen that she had once sacrificed her crown to Arthur, but now it was time to take it back.

That Mordred was dead.

That Gwendolyn was the real threat, and she must be stopped at all costs.

That Thorn's death was a tragedy, and she must be avenged.

It twisted a knot in Galahad's stomach to hear Zoe pretend that Thorn was an ally and a friend. The truth was, they were headed to the former elemental warlord's camp to do the same as Mordred had done—kill the upstart and remove another player from the board.

But Zoe no longer had any problem bending the truth, it seemed. And the frightened elementals drank it up, their nervousness disappearing with remarkable speed. They believed her. They wanted to follow her. They would pledge their loyalty to the Gossamer Lady.

And so, little by little, conversation by conversation, their army grew.

And little by little, Galahad's dread increased.

At the Gossamer Lady's request, he even approached his former knights. Bors, Gawain, and Tristan told him they were uninterested in fighting Mordred and wished to enjoy their lives of freedom and quiet. He did not press the matter, and neither did Zoe.

No small part of him had been relieved. He did not wish to put his brothers through more pain. But there was one to whom they had yet to speak. And one whose conversation he was dreading.

And it was him that they were seeking out next.

Conversation with the elementals concluded, Zoe opened a portal for them to travel through. And what greeted him on the other side was a modest home, tucked deep in the woods. He saw no other structure within sight in all directions. Whoever lived here wished to be left alone.

Galahad could not say he blamed him.

Dismounting his steed, he approached the door. Lifting his fist, he went to knock, only to have the door swing open before he could bring his knuckles down upon it.

It took everything in Galahad's being not to flinch when he looked upon the scarred and mutilated face of his former brother-in-arms. Mordred had not taken Percival's betrayal lightly, and had made sure that the act of removing his iron magic from the copper knight's chest had gone as painfully as possible.

"I heard your heavy boots, you walking beanpole." Percival grunted. "Why are you here? If Mordred wants something, he can suck off a goat."

Galahad frowned. "I am not here at the behest of our

former prince. Though I am here because of him, I suppose."
He did not want to do this, he realized. He did not want to rally
these forces and contend for the throne. He did not want to hurt
Gwendolyn.

But the die had been cast. His choice had been made. And
there was no turning back.

Percival narrowed his eyes—well, one eye. The other
seemed frozen by scar tissue. "Spit it out."

"Mordred is dead. Fatally wounded by the Gossamer
Lady." He stepped aside, gesturing to Zoe. "She has rebuilt
Caliburn and seeks the throne. We ask for your assistance. To
join us, in seeking the death of Gwendolyn and to stand against
any who might oppose the Gossamer Lady's ascendance to the
throne."

Percival paused. Then he burst out in laughter so hard that
he had to lean against the doorjamb. "You—*you*—have slain
Mordred?"

"He could not withstand the power of Caliburn." Zoe lifted
her chin in defiance.

"You attacked him from behind. You must have fought
cheaply, there is no *way* you could have bested him in combat."
Percival continued to chuckle before slowly calming his laughter. "But if you think I am deriding your choice, you are wrong.
I would have done precisely the same thing. Congratulations to
you, and good riddance to that rusted bastard."

Zoe's smile was tender. "Will you join us, then?"

Percival thought about it for a moment. "Yes. Perhaps I will
be given the gift of an honorable death in battle." A thin, cruel
smile twisted up the side of his lips that still moved properly.
"And I always hated that girl."

That broke his heart. But Galahad understood. Nodding
once, he turned from the conversation without another word.
He could not stomach it.

"We will rally at the keep within the week. Please attend if you are able." Zoe's voice was unwaveringly pleasant and sweet. "I expect Gwendolyn will pose little threat to us, but I would like to be overly cautious."

"A shame we elementals leave nothing but dust behind when we die." Percival's tone was cold. "I would have loved to have spat on his corpse. But I guess watching Gwendolyn die will be good enough. I will be there, Gossamer Lady. Knight in Gold."

Percival shut the door. Galahad was glad to be done with him.

"What is wrong, my love?" Zoe frowned at him. "It troubles you to see your old companion. And what has become of him."

"Yes," he admitted. It was easy to see, and while she may not have understood the depths and reasoning behind his distaste, it was still a fact.

"I know you were friends with Gwendolyn. But she chose her side, and you chose yours. There is no going back now." Zoe hugged him, her small, thin arms circling his waist. He held her back, kissing the top of her head.

"Let us go home, my love." Zoe held his hand, her fingers winding between his much coarser ones. "It has been a long day."

"Aye." Relief welled in him at the idea of home. What a simple yet powerful concept—home. Home, with her. He loved her. That was the unavoidable truth of it all. His Gossamer Lady was his life. His light. Without her, he would have nothing—no reason to be. He would follow her to the end, even if he disagreed with her choices.

He was her knight. He would protect her to the very end.

It was his sacred duty. No matter what may come.

No matter the cost.

For that was honor.

Was it not?

TWENTY

Mordred was dreaming.

Or, perhaps he had already awoken.

It was hard to say. The world around him felt detached from him—a step removed. He was standing at the edge of a clearing, though it took him a long time to realize that. Where he stood was the abyss of a moonless, starless night—nothing around him but the promise of emptiness. But in front of him was Gwendolyn—though he knew it to be only a vision. There was something empty about it—his love was not truly there. She was laughing and playing with Eod, tussling over a stick. They were happy.

Joyful.

And he was not there with them. He was watching, alone in the darkness.

Behold the light your shadow casts.

Whose was that thought? Not his, surely. But no one else was around. No one but the mirage before him.

In darkness, spare the sun.

The thought was not his own, but it did not feel foreign. He shut his eyes, blotting out the dreaming world around him. He repeated the words to himself, trying to find their origin.

Like the snap of fingers, something shifted. When he blinked his eyes open, the world around him was like nothing he had ever seen. Blades of grass, blue and translucent like the purest glass, shimmered in the moonlight as they swayed around him. Everything along the edges of his vision was a blur. He was still dreaming.

But this time, he was not alone.

He could not see them, but he could sense them. Or sense *it*, perhaps. He could not rightfully say. This simply did not feel like the magic that he had known all his life—it *was* the magic. This was Avalon. The heart of it. Or, perhaps, its dreams.

"Am I dead?" It was the obvious question. The Gossamer Lady had run him through with a remade Caliburn. He was dying, last he remembered, when he saw his keep and his feet touched the ground. He had kept his word—he had not lost consciousness on the flight back to his home.

No.

A thought. His and not his. Familiar and foreign. But a relief, all the same. He let out a breath, content with the fact that he still lived. For now.

More madness? Or, perhaps the presence of the gods of Avalon.

He found no harm in entertaining the possibility of the latter, given that offending them would likely spell disaster.

"Behold the light my shadow casts." He pondered the phrase—no, the *order*. It had sounded like a missive. He smirked. "Ah. I understand. You were the power behind that vision of Arthur, were you not?"

Silence.

He supposed it was the right of the gods to be mysterious. Especially when his query did not matter. What difference did it make now? He was at war. "If you are attempting to convince me to become this—this monster—you needn't. I have already made up my mind. I made that choice in the Crystal."

More silence.

But perhaps he misunderstood. Perhaps it was not here to convince him—perhaps it was here to console him? "The destruction of my honor, my soul, my—my light—will mean she will be happy."

Yes.

But he had not been there in the clearing with her. He had been alone, watching from the shadows. "Without me."

A long pause. Long enough that Mordred did not believe he would receive an answer.

In the light, alone.

It was not being mysterious; it was being *cryptic*. He pinched the bridge of his nose with his knuckles—he had long since learned not to do that with his fingertips while wearing clawed gauntlets—and fought down a sigh. It was worse than that damnable wizard.

In the light, alone.

A comfort, a warning, a gift? He did not know. And he knew perhaps he never would.

Shaking his head, he let out a slow breath. "Thank you."

No good comes in being rude to the gods.

He blinked his eyes open, light shining in them, streaming from a nearby window. He hummed and turned his head, though it felt like it had been stuffed with cotton. Ah, he knew this feeling well—waking up after being severely injured.

It was miserable every time.

His mouth tasted like blood. The room smelled of its metallic, coppery tinge and sweat. His sweat. With how much blood he knew he had lost, his heart would have begun to work in overdrive, sending him into a fever.

The wound should have been fatal, even to him. The Gossamer Lady was the only one who could heal such an injury, and there was no chance of that having happened. How was he alive? More importantly, *why?* Had the Ancients, had Avalon, resurrected him? For what purpose?

Behold the light your shadow casts.

And it was the light that was bothering him at the moment. Wincing, he turned his head back to the window, squinting at the bright sun. He wanted someone to draw the curtain. There was someone there in the bed beside him, and he felt the strain in his features relax at the sight of her.

Gwendolyn had been sitting at his side, holding his hand. She must have decided she needed to lay her head down for a second before she had fallen fast asleep, legs still dangling off the bed, tendrils of her firelike hair pooling around her.

She was so beautiful.

Behold the light his shadow casts, indeed. Reaching out, he gently stroked her hair with his other hand. The touch jolted her awake, and she sat up, lost for a moment.

He went to say hello, but found his throat was too dry to speak, and only managed to cough. The sound pulled Gwendolyn's attention to him. Her eyes were still red from what he assumed must have been crying.

"Mordred!" Frantically, she shifted closer to him, stroking his hair out of his face. "Oh God—Mordred." She kissed him, desperate but gentle.

How he wished he could return the gesture, far less gently. But he was in no shape to do anything of the sort. He gestured his hand at the dresser beside him where he saw a pitcher of water. Not so long ago, he had seen Arthur do the same...

"Oh! Right—right. Sorry." She filled a mug before helping him sip it slowly. Every drop of it felt like heaven. "I hope you weren't awake long without me, I just—I guess I was really tired."

He could not imagine why. "Firefly," he finally managed to

say, though it felt as though he had eaten a few fistfuls of gravel for dinner.

"It's all right." Gwen stroked his hair again tenderly. She was smiling at him, but there was a deep sadness in her eyes. Something that her relief could not touch. And deep within it, a tinge of fear.

There was a cost to his recovery. There was a price to be paid for his life. What had Gwendolyn sacrificed? She had already forsaken her home. She would never see Earth again, when she could have been free.

What else would she have to surrender because she loved him?

Carefully lifting his hand to her cheek, he rested his palm there. She leaned into his touch, eyes shutting. He saw the exhaustion. Grief. He wished to ask her what had happened.

No, he should wait. His focus had to be upon healing, for their time was short. The Gossamer Lady had declared war. Though they would believe him dead, they would come for Gwendolyn in his keep.

Although he did deeply wish to know.

"You—you should rest." She sat back, gently placing his hand down. "Get some sleep. We'll talk when you're back on your feet."

Curiosity got the best of him. "What... trade?" he managed to choke out.

The flicker of pain and fear on her face looked as though he had struck her.

"I—of course, you'd know. Somehow." She sighed, her shoulders slumping. "I couldn't let you die. I tried to heal you, but then... well. I'll tell you the whole story when you're up and about. If you try to throttle me, you'll pop a stitch and Mae will be *livid*."

That made sense, he supposed. Nodding weakly, he rested his head back into the pillow and let out a long, ragged breath.

Sleep sounded wonderful, especially as breathing was currently a rather painful endeavor. The bitch must have collapsed his lung with the blade. He would have to be sure to return the favor.

"Goodnight. I love you." Standing from the edge of the bed, Gwendolyn kissed him again before she headed to the door. She was partway through shutting the door when she paused and looked back at him.

"I'll tell you this much—I finally met Merlin."

The door shut behind her.

And Mordred knew no good would come of this.

None at all.

* * *

"Explain it to me again?"

Gwen sighed and rested her forehead on the edge of the dining room table. She didn't blame Mordred for not quite getting it. She didn't get it either. It had only been a day since he insisted on walking around the keep and sitting down at the table for dinner. Part of it was the fact that he healed fast. Part of it was the fact that he was a stubborn bastard.

But he wanted dinner. At the table. She understood, honestly—Mae was a lot when she *didn't* have a patient to fuss over. When she felt like she had a mission, she was unstoppable.

"The young wizard was actually the old wizard, but not yet. He traveled back in time and became the old wizard you knew as Merlin."

"But it was the same man."

"Yeah." She had been dreading this conversation the entire time. It had been like walking on eggshells around him. Every moment he was awake, he was watching her, waiting. Waiting for the other shoe to drop. And she could sense it coming.

"His future created the myth that his past was built upon."

Mordred hummed. "I cannot say I am entirely surprised. He was always infuriatingly abstruse. It is suitable that his life be the same." Picking up his goblet of wine, he took a sip from it.

She had tried to keep him from drinking. That went over about as well as she'd have expected.

"I am more annoyed that I did not see it." He sat back in his chair, spinning the goblet idly between the tips of his claws on one hand. "Although I suppose it serves me right. I never paid him much mind."

Lifting her head, she decided she wasn't sober enough for this herself, either, and swallowed half the goblet of wine in one go before refilling it from the bottle.

"Will you tell me what transpired?" Mordred's molten, rust-colored eyes were boring into her. "Or, are you still frightened that I will 'pop a stitch'?"

He learned fast. She'd give him that. "I mean, it's... It's fine." Standing from the table, she couldn't help but pace. There was no point in trying to hide her nerves. "It's going to be fine. You just can't be pissed—I had no choice."

"I feel as though you did."

"Yeah, I could've let you die. That was the other option." She rolled her eyes. "Which isn't a choice."

"Ostensibly, yes. It is."

"Well, it's a shitty one, okay?" She didn't know why she was getting frustrated. Taking a breath, she held it for a second before letting it out, trying to calm down. It mostly worked. Kind of. Maybe. A little.

"Gwendolyn." There was that tone. The disappointed voice that made her want to throw something at his head. "Tell me."

This was not going to go well. This was not going to go well at all. Cringing, she braced herself for his outburst. "The island wants me to become queen. Doc—Merlin—whatever—he gave me the crown. Said that if I stopped pursuing it, or if I ever gave up the throne, you'd die."

Mordred was silent for a long moment. "And what happens if you try but fail to become queen?"

"I..." That was a good question. Merlin hadn't said. "I don't know. He just said I can't stop trying, or once I'm there I can't give it up."

Mordred hummed but said nothing else. Simply looked off into the distance, his expression unreadable.

When he didn't say anything for what felt like minutes, she couldn't take it anymore. "Mordred?" She could see the wheels turning, but she couldn't predict what he was thinking. It could go any direction.

"Who am I to argue with the Ancients?" He sipped his wine. "They have chosen you."

"I—I mean, let's be clear here, I don't *want* to be queen. I didn't *want* to be chosen." Shaking her head, she went back to the table, sitting in the chair next to him. "I'm going to be a shit queen."

"I do not think so. You care as deeply for this world as I do. And you are something I am not."

"What?"

He smirked. "Liked by others."

That had her slapping her hand over her eyes. "You're liked by others, just, y'know...?" *Not a ton of them?*

"I have your love. All other fondness paid to me is by those creatures that I created. Galahad is now my enemy. The other knights bear me no love, nor should they." Mordred shook his head. "I find myself very much alone. But do not mistake me, this suits me fine. I think I have given up this foolhardy quest to be *respected* or *liked*. I think I will finally comfort myself by settling for that which I garner best." His expression turned just a little wicked. "Fear."

"I don't think..." She paused. What good was it to argue with him? Besides, she hated to admit it—but he was right. He was really damn good at being terrifying. "But I know you want to be king, and—and this—I didn't want you to be mad."

"You said it yourself. You do not wish for this. You chose to save my life. I could hardly become king if I were dead." He reached out a hand and combed his claws through her hair, gently tucking a few strands behind her ear.

He wasn't mad. What a damn relief. "I should have trusted you not to be angry, I'm sorry. I didn't want to tell you earlier because I didn't know how you'd react."

"I understand." He finished his goblet of wine before pressing up out of his chair. She didn't miss his wince as he did so. "I think it is best if I retire early. This wound seems to have at least temporarily cured me of my insomnia."

"Silver linings, I guess. Do you need a hand?"

"No. But thank you." He tipped her head so that he could bend down to kiss her, his lips lingering on hers. "Goodnight, my firefly."

"Goodnight." She smiled and watched him leave the room. If she didn't know him, she wouldn't have known anything was wrong. Dozens of wars and countless injuries would do that to a person.

The silence that followed settled over her like an unwelcome blanket. He didn't seem angry with her for needing to become queen. But he hadn't exactly been enthusiastic either. What had she expected? For him to be *happy* for her?

It all just left a strange feeling in her stomach. Something wasn't right.

* * *

How *dare* they.

How *dare* the Ancients subject him to this!

This humiliation. This degradation. The throne should be *his*. His! He loved Gwendolyn, but she had no right to the crown. None. Arthur passed Caliburn to him, and it was stolen by the Gossamer Lady. Now Gwen would steal his reign as king?

No.

This could not stand.

He loved her. He loved her more than he loved life itself. There was no harm he could bring to her—that was out of the question. But something *must* be done.

Pacing back and forth in his bedroom, his blood was boiling from the rage. From the indignation of it all. It was his right to rule! Not her!

Staring down at his palms, Mordred clenched his fists and forced himself to slow his breathing. His heart was pounding, and it was giving him a headache. He could not push himself too hard as he was still injured.

But he would have to act soon.

The crown would be *his*.

TWENTY-ONE

Galahad watched the keep from the cover of the woods, and reflected upon how, not long ago, Lancelot had stood in this exact place, planning to do exactly the same thing.

But without the iron army and Mordred, the keep would fall much faster. He frowned at the idea of having to put Gwendolyn to the blade. It hurt him deeply. She did not deserve to die. But that was war. That was what happened when forces fought for power.

The fires flickered in the woods around him, where the elementals had set up camp. Their light would warn the denizens of the keep, whoever was left. And that was very much by design. He knew the villagers had rallied to Gwendolyn's cause. He knew that upon seeing their encroaching force, she would send them away. She would seek to spare their lives and likely surrender herself to them.

That was his sincerest hope.

"I know you feel this is wrong," Zoe said as she approached, hugging his arm and leaning her cheek against him. "But it must be done."

Galahad merely sighed in response.

"I will ensure her death is quick and painless. I do not wish for her to suffer. I am so very sorry that you have had to endure the loss of your friends. But you know quite well what Mordred would have done to this world, should he have been allowed to live."

"I do." Galahad shut his eyes.

"We will approach the keep at dawn, in hopes that you are correct—that she will surrender."

She would.

Then she would die.

And Galahad would be left to wonder if he could live with himself and his deeds.

* * *

Mordred smirked as he saw the fires flickering in the distance. It seemed Galahad sought to repeat recent history.

"What do we do?" Gwendolyn asked from beside him, hugging his arm as she watched the field as well. "And... they told us they were here. Wouldn't a surprise attack have been better?"

"They believe me to be dead. They will think you are here alone with your army of villagers. If I know Galahad, he is hoping to procure your surrender." Mordred huffed a laugh. "Which, if the facts he believes were true, I am certain you would."

"Probably." She paused. "Yeah. I would. To spare the villagers. Even if Bert would be super pissed about it."

She had a noble heart. And such a thing was easily used and manipulated. Mordred knew that from personal experience. To think that he had submitted to the *laws* of those who sought to harm him. Never again.

Nor would he allow Gwendolyn to take from him that which was rightfully his. He adored his firefly. And he would cherish her for all the time they had to share. The discord between the two truths was churning in his mind. He had a solution to the issue, but to say that it would strain their love would be putting it mildly.

Perhaps it was his turn to betray her. The Ancients knew how many times he had forgiven her for the same. Love was eternal, but anger was temporary—she would forgive him in time. And time was something they would have in abundance once his work was done.

"Y'know," she interrupted his thoughts. "If I become queen, and we get married... you still get to be king."

"King consort. It is different." He placed his hand atop hers where it rested on his arm. "But I understand your meaning, and I appreciate it." Pausing, he turned to her. "Did you just casually agree to marry me?"

"I mean, yeah." She smiled up at him, shrugging shyly, as though it were no matter worth discussing. "I figured that was obvious."

His heart soared and fell into oblivion at the same moment. "Then I believe the modern custom is to provide you with a ring, is it not?"

"Sure, but it's not a big deal."

Holding his hand up, he closed his fingers into a fist, and summoned his power, weaving an intricate ring of iron. He pulled magic from himself, just a thread—just *enough*—and created a shining, faintly glowing shard of crystal to sit in the center of the band. When he opened his palm, her eyes went wide, her smile broadening.

Mordred knelt. "Will you be my bride, Gwendolyn Wright?"

"I—I already told you," she murmured, staring at the ring in awe and disbelief.

He chuckled. "Then do me the honor of saying yes, will you?"

"Yes." She laughed as if she did not quite believe it. "Yes! I'll marry you. I love you."

Standing, he kissed her. She jumped, wrapping her arms behind his neck, and he took her weight easily, her feet no longer touching the ground.

When he released her, she took the ring from him and studied it, turning it over in her palm. "What's making it glow, your magic?"

"Indeed. A piece of me." He was almost proud of her for recognizing it and growing suspicious. He could hear it in her voice. "So that I will never leave your side."

There was a smile on her features as she turned the ring over in her hand, inspecting every delicate curl of iron that grasped the shard that resembled opal. There was a moment when he thought she might reject it—when she thought she might see through his scheme.

But she trusted him.

For now.

She slipped the ring on her finger.

When nothing happened, she smiled, laughed, and studied it. "I—I love it. The glow is subtle enough that it won't keep me up at night."

"Hm. I did not think of that." He combed his talons through her hair as he held her close. "Gwendolyn, they will strike in the morning. I need you to stay in the keep. I need you to stay out of the way."

"Why?" She furrowed her brow as she looked up at him. "You think I'm going to stop you from killing them?"

"At least Galahad, yes. I know you. And I know your bleeding heart." He crooked a claw beneath her chin. "You will wish to spare him, no matter what he has done or vows to do. Galahad *will* die by my hand. I will not tolerate your meddling, too much is at stake."

"I..." Her shoulders slumped. "You're right. I don't think I can watch him die. Lancelot was bad enough, and I really like Galahad."

"I appreciate that you did not attempt to lie to me this time." No matter what he did, he could not suppress a smirk. "And you believe I had enchanted the ring."

"Yeah. I did. I mean. You're taking this whole 'the island decreed it wants me to be queen' thing really well." She stared down at the ring again, clearly fascinated by how it looked on her finger. "I guess I expected you to be mad about it."

"I have two responses to that. The first is that my goal in all this is, and forever shall be, to keep you safe from all those who would see you harmed. This includes our former friends, the elementals, and any new threats that might arise." He leaned down to kiss her, hovering his lips just over hers, before pausing. "And the second... is that you are right."

"Wh—" Gwendolyn's eyes rolled back into her head, her knees giving out as she fell asleep. He caught her as she fell, lifting her easily in his arms. When she woke, all the dirty business of Avalon would be concluded. Galahad, Zoe, and all the other elementals would be long dead.

She would wake with him having taken the throne. *And* Caliburn. Both of which were his by right. And he would leave her there in her dream until everything was secured. He would endure her wrath, but it would be worth it in the end.

Worse yet for her would be her discovery that the ring was impossible to remove. It would be his insurance that she would never be able to stand against him.

"The Ancients decreed that you must not give up your fight to become Queen of Avalon. And you never shall—but neither shall you succeed." He carried her into the room, placing her down on the bed. He stroked her fiery hair before kissing her and pulling the blankets up over her. "We shall exist until the stars burn away as the King in Iron and his Queen in Chains."

Eod, who was curled up on the rug by the fireplace, lifted his head and whimpered quietly.

Mordred patted the bed. He did not usually allow dogs to sleep there, but he would make an exception this time. Though, he suspected an exception once made was an exception no longer, but now the rule. But he would make that a gift to his firefly.

The hound jumped onto the bed, turned around a few times, sniffed Gwendolyn, then collapsed in a heap beside her, resting his head on her legs. He was a good and loyal animal.

Mordred petted the dog, seeing worry and concern in those big, doleful eyes. "It will be all right, I promise. She will understand."

The dog's ears drooped as if he questioned the validity of that statement. But Mordred was certain that Gwendolyn would forgive him. She *must.* There was no option.

Standing, he headed for the door. There was work to be done.

* * *

Gwen was back in senior year of high school, sitting on the field, staring out at the baseball diamond. It was a championship game, and her boyfriend Mick was shortstop. So here she was, cheering him on, with her bag of kettle corn and diet soda.

Wait.

Ex-boyfriend.

Mick was her *ex-boyfriend.*

All at once, she realized she was dreaming. And the moment after that, she remembered what had happened to put her here. Her first reaction had nothing to do with her dream. "*Fuck!*" she growled, placing her hands over her face. "I should have known—I should have known! Fucking *damn it!*"

Mordred had tricked her. The ring wasn't just enchanted, it

was cursed. But cursed how? That remained to be seen. She was going to beat the *shit* out of him. Or rather, she was going to *try*. Maybe Maewenn would loan her a frying pan.

The last thing she remembered was putting the ring on her finger, and then she was here. She knew why he'd done it. He wanted Galahad and Zoe dead—and while she agreed about Zoe, she was on the fence about Galahad. More important-ly... *he* wanted the throne.

Something told her she was going to have a hard time getting the ring off her finger when she woke up. "Fuck-fuck-fuck-*fuck-fuck*—" She knew swearing wasn't going to get her anywhere, but it made her feel better.

He'd betrayed her. She was furious. But at the same time, she wasn't *surprised*. And, to be fair, she'd done it to him a half dozen times so far. It still made her want to scream. Given that she was alone in a dream, she did. Nobody around her even registered her outburst.

She knew what he was up to. It wasn't enough that Mordred was going to kill Galahad and Zoe and take the throne for himself—it was what he was going to do the day after. Namely, slaughter all the elementals and place all of Avalon under his thumb. He was going to take the throne. Technically, the Ancients had said she couldn't give up trying—not that she had to succeed.

He'd found a loophole. Great. A murderous loophole.

But how could she stop him? What could she *do*? If the ring made her fall asleep on command, he effectively had wired her with a goddamn off switch.

Even worse, she was trapped in a dream. She couldn't do anything from here. That was her first step—get out of the dream.

"Wake up." She slapped her palms against her temples. "Wake up, stupid. Wake up!"

The dream baseball game continued, the crack of the metal

bat against the ball echoing across the field. She sighed and lay back on the grass, staring up at the blue sky of her dream. "This is stupid."

There was no way Mordred would leave her asleep like this. Not forever. But just long enough to have finished his murder spree and take the throne. If she didn't wake up now, Galahad and Zoe would be dead, and who knows how many with them?

"Wake up. *Wake up wake up wake up!*" She screamed at the sky, but nothing but the cheer of the crowd around her responded.

It was a statement she'd made a thousand times since coming to Avalon. And she had the feeling she'd make it a thousand more times before this place was done with her.

"This fucking *sucks*."

* * *

History would repeat itself for Galahad, Mordred would see to that. But perhaps not in the way that the Knight in Gold would predict.

They believed him to be dead.

And that would work very much to his advantage.

"When dawn breaks, Galahad will ride forward and ask for the surrender of Gwendolyn. You must tell him that in a fit of grief, she has killed herself." Mordred did not take his eyes off the campfires at the edge of the forest.

"Um...," Bertin—Mordred refused to address or think of the scarecrow as *Bert*—was clearly not a fan of the plot. "Why? Where is she?"

"Gwendolyn has opted to stay in my chambers for the duration of the fight. The death of her former friend and ally will hurt her too much to witness. Her sympathetic heart is what we all adore about her—but it brings her untold harm." Mordred placed his hand on the hilt of his sword. It was not meant as a threat, but if Bertin took it as such, all the better.

The scarecrow sighed. "I'd like to talk to her."

"She is resting."

"Right." Bertin walked away, thinking better of questioning Mordred's obvious lie. He paused before leaving. "And my soldiers?"

"They will wait here in the keep. When I spring my trap, the other elementals may panic and rush forward in an attempt to seize the keep. If that is the case, you will need to defend your future queen."

"Hm. Fine. That's a decent plan." With that, the scarecrow left.

Good. He did not need Bertin to like him or trust him—simply to obey him. This moment was crucial. Mordred could defeat Galahad on his own, but with the addition of the Gossamer Lady, of Caliburn, and of an unknown number of elementals... the situation was still a roll of the dice. He would need every advantage he could gain.

His jaw ticked.

How many times had he stood on the ramparts and defended his home from those who wished to see his head on a pike? How many times had his former companions been the ones to greet him?

It did not matter.

This would be the last.

He would see to it.

TWENTY-TWO

Gwen had no other brilliant idea except to just *walk*. She didn't know where she was going, she was doing some weird kind of lucid magic-dreaming by herself. But she didn't have anything else to do. So she picked a direction and just went.

And with nobody else to talk to, she did the most logical thing. She talked to herself.

"All right. So. I need to wake up. But then what?" The dream landscape had taken her to the parking lot of a mall that she used to frequent. She kicked a small, loose chunk of sidewalk, sending it skittering in front of her. "How do I stop Mordred? Do I even *want* to?"

That was silly, of course she did.

"I get it. Zoe probably has to die. Probably." There was likely no way around that one. The Gossamer Lady had skewered Mordred like a kebab with what had *theoretically* been his own sword at one time. If pressed, Gwen would admit it was the right call, even if she hated what it would do to Galahad.

It was the Knight in Gold whose death she didn't think she could stomach. Mordred had been right about that—if she had to watch it happen, there was no way she couldn't get involved.

There was a good chance that Galahad would prefer death over living without the love of his life.

But it just didn't *feel* right.

As for all the other elementals? They probably viewed Zoe with a mix of fear and loyalty. And Gwen had to admit that she herself hadn't won any favors with them since her time in Avalon. Siding with Mordred would do that.

But that didn't mean they should all die.

If she did manage to become queen, though, that would be her problem to solve. She'd need to find some way to try to keep the peace without damning everyone to an eternity trapped inside the Iron Crystal or sentencing them to death.

There had to be a way. There *had* to be. That was why Avalon had chosen her, she was sure of it. If anybody was going to be able to figure it out, it'd be her. Not like she had any clue about where to start. Hopefully, it'd come to her when she needed it.

That didn't solve her immediate problem, though. She was asleep. And if she waited for Mordred to wake her up, the massacre would be done. Walking through the dream, she transitioned from the mall parking lot to a campsite she used to frequent with her family. There was a small river with a rocky cliff along one side, and she used to love to follow the trail along the river, skipping stones across the surface when it was calm enough.

She felt like Winnie the Pooh. "Think, think, *think!*"

A heavy, beleaguered sigh came from the cliff above her. "I'm afraid to say that's something you're clearly not capable of doing. You might as well give up."

She knew that voice. Stopping in her tracks, she looked up. And there, perched atop the cliff, lying like a panther on a branch, was a huge, catlike demon. Two glowing red eyes peered down at her.

Grinn.

It was *Grinn*.

But he was whole. He had his horns, his eyes, his fangs. His lion-esque tail flicked in annoyance, the tuft of hair at the end thumping against the rock.

"This—this isn't possible. You're not real. This is a dream."

The demon shrugged and peered off into the dream, his lip curling in disgust. "Certainly not one of mine."

"You're dead."

"I died. That part is accurate."

"Are you—are you really here?" Gwen couldn't help but gape in disbelief. Even in the dream, she felt her heart race. Was it possible? "Did you make it back to hell?"

"If I said I did, would you believe me?"

Thinking about it for a moment, she shook her head. "You could just be my mind telling me what I want to hear."

"And if I told you I was just a figment of your idiotic mind, what then?"

"I'd probably think you were really Grinn but that you were fucking with me." She shrugged. "So I guess it doesn't matter if you're real or not, I wouldn't believe you."

"Exactly. So don't waste my time on stupid questions." He stood, stretching, his long claws digging into the rock, leaving trenches in the stone. "What foolish mess have you gotten yourself into this time?"

"Mordred has lost his mind. He—wait—wouldn't you already know this if you're part of my dream?" She narrowed her eyes.

"Or, you think I wouldn't know, so I don't." He shook his head with a heavy sigh, smoke curling from his nostrils. He sat, wrapping his tail around his front feet. Paws? Hands? They were kind of both, she supposed.

"Right." She placed her own hands over her eyes. "I'm betting this is just my inner sarcastic self-loathing taking the shape of the asshole demon to talk myself through what's going on."

"Whatever makes you happy. Now, will you hurry it up? I hate you, and I want to be done with inane conversation as soon as possible." That sounded like Grinn, all right.

"After you died, Zoe took Mordred prisoner. He stood trial. And was condemned to being imprisoned in the Iron Crystal."

Grinn burst out laughing. A kind of real, jovial humor that she'd never heard from the demon. But she supposed that tracked. He'd love Mordred's suffering, that was easy to predict. "That is *amazing*. Of course I wasn't around to see it. Avalon wouldn't do me that favor. Instead, I had to die with you slobber-crying all over me."

Rolling her eyes, she tried not to be offended. "Yeah, sorry I felt bad that you died."

"You should be."

Yeah, he made her want to scream. "If you're an illusion, I've really got your personality pegged. Couldn't I have dreamed up a slightly nicer version of you?"

He huffed. "You're a moron, but you never were good at lying to yourself."

"Thanks?" Why did she have to summon up the vision of the asshole demon? Now and then, she had to admit, he gave decent advice, even if he did it in the worst way possible. "Anyway. Mordred was losing his mind in the Crystal, so I went off to free him. In the process I managed to piss off Zoe and Galahad. Zoe wants to be queen because, apparently, she was the ruler here before Arthur arrived."

Grinn waved a hand, indicating she needed to speed up.

God, she wanted to throw a rock at him. "I freed Mordred, but now he's intent on murdering all the elementals on the island. Zoe almost killed him with Caliburn—"

"I thought I destroyed that damnable sword."

"You did. She brought it back."

Grinn huffed. "Nothing ever stays dead around here." He lay back down on the edge of the rocky cliff with a *thwumf*. "Except for me. Proof this island truly has a grudge."

She picked up where she left off as though he hadn't interrupted. "Zoe almost killed Mordred with Caliburn, and I had to make a deal with Avalon. I agreed to become queen if they saved him."

He snorted. "Never mind. I'm glad I died, if this place wants *you* in charge."

"I wish I knew if you were really here or not." She frowned, tucking her hands into her coat pockets. "I'm sorry you died. I know it's stupid, but I kind of miss you. I guess I can only hope you made it back to your family."

"You're right. You are stupid. But this isn't news."

Whatever. "Mordred betrayed me. This ring is enchanted." She held up her hand, showing off the cursed item in question. "He knocked me out and trapped me here while he goes off and massacres everyone."

"And you, predictably, want to stop him." Grinn sighed in annoyance and rolled onto his side, not even caring enough to talk to her while upright. "Have you ever stopped to consider that he might be right?"

"Yeah. I have. And I still think he's wrong."

"Because a child knows better how to rule Avalon than a man who has lived here for over a thousand years."

"I thought you hated him?"

"I can hate you both."

She shook her head. "I clearly need therapy if my brain made you up." She started walking away from him, not wanting to continue to stand there and be berated by the ghost of Grinn, whether he was in her head or not.

There was a rustle from behind her, and the *ka-thud* of a heavy animal landing beside her told her that Grinn wasn't done mocking her.

"If you're going to be an asshole, can you at least be a useful asshole and help me?"

"Cranky, aren't you?"

"I've had a bad time of it lately. Honestly? Ever since you brought me to Avalon, things have been a shitshow. I love Mordred. I really do. But all my friends are dead, or gone, or probably about to die. And it's all your fucking fault."

"Would you trade it all to go home again?"

It took her a second to admit it out loud. With a heavy sigh, she replied, "No."

"Then quit whining."

Maybe she didn't miss Grinn at all, now that she thought about it. Picking up a handful of pebbles from the riverbank, she started tossing them into the water idly as she walked. They went in silence for a while, Gwen having to glance over her shoulder occasionally to see if he was still with her.

"Why're you following me?" She raised an eyebrow. "If you hate me so much."

"What, I can't amuse myself by watching your failures?" He smiled, revealing his fangs. "Call it for old times' sake."

She whipped a pebble at him. It bounced pointlessly off his fur. But it made her feel a little better. "If you're going to be here, can you at least help me come up with a plan to wake me up?"

"Hm. No."

"Why not?"

"I simply don't care."

She threw another pebble at him. It did about as much good as throwing a snowball into the sun. But whatever. It gave her something to do—like walking pointlessly through her dream landscape.

"Besides," Grinn began, his voice growing quiet in a way she didn't like. "I've come up with a new way of amusing myself, I think."

Stopping, she turned to face him. "What do you mean?"

"Well, I have an opportunity to do something I've been wanting to do for *years*." He walked up to her slowly, resembling a panther, until he loomed over her. His glowing red eyes flickered like fire as he let out a puff of dark smoke from his nostrils.

"Which... is...?" This was starting to make her nervous. He couldn't hurt her—right? It was just a dream—right?

"I think I'll start by breaking your wrists and your ankles. Shatter them at the joints, so you can only crawl and whimper and flop around like a dying fish as I go about doing the same to your knees, elbows, shoulders—human skeletons are so *fragile*." His smile grew vicious and cruel as he lowered his head closer to hers. "I've had to put up with your voice for over a decade, quacking away at me. Now, I want to finally hear it *scream*."

"But—I—" She took a step back. He took a step forward. "Wait—"

"Then I think I'll cook your limbs. One by one. Let you watch your skin turn black and crumble away."

"You—you can't, I'm immune to fire."

"In the waking world, sure. But this is a dream, isn't it?" He laughed, and the sound sent a shiver down her spine. "I'm about to turn it into a *nightmare*."

"Grinn, look—I'm—I'm sorry—" She put her hands up in a show of harmlessness as she retreated from him, glancing down at the ground occasionally to make sure she didn't trip over a rock or a root. "You don't need to do this."

"I know. But I *want* to." He readied to pounce. "If you know what's good for you... you should be running."

Yeah, it was hard to argue with that logic.

With fear pounding in her heart, even in her dream-turned-nightmare, she turned and ran. Grinn's cruel laughter was followed by the sound of him giving chase.

She didn't know what happened if you died in a dream in Avalon.

And she really, really didn't want to find out.

* * *

Mordred watched from where he was waiting in the shadows of the parapets of his keep as the sun began to rise over the line of the trees. And just as he predicted, he saw a golden steed break from the treeline. Galahad sat atop the horse as he headed toward the keep at a walk. He was in no rush, it was clear.

Not ten paces behind was a copper horse. Atop it, another familiar man in armor. Percival, the Knight in Copper. *Of course.* The bastard would not hesitate at the chance to watch the downfall of a man he hated so very much.

Behind them, staying about a hundred paces away, came the elementals. Mordred counted about thirty in all—not a poor number, considering the Gossamer Lady's lack of time in entreating them to join her. And he saw the lady in question, hovering over the grass, leading the elementals. They would want their forces known.

It was clear Galahad wanted to give Gwendolyn time to consider her options and to surrender. It was a good scheme—and if the facts had been as the knight understood them, then it would have been successful. But there was a cruel twist waiting for his former friend the moment he drew close enough for Mordred to spring the trap.

There had not been any time to hide his iron army in the field as he had done so many centuries ago. Instead, they would pour from the sides of the keep and flank the elementals, while Mordred attacked from the front and his dragon came from above.

The timing was key. Spring the trap too soon, and the elementals would have time to flee into the woods. Too late, and they might storm the keep. Only the villagers stood in the way, and he had no faith in their ability to withstand a drizzle of rain, let alone the force that was standing against them.

Mordred had three targets in the fray. The traitors. His so-called *allies*.

Percival, Mordred was not surprised about nor did he particularly care. The Knight in Copper had always been an insipid bootlicker, only looking out for his own self. Nor did he care overmuch about the Gossamer Lady's betrayal. She was an elemental. It was to be expected.

It was Galahad that hurt. That stabbed at what was left of Mordred's heart.

His so-called brother-in-arms.

Galahad would die by his hand this day, as would his beloved. In what order they would fall, Mordred could not say —his focus would be on neutralizing the Gossamer Lady and retaking Caliburn. That would give him the advantage he would need over the remaining forces.

But first, the scarecrow must play his part. Mordred disliked putting so much faith in someone—let alone an ally of his soon-to-be wife. Bertin's loyalty was elsewhere. He could only hope that the villager would understand that what aided Mordred in this case would aid Gwendolyn.

If not, he would deeply enjoy ripping the scarecrow's metal head from his shoulders and melting it down in his forge. He suspected Bertin knew that would be the cost of betrayal.

This day would be a day of bloodshed. A day of glory. A day of vengeance.

This day would live in the history of Avalon for a thousand years to come—for this was the day he would take his rightful place upon the throne.

The Prince in Iron would cease to be.

And the King in Iron would rise.

TWENTY-THREE

Galahad slowed to a stop in the shadow of the keep.

Behind him, just at the edge of the woods, was their elemental army. All but a few had answered the call to put a stop to Mordred—even if he was already dead, they needed to make sure of it. They had united behind Zoe, as the Gossamer Lady had predicted they would. Creatures and monstrosities of every shape and form. Fire, stone, tree, river, ice, lightning—all in service to the Gossamer Lady.

They itched for revenge. To see the keep sundered and destroyed, a surrogate for their rage against the fallen Prince in Iron.

It felt so strange, coming back to what had been his home, now as an enemy. Galahad had spent centuries in this place. He knew every nook and cranny, every door, every notch in the wooden beams. He knew the names of the servants who must now be nothing but rubble on the floors, fallen when their master Mordred died.

Now, he had come to kill a young woman who did not deserve it.

It felt wrong.

Endlessly wrong.

But what was he to do? He could not betray the woman he loved—the one he had sworn his soul, his heart, and his fealty to. And he could not say he disagreed with Zoe's logic either. Gwendolyn was nothing but unpredictable—would she seek to avenge Mordred's death? It would be what he would do in her situation.

It would be a quick and painless end to her suffering. It would be the kindest act he could give her. With her love dead, she must be agonized in his absence. Perhaps she would go willingly into the ever after to be with Mordred. Not that Galahad could say what happened to elementals—or witches—after death in Avalon.

There were figures on the wall, watching him. That was surprising. Even more so was how varied they were—men and women, creatures with horns, creatures without. They were mortals. Villagers.

"Who are they?" Percival asked from behind him.

Galahad did not turn his head when he responded. "Gwendolyn's army."

Percival snorted in laughter. "A collection of scrawny, feral cats would be more imposing."

The doors to the keep opened and a single figure walked out to greet him. A man with a rusted metal pumpkin for a head, carved with the crude visage of a face, like one of those made to entertain and ward away his people, the fae, during the autumn months. His body was haphazard. Straw was shoved into clothing to make up his limbs, and he had a broom handle for one leg beneath the knee. A sentient scarecrow. How odd.

Keeping his guard raised, Galahad rested his hand upon the hilt of his sword. Simply because the scarecrow did not *seem* to pose a threat to him, did not mean there was no danger in the situation. He did not dare glance over his shoulder at his

Gossamer Lady and the collection of elementals who waited for her orders.

"I do not know you," he called to the scarecrow when he was within earshot.

"But I know who you are," the scarecrow replied as he walked closer, seemingly unconcerned by the force at the door. "I'm Bertin. Gwen's—" He broke off. "I knew Gwen."

Knew. Past tense. "I am here to demand the surrender of the lady of the keep. Her life is forfeit. If she surrenders, all of you will be spared."

The scarecrow's shoulders slumped. "I'm afraid you're too late for that."

Galahad pulled his helm from his head, wishing to study Bertin without the restriction of his visor. "I do not understand."

"She—" The scarecrow shook his head. "She jumped from the tower. Off the cliff. Killed herself. Because of what you and your lady did. Couldn't go on without the man she loved. This place is ours now. Our home. She left it to us. Go away. *Now.*"

It did not sound like a threat. For what threat could a small pack of villagers pose to thirty-odd elementals? No, it was not a threat. It was... a warning. He furrowed his brow.

Zoe floated up beside him. "Her promises to you are null and void. This place is a travesty—a corruption upon this land. We plan to raze it to the ground. If you all value your lives, you should leave immediately."

"My love." Galahad turned on his horse to address her, all thoughts of the strange warning fleeing from his head. "Is that not rash? Allow them to have this place—it is a secure fortress. Given what Thorn did to so many of their homes, it seems only fair."

"I am not Thorn, and the violence afforded Mordred's people ends today. If what you say is true, scarecrow." Zoe lifted her head in defiance. "I wish to inspect the keep to ensure she is not hiding in some darkened corner. This could easily be a ploy."

Bertin sighed. "I—just—I think you should both go. Now. Take your army and leave. Galahad, you are a good man. A *good man.* Those don't come around often. You should all leave. *Now.*"

There came the warning again. It unsettled him. What did the scarecrow know?

But his wife was the one in command. Zoe smiled gently at Bertin, clearly trying to soothe his worries. "You have every right to be frightened and concerned. We mean you and your friends no harm. Let us inspect the keep—simply the two of us. Then you will be allowed to leave with your people at your own pace."

"Right." Bertin paused to think. "Fine. But only you three. Your friends stay out here, where we can keep an eye on them. You'll forgive me if there's no love lost between my people and yours."

"Of course. I—" Zoe paused.

There was the sound of a flap of wings. Deep and resonant. Powerful enough that it made Galahad's ears pop with a pressure change.

That was a dragon.

But not just *any* dragon.

"I told you to leave." Bertin retreated into the safety of the walls of the keep. "I tried. I'm sorry."

Galahad looked up.

As an enormous iron dragon came down behind him. It was not targeting him—it was targeting the elementals. That was the only reason he was still alive and not flattened underneath its enormous claws. The sound of its screech made his ears ring. It sounded like sharpened nails on metal.

He turned his horse to see the familiar and terrifying creature tearing into those who had sworn fealty to the Gossamer

Lady. Zoe screamed, her hands covering her mouth. But neither he nor his Gossamer Lady could spare any concern for the elementals now scrambling to defend themselves.

Explosions of fire and the crackle of lightning echoed through the field as the elementals warred against the great iron dragon. An enormous boulder hurtled through the air, sending the dragon staggering, but it did not even dent the panels that made up its body. Nearly every elemental on the island stood against that creature—and it would take them all to destroy it.

"Archers, at the ready!" Bertin shouted. "Soldiers! Be ready to defend our home!" The scarecrow shook his head and hollered at Galahad. "I'm sorry. I didn't want to have to do this."

Movement at the top of the walls caught Galahad's eye. He looked up to see the villagers pulling off their cloaks to reveal the iron armor they had been hiding beneath them. Soldiers put metal helms upon their heads—more iron.

Galahad wanted to laugh. *Well done, Gwendolyn. Well done.*

Regiments of iron soldiers were approaching from the left and the right, coming from around the sides of the keep, flanking them. The dragon was cutting Zoe, Percival, and Galahad off from the elementals. The iron soldiers were about to end them if they did not act quickly.

He grabbed Zoe by the upper arm, hating that he had to manhandle her in such a way, but there were no other options. He hefted her up onto the saddle in front of him, and kicking his golden steed as hard as he could, rode it in the only direction he could.

Into the keep. But the other option was worse—certain death under a hail of arrows.

Unfortunately—many of those archers were now pointed *inward* at them instead. But they seemed either under orders not to fire... as though...

This was a trap.

Galahad dismounted his horse, drawing his sword, and stood to face a far more present danger that was waiting for them at the top of the stairs into the building proper. He heard Percival follow suit.

The gate creaked and slammed shut as the villagers pushed it closed, muffling the sounds of the battle outside. What sounds of archery he could hear were pointed outward, protecting the keep from the fray.

Zoe stood beside him, wings unfurled, Caliburn floating in the air nearby, ready for battle.

The screams of battle had begun behind them and outside the walls—the clash of metal, the roar of fire, the heavy *thud* of the dragon's steps. It did not matter. None of it mattered.

The iron dragon. The soldiers. It was far too much for Gwendolyn to command. Soon, he had his answer—soon, the severity of the trap that had slammed shut around them became clear. Like a nightmare, like a demon from hell—against all odds.

He was alive.

Mordred.

Wearing his full armor, complete with the helm that resembled a dragon, its horns jagged and dangerous like the rest of him, Mordred watched them.

Gwendolyn was nowhere to be seen. Half the archers were aiming inward—at Galahad, Percival, and Zoe.

"Before we begin." Mordred began to walk down the stairs, slowly, taking his time. Savoring the moment. His cape whispered against the stones behind him, following him like a twisted shadow. "I would like to assure you that Gwendolyn is very much alive. She will not be waiting for you in whatever afterlife is bound to greet you when I remove your heads from your shoulders."

Galahad narrowed his eyes, placing his own helm back over his head. "Where is she?"

"Resting."

That was not likely. "What have you done to her?"

The Prince in Iron laughed, tinny and hollow from within his helm. "You came here to kill her! And now you wish me to believe you are *concerned* for her *safety?*"

Galahad had to admit it was a bit farcical.

Mordred shook his head. "Tell me, *old friend*, how many times have we sparred, you and I?"

Galahad gritted his teeth. "I have lost count. But I do know I am more often the victor."

"True, true." Mordred cracked his neck and rolled his shoulders, readying for a fight. "And tell me, Gossamer Lady—are you willing to fight fair, this time?"

"I will not dignify that with a response." Zoe showed no fear in her voice or her demeanor, if she felt any at all.

"Suit yourself." Mordred shrugged idly. "Simply attempting to make conversation."

"Why?" Galahad could not help but wonder aloud.

"Hm. I suppose, in some small way, I am sorry to have to kill you. As for Zoe, I could not care any more or less about her. We could have been allies, perhaps even friends—but she saw the quick end to that. But you, Galahad." Mordred's voice grew sad. Almost regretful. "I am sorry to see your life end."

"It is not over."

"Yet." Mordred chuckled.

"You will die for your crimes, Mordred," Percival interjected.

"Oh. Hello, Percival. When did you arrive?" Mordred chuckled. "Forgive me for overlooking you. You never were of much consequence."

Percival growled and took a step forward. Galahad raised his hand to stop the Knight in Copper before he did anything foolish.

"You cannot stand alone against the three of us," Percival snapped.

"Three? Two and a quarter, at best," Mordred taunted the knight, waving his hand dismissively. "And I am being generous."

This was a breed of cruelty that Galahad had never before seen from Mordred. He had been a great many things, but never *flippant*. It made him deeply nervous. What had happened to the Prince in Iron in the Crystal? Who, and what, were they fighting against?

This would not go like their sparring matches, of this Galahad was certain.

Zoe took a step forward in defiance, her hands clenched into fists at her sides. "There are *three* of us, and you have no other allies. You are alone. You will die here. Arthur would spit upon you if he could see you now. Who are you to stand against us?"

"Who am I?" Mordred began to laugh, a quiet, sinister sound that poured ice water into Galahad's veins. He held his arms out at his sides, palms up, as if to say *behold*. "I am the shadow of Avalon. I am the wrath that lurks in the darkness. I am finally that which I was meant to become so long ago. I refused to accept it, but now I can see the truth." He drew his sword.

The sound of the metal shrieking against the sheath set Galahad's teeth on end.

"Who am I? I am Mordred. I am the cruelty of Avalon. I am the King in Iron." Mordred aimed the tip of his blade directly at Galahad. "*And I will be the ruin of you all.*"

* * *

Gwen was running for her ever-fucking life. In a dream. Being chased by Grinn. Who may or *may not* actually be real, or just her version of dreaming up the murderous, mouthy, bitter demon.

Who was trying to kill her. Slowly. Painfully. Torturously. And who was mocking her, every step of the way.

She was glad in a dream she didn't get out of breath. But unfortunately, the logic of her dream world wasn't helping her out at all. She was lost inside her high school. Well, a building that looked like her high school, if it had been designed by a total nutjob. Twisting and turning through the hallways, she kept skidding across the tile floor and crashing into the lockers.

It slowed her down just long enough for Grinn to catch up, his claws ripping through the flooring, the heat pouring off him causing the overhead lights to flicker and the ceiling tiles to char. The air around him was wavy. She'd never been afraid of him before—not really—because they were linked together, and he couldn't hurt her without hurting himself.

But now?

Now, it was a crapshoot and anybody's game. "Stop!"

"Why?" Grinn cackled. He balled up a fist and smashed it into a row of lockers, crumpling them in the middle until they looked like they had been hit by a truck on the highway. Papers, books, pencils, and the like spilled across the tile before blackening and charring with his presence as he approached. "I am having so much fun! I haven't been this entertained in *years*."

"Grinn, please—I—I thought—I thought we were friends!"

"Don't insult me." He grunted. "I'm going to eat your fingers one at a time because of that."

"You wouldn't. You wouldn't! I know you wouldn't. You're a—"

"Don't you *dare* say anything about me being 'good.' I am a demon, you incomprehensibly mountainous moron." The sparks that fell from Grinn's maw seared into the floor. "You shouldn't have stopped to chat. You're trapped."

"Wh—" She glanced behind her. She had been in the

middle of the hallway leading to the cafeteria, there was, like, four hundred more feet of identical hallways and—

No.

No hallway.

Just a brick wall. "Shit!" She ran at it, slapping her palms against the brick. She'd already tried changing the world around her a few times, and it hadn't worked. "Shit, shit, shit!" She pushed on the wall. It wasn't going to budge.

Grinn laughed.

Turning back around, she watched as he slowly prowled closer, lowering his head, shoulder blades protruding from his back as he moved like a lion readying for a kill.

The heat pouring from him melted the glass bulb in one of the overhead lamps, casting him in darkness. She could only see his silhouette and the glowing, terrifying, red eyes and the flicker of the fire inside of him.

This was it. He was going to rip her to pieces. Panic welled up within her. Grinn was really going to break her joints one by one and then cook her limbs and eat them. And only then would he kill her.

"Please—" She started to cry. She was shaking. She wanted to go home. She wanted to wake up. She wanted Mordred to save her from this nightmare.

All Grinn did was laugh.

Before he raised a claw and brought it down on top of her.

Gwen screamed.

TWENTY-FOUR

Gwen sat up in bed, her heart pounding in her ears, panting for air.

She was covered in a cold sweat. Every nerve in her body was electric, and she was on high alert from all the adrenaline pumping through her like wildfire.

Eod army-crawled across the bed on his belly so he could flop his head down onto her lap, looking up at her with giant, concerned eyes. *"Mom okay?"*

Taking a deep breath, she shut her eyes to count down from ten. She was going to have her first panic attack in a long time if she wasn't careful. It was right there, shrinking her vision. Digging her hand into Eod's fur, she petted the animal, using him to help calm her down.

Maybe it wasn't magic that was curing her panic attacks.

Maybe it was the dog.

I told Dad he should have let me get a dog.

The thought made her laugh weakly. Leaning down, she kissed Eod's head. "Mom's okay. Mom is going to have to shout at Dad, though."

"*Uh oh.*" He lifted his head and licked her cheek. "*But dog love Dad.*"

"I love Dad too." Eod's worried and sappy tone of voice was going to make it very hard to stay pissed at Mordred. But she was sure he'd remind her really quickly exactly why she was so mad. "It'll all be all right."

Taking a breath again, she let it out in a rush, her panic quieting down enough to let her remember what had just happened. Grinn had terrorized her so badly it... must have forced her awake through the spell that Mordred had placed her under.

Holy shit, my panic attacks finally serve a purpose. How nice.

But that made her wonder—had Grinn done it on purpose?

Had he really been there and known that was going to work?

What if he was just a figment of her imagination, and that meant *she* knew somehow it would wake her up?

Or, maybe he had been there but actually wanted to maim her, and it was a happy accident?

Option four was that he *hadn't* been there, and she was just terrorizing herself for shits and giggles.

All options were deeply and equally ridiculous, but one of them had to be true. She supposed it didn't really matter either way. It'd be nice to know if Grinn was really alive and back in hell with his family, she supposed. Even if he was a total asshole.

"I—"

She paused as the sound of a dragon flying overhead, the heavy *whumf* of wings, was followed by a dark shadow blotting out the sun for a brief moment. A heavier *ka-thud* and the screech of metal that was Tiny's shriek told her that she had woken up either just in time or too late.

"Eod, you have to *stay*. This is dangerous. I'm serious." She pointed at him sternly.

The dog whimpered but laid his head back down and seemed like he was going to obey. But she had a feeling it wasn't going to last. With a sigh, she shook her head. "Fine. Stay with Mae."

"Dog protect food lady!"

Smiling despite the situation, she jumped out of bed, still dressed from the night before. She looked down at the ring on her finger. She had to get it off. It was an emergency. Yanking on it with her other hand, it didn't budge. It wasn't too tight; it should come off easily—but it was stuck on her as if built into her hand.

Maybe she could melt it. Holding up her hand, she ignited it. Focusing on her power, she tried to burn as hot as she could. She watched as the fire shifted colors. Red, to orange, to yellow. She gritted her teeth. It needed to be hotter. Picturing her frustration and her anger, she watched the flame turn white. Then blue.

The iron ring was unchanged. It should have at least heated up, changed colors—something. *Anything.* Putting out her flame, she touched the ring. It was cold.

Fuck. Fuck, fuck, fuck!

A magic ring that wasn't meltable, removable, and was a glorified Gwen off switch. Great. She figured it wouldn't be that easy, but she had to try. Shutting her eyes, she sighed. She didn't have time to fart around with trying to un-magic it off.

And that left only one option.

This was going to hurt.

A lot.

"Fuck you, Mordred. Fuck you."

* * *

Galahad had battled Mordred a thousand times. He had seen what both the mortal man and the elemental had been capable of in combat.

This... was like fighting a stranger.

The odds were against the Prince in Iron. Three against one. But it was like battling a force of nature. The man Galahad called friend had fought with rigor but with restraint—with a calm that had been pervasive and brought from discipline and practice.

This Mordred fought with a wild and unhinged fury. Galahad was driven back by the brutally painful impacts of Mordred's sword against his, the *clang* of metal sending a reverberating jolt up his arm. But he was not simply fighting with sword and steel—he was fighting with iron.

All the while, the sounds of chaos and war raged outside the castle. An army of iron versus an army of elementals. The elementals would win—eventually—but could they do it in time before it was too late? He had to push his thoughts to the background. This fight was taking all his focus.

Zoe dashed out of the way, barely avoiding being cut in half as Mordred hardened his cape into iron panels and swiped at her, the heavy *whoosh* at odds with how fast it moved.

But that was not all. Metal spikes—jagged, rusted, and cruel —shot up from the ground at them. The Mordred of old might have demanded a fair and honorable fight to the death. Not engaged in such chaos with all the mannerisms of a rabid animal.

Galahad was bleeding from a wound underneath his shoulder pauldron. Percival was limping. Zoe was unharmed, but her expression revealed how frightened she was. Her ability to pull the life out of the air around Mordred did little good when the man was encased in iron.

This was the creature they had feared all along. This was

the man they had sought to keep from rising to power. And in doing so, they had released him.

What fools we have been.

But Galahad could not think of regret. He could not think of how he had created the monster before them—this rampaging nightmare. Because one wrong move, and it would all be over, and he would be left to reminisce over his decisions in the ever after. If one waited for him.

The sound of metal on metal was deafening. No one could manage to gain ground. Only Caliburn gave Mordred any manner of trouble, as the impacts from the blade sent him back a step. But it seemed that the Prince in Iron had a solution to the issue.

"Enough of this!" Mordred snarled as he gestured at the blade, clenching his clawed gauntlets into a fist. Iron shot up from the ground, wrapping around the blade like vines, dragging it to the dirt. The blade struggled to be free, but the laws of Avalon were clear.

Iron defeated all. Contained all.

Such power was never meant to be wielded in such a way. And this was why.

Percival took the opportunity to seize on Mordred's apparent distraction and dashed forward, swinging his own blade for the prince's neck. But the decision was rash.

"No!" Galahad jumped forward, but it was too late.

Mordred caught Percival's blade in his metal gauntlet. Percival gagged in pain as Mordred tightened his fist. The metal creaked, bent, then shattered, leaving Percival only holding onto a splintered shard attached to a handle.

The Prince in Iron was not done. He grasped Percival around the throat, tightening. "You were always such a *waste of time.*"

It seemed Percival was not to be without a last word. He

drove the shard of his sword into Mordred's side, finding a gap between two of the armored panels.

Mordred snarled in rage. Dug his claws deep into Percival's neck. "You shall die as you lived—as a thorn in my side."

He tore out the Knight in Copper's throat.

Zoe screamed and moved to aid the fallen knight, but Galahad stopped her. "It is too late, my love."

"But—"

"No." He would not let her draw too close to the murderous prince.

Mordred released his grasp, his hand dripping in gore, his nightmarish armor spattered with the spray from Percival's wound. The Knight in Copper slumped to the ground, blood pooling on the dirt around him, his expression hidden behind his helm the only remaining dignity afforded the dead man.

Galahad felt his stomach churn. He had spent over a thousand years with Percival. They were not friends, but they had been like brothers. "Enough, Mordred. Enough."

"Do you think I will mourn him?" Mordred laughed darkly. "Please give me more credit than that."

Zoe was crying silently, tears rolling down her cheeks as she looked upon Percival. "Let this end, Mordred."

"Yes." The Prince in Iron yanked Percival's broken sword from his side. It was tipped in blood, but it had not bit deep enough to even slow him down. Mordred tossed it aside as if it were nothing more than a toothpick. "You are right. It is time to end this."

The time to mourn Percival was over. Because if Galahad did not focus, he would quickly be joining his brother in death. Galahad readied his stance.

Mordred took a step forward. "And then there were two."

* * *

"There has to be another way!"

"There isn't, Mae." Gwen was already trembling at the idea. "Trust me, I don't want to do it either—but I don't have a choice. I can't go out there with this thing on my hand, he'll just knock me out again. And if I don't hurry up, everybody'll already be dead."

The cook wailed, and shook her metal head, pacing away. "I can't! I can't. I can't do this."

"I know, Mae—I know." Gwen smiled at her, trying to be as reassuring as possible. "It'll be okay. I'm asking you to do this. It'll be a favor."

Gwen put her left hand on the chopping block, curling all her fingers in except the one wearing the ring. It wasn't exactly easy, folding her hand in such a way, and she had to cram her fingers against the edge of the chopping block so hard it was painful, to give Mae a clean shot. Or, at least, her best chance at a clean shot.

She held the butcher's knife out to Maewenn, handle first.

She wanted to puke.

But this had to be done.

With a choked sob, Maewenn took the handle in her shaking hand. Gwen really hoped Mae didn't miss. The cook took a deep breath, held it, and let it out. "Are—are you sure? You... you could ask Mordred to simply take it off."

"He's in the middle of murdering Galahad. I'm pretty sure he's busy." This was the last thing she wanted to do. But she didn't have a choice. "Please. I have to stop him. He's out of control."

Mae nodded. "Okay. Okay." She put her metal hand on Gwen's wrist, holding her steady.

Gwen shut her eyes and braced herself.

There was a pause.

"I'm so sorry, I can't!" Mae put the cleaver down on the

block with a *clunk*. She walked across the kitchen to hide her sob.

A metal hand rested on her shoulder. Tim. He had been hovering near her, nervously watching the whole scene play out. Then he reached for the butcher's knife.

"Oh no, no, no, no—" Mae waved her hand at the rusted half-finished guard. "That's worse!"

"I trust him." Gwen smiled up at Tim. "Go ahead."

Tim nodded, squeaking as he did. It was clear he wasn't enthusiastic about the situation, but he took the cleaver and moved to a better position.

Gwen took a breath. It was weird, loving someone you couldn't trust. But she supposed Mordred was already living that life. Turnabout was fair play, yadda yadda.

Mae twisted her hands as Tim readied himself. "You're sure?"

"I'm sure." Gwen shut her eyes. "Just don't tell me when he's going to do it, I'd rather not kn—"

Her mind flashed white.

The pain was total, instant, and overwhelming.

Her stomach flipped. She felt woozy. The floor rushed up to meet her, but somebody caught her. Her head felt fuzzy and a thousand miles away. She barely felt the burning-hot end of a kitchen tool pressing against the stump of where her finger had been a second before, cauterizing the wound and stopping the bleeding.

She'd heal fast. She was a witch of Avalon.

But it wasn't like it'd regrow.

Shutting her eyes, she tried desperately not to pass out. Tim was the one who had caught her. Mae was talking to her gently and stroking her hair. Eventually, she could make out what she was saying.

"You're okay. It's done. It's all over. It's gone."

"Not over," she muttered as she tried to blink her way back

to reality. Mae was cleaning the chopping block frantically, scrubbing at what must have been her blood. "Only just begun."

Tim reached up and took a goblet of water from the counter and helped Gwen drink it. It did wonders to settle her stomach, even if she did wish it were wine at the moment. But that'd come later.

Finally, she worked up the nerve to look at her left hand. Her ring finger was gone. Just a stump, right below where the ring had sat. It was a good shot, honestly. "Thanks, Tim. Thanks, Mae."

Tim shook his head forlornly. It clearly wasn't a favor he was proud of. He helped her stand up, sitting her back on the stool. Mae began wrapping her hand in gauze.

There it was.

Her finger.

Sitting on the counter.

Ring still stuck on it.

It should have been upsetting, seeing it. She should have puked. But instead, she felt... nothing. It wasn't hers anymore. It was just a thing.

But that wasn't true. She didn't feel *nothing*.

She felt something all right.

Rage.

Anger, plain and pure and total, was burning in her chest. She didn't think she'd ever been so furious in her entire life.

"Enough." Her one word stopped Tim and Maewenn. They stared at her. Maybe it was the way she had said it. She didn't know.

But what she did know was what came next. "This ends *now*."

Grabbing some of the gauze, she wrapped up her severed finger, and headed for the door.

This ends now.

And Gwen was going to be the one to put a stop to it.
One way or another.

TWENTY-FIVE

Mordred had felt nothing at the death of Percival, except perhaps some minor relief. But not because a so-called threat was dead, but because he finally knew he was *free*. Free of the laws that he had bound himself in, tighter than any chain and more maddening than any cage of his creation.

Not so long ago, he had spared Percival's life. He had ensured that the traitor had suffered for his betrayal, but the Knight in Copper had survived. Why? So that Mordred would not incur more wrath from the supposed rules held sacred by the elementals. The law of hospitality. The law that barred death of another elemental unless it was unanimously decreed.

None of it mattered now. It was all stripped from him, like a weight that had been carrying him to the bottom of the ocean's crushing depths.

Mordred was free.

Free to do what was his birthright.

Galahad and the Gossamer Lady were putting up a valiant fight. But in his new world of broken restraints, he did not fight with the honor and dignity that he had been trained to conduct himself with. No. This was about violence. About wrath.

And it was *glorious*.

He barely felt the strikes of Galahad's sword, or the blasts from Zoe's pathetic magic. Encased in iron as he was, there was no damage the Gossamer Lady could do to him that would matter. Especially not since he had removed Caliburn from the equation. Once her head was cut from her shoulders, he would reclaim the sword as his own.

But for now, he wished to rip the two remaining usurpers apart with his claws.

The Knight in Gold always fought with a speed and surety that was surprising for someone his height and age. But there was a weariness in him that Mordred could sense in his swings, in his stance. Galahad was not simply tired—it was as though his heart were not fully committed to the fight.

Shame.

It would not spare him.

Mordred idly wondered, through the crash and clang of metal and the scrape of claws on golden armor, if Galahad was even aware of this difference in fervor. He was fighting to spare his own life, and yet seemed lackluster over the topic.

It was almost disappointing, now that Mordred thought about it. This was to be their last sparring match, and this would be how he remembered the golden fae warrior.

There was an easy way to see if he could spur the old beanpole into a more passionate fight. Perhaps he should kill Zoe *first*. He had been trying to do the fae a favor by taking his head before that of his love.

Now, he wanted to see if it might inspire his old "friend" to put up a proper fight.

He turned his attention toward the Gossamer Lady. The reaction from Galahad was instant and palpable.

"Your fight is with *me*, Mordred." Galahad moved to cut him off from advancing toward the butterfly-winged woman.

Galahad swung his sword, causing Mordred to deflect with his own blade and step aside.

"My fight is with you both." Mordred laughed. "Or, have you forgotten who ran me through with my own blade?"

"It was never yours!" Zoe fumed, blinking out of existence where she was and reappearing across the dirt of his courtyard. It was difficult to catch a woman who was as constant and predictable as bolts of lightning. One moment here, the next there.

"It was given to me by Arthur. I was his proper heir. The last words upon his lips before he died charged me with the protection of this place." Mordred was tired of making the argument—this would be the last time he bothered to speak it. "It is *you* who have taken that which does not belong to you."

"Is this how you protect Avalon? By destroying it?" Galahad charged toward him again. Mordred was sick of the interruptions. Gesturing his hand, a thin and rusted spike of iron shot from the ground, skewering Galahad through the calf.

The Knight in Gold shouted in pain and went to move forward. But the spike was barbed and jagged, and any movement on his part would rip his leg to shreds. His other leg buckled as he fell to that knee, his sword hitting the ground with a thump.

It was a dirty trick. A coward's ploy. Something Mordred would once have loathed to resort to. But now? Now, it felt... so easy. So simple. Why would he *not* use his power to its fullest extent?

Arthur was not watching him. No judge and jury were waiting that had power over him.

"Galahad!" Zoe cried and rushed to his side, wrapping her arms around the man she loved. "Let him go, Mordred!"

"Why?" Mordred took his time approaching the pair. "Give me a reason, and I will consider it."

"This is not right." Zoe's eyes were wide, and he watched as tears began to fill them.

"I will amend my statement." Mordred stopped a few paces away. "Give me a *good* reason."

Zoe's lips twisted in a grimace, and he watched as her eyes slowly grew black from lid to lid. Her voice echoed with another, deeper voice. "Release him, or I shall end all those within this keep."

"You mean them?" He gestured at the villagers on the walls of the ramparts. They were still fighting the war outside, firing arrows at any of the elementals who drew too close. Those without bows were waiting for their chance to battle. "Go ahead. I do not care."

Zoe continued. "I will wither and rot every living thing—"

"As you wish. You cannot harm me."

"Run, my love—" Galahad pulled his helm from his head. Sweat matted his brow. A bruise was forming on his jaw from where Mordred had punched him. "Run. I am lost. Go and save yourself."

"I would hunt you down, Gossamer Lady. I will not stop until you are dead." Mordred kept his voice even. It was not a threat. It was a simple fact. "There is nowhere you can hide. No shadow in which you might cower that I would not search to find you."

"Let her live. Spare her. If our friendship meant anything to you, spare the woman I love." Galahad struggled to stand, but it was no use. He collapsed a second later.

"It hurts me to see you like this. Weak. Tired. You need a rest, old man." Mordred took another step forward.

Zoe blocked his path, standing her ground, the darkness of her eyes swirling like an oil slick.

Mordred lifted his blade and pointed the tip at her throat.

"One touch from me and you will be dead." Her voice was like the rumble of thunder upon the horizon.

"You will be dead before you have the chance to try." Mordred smiled underneath his helm. She would be a proper challenge.

"I—"

Fire roared through the air, making it suddenly difficult to breathe. It blotted out the sky. Turning, Mordred felt his heart skip a beat.

A woman whose hair was a pure fiery blaze stood atop the stairs to his keep, wings like those of a dragon spread behind her. It was from her that the explosion had come. A terrible, beautiful, force of nature.

Mordred paused. As did the others.

"*Enough.*"

* * *

Gwen stepped out onto the top landing of the stairs that led from the door of the keep down into the courtyard. The fire she had sent rushing through the air had been a warning shot. Her wings unfurled at her back, spread wide in threat. Her hair was made of fire, and it curled around her as she walked. But it did not singe her clothing. Funny, how she could control her power better when she was *pissed*. She was in no mood to play.

"*Enough.*" She didn't shout. She didn't need to. With that one word, everything seemed to pause. There was a crumpled body in copper armor bleeding into a puddle of crimson. Percival.

Galahad was skewered to the ground on a nasty and rusted iron spike.

Zoe had gone "dark," her eyes black from lid to lid, her skin pale, veins the color of ink. Her wings were no longer that of a summer butterfly—but somehow seemed rotted and corrupted.

And judging by the sound and the movement outside, the elementals and Mordred's army were still at war.

But with that one word, there was a skip in the beat of the action. One moment when everything seemed to hang as all focus turned on her. She was too furious to care.

On either side of her, walking from the keep, were Tim and Bert. Maewenn followed close behind. Even Eod was with her, staying close to Mae as Gwen had told him to. And, more importantly, far enough back to keep from getting scorched.

Her hand hurt like hell.

But it gave her a strange kind of clarity.

Mordred had turned to her, Zoe and Galahad forgotten. "Gwendolyn—how—"

She tossed him the gauze-wrapped "package" she was holding in her injured hand. He caught it, looking down at it in his palm. She could not see his face. Hopefully, it was a look of pure horror as he realized what it was. "I got you a wedding present." There was a shocking amount of coldness in her own voice. She was almost proud of it.

"I—" Mordred stammered. He sheathed his sword before slowly unwrapping the gauzed object that she had thrown to him. Upon seeing her severed finger, he looked away from it, closing his hand around the piece of her. "Gwendolyn—" His voice cracked. "Why? I love you. I was going to wake you. *Why?*"

"Are you serious?" A laugh of disbelief burst from her. "You were going to wake me *after* everyone was dead! And would you have ever taken that cursed ring off? Or, were you going to keep me on a leash for all time?" Lifting her good hand, she summoned the crown that Merlin had given her. "All because you want *this* so very badly?"

Mordred said nothing. Simply stood there in silence like an iron statue.

Gwen didn't care. She'd deal with him later. She had other issues to contend with. Passing the crown to her injured hand, she walked up to where Caliburn was trapped in iron. She had no idea how she knew what to do. It was just in her, shining through the anger. A wonderful clarity that she was so very grateful for.

Grasping the hilt of the sword, she commanded the iron to dissipate. The sword hummed in her grasp—it almost seemed to vibrate with power. Before her very eyes, the blade *changed*. No longer the huge broadsword that Mordred had used, or the slightly smaller blade that Zoe had recreated.

Caliburn wasn't simply one blade. It was whatever its owner wanted it to be. Whatever they needed it to be. She could feel it there, almost a sentience—calling out to her. And she answered it.

The blade shifted until it was something far more *her* size. The blade was decorated with twisting, swirling flames that climbed from the crossguard and up the flat of the shining steel. The crossguard itself took on the appearance of a dragon's wings. And the pommel was a roaring head of the same lizard-like creature.

Caliburn was hers. Because she took it. Because it *wanted* to be hers. It was beautiful. And it sang, shining in the light.

"You have no *right*—" Zoe protested. "I am of Avalon, and I ruled here for a thousand years before you fools came to its shores. That crown and blade are mine!"

"You couldn't just let me enjoy the moment, could you?" Gwen rolled her eyes before turning to Zoe. She was still standing in front of the wounded Galahad. Gwen could free the Knight in Gold—but he was also trying to kill her and Mordred, so... maybe it wasn't such a good idea.

Zoe furrowed her brow. "You commanded the iron. You share in Mordred's power?"

"I share in all the powers of the elementals. Maybe even yours." Gwen smiled in false sweetness. "Wanna find out? Come here."

The Gossamer Lady froze. Real fear flashed over her

features. "We will rule together. Split the kingdom. You will take half and I will take half—the Queens of Avalon. I will teach you."

"Let me think about that." Gwen walked over to her, keeping Caliburn down at her side. She stopped, a few feet away from the other woman. "No." She swung her sword for Zoe.

The Gossamer Lady disappeared in a blink. Which Gwen was counting on. She let go of the handle of the blade and commanded it to whip through the air.

She didn't know *how* she knew where Zoe was going to reappear.

But she did.

And therefore, so did Caliburn.

Zoe reappeared the moment the sword pierced through her stomach. Just as it had pierced Mordred.

Galahad roared. "*No!*"

The Gossamer Lady's feet touched the ground. Then her knees, as she knelt, the blade still protruding from her body.

Flicking her wrist, the blade returned to Gwen. She'd reflect on how awesome that was another time. Looking over at Galahad, she frowned. "I'm sorry." She dissolved the iron that held him in place and jerked her head for him to go to his wife.

Limping, but moving, the Knight in Gold went to the side of his wife. Crimson was flowing from her as she pressed her hands to the wound. She collapsed into Galahad's arms as he knelt beside her. "Shush, my love, shush—" He kissed her, cradling her gently.

Mordred had yet to move. He was still standing there, staring at the severed finger in his palm. If he was aware of what was happening, he made no sign of it.

Gwen watched as Zoe lifted a bloody hand to touch Galahad's cheek, but her strength was quickly waning. "My love. My sweet, my knight..."

"We are threads of silk and gold." He grasped her hand and held her palm to him. "Wound together, now and forever. Death shall not separate us. Your soul and mine are one."

Zoe's smile was weak and forlorn. "I—I am so very sorry."

"We are past regret. Think only of peace. And my love for you. Let it carry you to the stars, gold and silk together. We will be together soon." He kissed her, holding the embrace, until Zoe's hand went limp and slipped from his.

Clutching her close to him, Galahad let out a sound that broke Gwen's heart. She was gone. Not even the elemental of life could stop her own death.

Gwen shut her eyes and wiped at the tears that threatened to slip down her own cheeks. This had to stop. All of it. The Knight in Gold had betrayed them, but she understood why. And he was still a friend in pain. Sniffling, she decided she was on to the next thing. There was a war to stop. She'd deal with the two men later.

She gestured her hand, and the villagers quickly worked to open the gates. "Bert. With me."

The scarecrow went into action silently, the villagers filing in behind her in rows. Her soldiers, adorned in iron armor.

Heading out of the gate, she saw the mayhem in front of her. Elemental corpses and the remains of iron soldiers were strewn about. Sticking the pointer and thumb of her good hand into her lips, she let out a sharp whistle. Tiny was causing most of the mayhem, screeching and swiping at the elementals that were blasting it uselessly with their magic.

Her own obsidian dragon flew overhead, screeching loudly, before descending on the battle. He—no, *she*—crashed down right in front of the iron dragon. Her dragon was smaller than Mordred's enormous creation. But her dragon, like Gwen herself, was *pissed*.

Her dragon roared in Tiny's face. The iron monstrosity took

a step back before... sitting down. It would have made her laugh if she hadn't been so damn angry and in pain.

Their sudden arrival had stopped the fight in its tracks. Gwen let go of Caliburn, watching it float idly in the air beside her, waiting for a command. All the remaining elementals—maybe thirty—were watching her.

"I don't want this!" She held up the crown in her bandaged hand. Blood was seeping through the gauze in places. It was weirdly fitting to see the delicate jewelry and crimson together. "I don't. I didn't ask for this. But I am *sick* of this. Sick of listening to all of you fight and moan and kill each other. People are *dying*. Love is *dying*." She pointed behind herself back to where she knew Galahad was still holding Zoe in his arms. "And it ends here. It ends now. No more."

Silence.

"Peace. This is what I decree. No more warmongering. No more squabbling over who owns what and where. You will come to me to settle these disputes." She took a breath and let it out. There was no going back. "I am Queen of Avalon. Chosen by the island. By Caliburn. And by Merlin. Will any of you stand against me?"

Silence for a long moment. A few of the elementals glanced at each other. One, who was made of ice, took a step forward. "Why should we follow you?"

"None of you know me. None of you have had a chance to know me." Gwen also took a step forward. She still refused to put the crown on her head. Holding it was good enough for now. "I'm not cruel. I will be fair. I will be kind. But this death, these wars, it ends now, once and for all. If you stand against me, I'll send you from the island to a slow death. Or, you can have a fast one by the sword. Your call."

"And what of *him?*" The ice elemental pointed behind her. "Is he to sit at your side?"

Gwen turned to see Mordred standing some ten feet away.

She knew what she had to do. She loathed doing it. But there was no choice. "No. He... is exiled from Avalon."

Mordred jerked his head again as if he had flinched from a physical blow. But he said nothing.

The ice elemental considered their answers, then nodded once. "Peace. Peace sounds... good."

"Will you reign here?" said another elemental, this one made of rock, as he gestured up at the keep. His voice sounded like gravel in a tumbler.

Gwen thought about it for a moment, then smiled slightly. "No. I will rebuild Camelot." That sounded fun. She was sure Bert and his friends would help her, especially for the right pay. "Now go. Go home. Go back to your loved ones. Tell the others what has happened here."

The survivors didn't wait long to disperse, heading back to the woods on foot, by flight, or simply disappearing into the ground, or the air, or into a swirl of greenery or leaves.

That left the iron army and two giant dragons. Tiny was staring at her obsidian dragon strangely.

"Don't you go getting a crush," she said to the enormous animal. "I don't want to see what happens if you two get it on." She headed back into the keep, ignoring Mordred.

"Gwendolyn—" He reached for her as she passed.

"Not now." She brushed him off. Arguing with him was the last thing she wanted to do at the moment. Galahad was still holding Zoe's lifeless body in his arms, rocking her back and forth and crying into her dark hair.

Before their eyes, she shimmered, and disappeared into dust that glittered in the fading sun. Galahad doubled over, weeping, his head in his hands.

Gwen knelt beside him. "I... I'm sorry."

"You did not have a choice. To bring peace to this world, I knew a life must be sacrificed. As much as I love her, I—" Galahad grimaced. "I knew that this could happen. I saw her going astray. But I could not leave her side."

"She was trying to do what was right in the end. By any means necessary." Gwen glanced over at Mordred. "Which seems to be a theme around here."

Galahad took a breath and nodded before letting it out in a long, broken sigh. "So it seems."

"Can... you forgive me for this?" Gwen frowned.

After a long pause, Galahad shook his head. "But neither can I hate you for it. We are at peace, Lady Gwendolyn, for the brief time I continue to live."

That was good enough. Reaching out, she pulled him into a hug. The love of his life was dead. Galahad allowed her to hold him and leaned against her. Mordred stood some ten feet away, staring. Waiting.

When Galahad's tears dried, he wiped his face before gently pushing out of Gwen's grasp and hefting up to his feet. He faced Mordred, approaching the Prince in Iron before kneeling and bowing his head. "Take my life."

Mordred pulled his sword from his sheath.

Gwen wanted to stop him. Wanted to spare Galahad. But what was the point? What reason would he have to go on? Zoe was dead and dust. This was a mercy, of sorts.

Mordred raised his blade, ready to cleave the Knight in Gold's head from his shoulders. He paused. Then slowly lowered the blade back to his side. "Stand, old man."

Galahad looked up, grayed brows furrowed in confusion. "What manner of cruelty is this?"

"You will not die by my hand." Mordred turned from them and headed into his keep, ignoring the stares of everyone as he disappeared inside.

"I do not wish to live without her, Lady Gwendolyn," Galahad said from where he knelt, pleading with her. "End my life. It is a mercy."

Gwen sighed and shut her eyes. She didn't want to kill Galahad any more than Mordred did. Then it hit her. "Take the skiff and go home."

He watched her in disbelief. "I have raised my sword against you."

"Yeah. But you did it out of love." Gwen shook her head. "I can't kill you. I just can't. You don't deserve to die like that. You've... you've been such a good friend. But I can't let you stay either. So..."

He nodded in understanding. "Home. Yes. I will return to my people in Tir n'Aill. Perhaps the trees will take me, and I will grow as one of them. Perhaps my soul will be free to join my beloved." The act of getting to his feet looked painful. He seemed so very tired. She knew he wouldn't last long, away from Avalon and its magic that was keeping him alive. "I will depart in the morning."

"I'll send you off." She smiled faintly. "Like you did for me."

He nodded once. "May I... sleep the night here?"

"Of course."

Turning, Galahad walked away, each step looking painful.

With a weary sigh, Gwen walked back up the stairs and knelt down by Eod to pet him. The dog licked her cheek, sensing her sadness.

'What's next, boss?" Bert asked. She didn't miss the excitement and happiness in his voice, even if he was doing his best to hide it. His side had won, after all.

"I need to settle things with Mordred before I exile him from the island. Anyone who wants to come with me to Camelot is welcome to join. There's a lot of work to be done."

"What will become of the iron soldiers without Mordred?" Bert shook his head. "I'd... hate to see anything happen to them." The silent subtext was Maewenn and Tim, both of whom were standing nearby.

"I can command iron, the same as him. I can keep them

alive." She knew. Just *knew* she could. It was bizarre, being so tapped into the island. She laughed quietly. At the look of confusion at her laughter that she got from those nearby, she shook her head. "Sorry. I wanted to meet Merlin, and then I became him." Pushing to her feet, she looked over at her friends. "Who will come with me to Camelot?"

Tim nodded with a *squeak-squeak-squeak*. He was clearly on board, even if he was one of Mordred's creations.

Maewenn twisted her hands in front of her. "I—well. What would you do without a good cook?"

"I don't know what I'd do without my good friend." Gwen smiled at her. She patted Eod on the head again before walking into the building.

There was one last fight to be had.

And it was the one she was looking forward to the least.

TWENTY-SIX

Mordred did not know what to think.

He did not know what to do.

Gwendolyn... had mutilated her hand. He had not even considered that she would do such a thing. To remove her own finger? It was beyond what he had thought her capable of. But perhaps that was his own lesson—to never underestimate his firefly.

But was she his firefly no longer?

Had he broken their bond in an attempt to seal it in his own selfish way, for his own means?

He is exiled.

The door opened and shut behind him. He did not need to turn to know who it was. He vanished his armor, letting the weight dissolve from him. If she meant to kill him, he would accept that fate. He would not fight her.

Neither of them spoke.

Gwendolyn approached the table and picked up the gauze-wrapped piece of herself. With a gesture, she lit the fire in the hearth ablaze, and tossed the digit into the flames. Hopefully, it was no longer immune to the heat like the rest of her.

"I would have woken you." It was a paltry excuse.

"But you wouldn't have set me free." Her tone was cold but not harsh.

That was true. He walked to his bar to pour himself some whiskey.

"Make me a double." She walked to one of the chairs by the fire and sank into it.

A small smile graced his face as he obeyed. "Do you intend to kill me, Gwendolyn?"

She paused for a long moment. "No."

"Do you intend to forgive me for my transgression?"

Another long pause. "No."

That was fair. He brought her the glass she asked for, and sat in his own chair, but not before placing the bottle on the table between them. He had the feeling it would be mostly gone before too very long.

"Fuck you." Gwendolyn stated after a long pause.

"I deserve that." He sipped his whiskey. Another long stretch of silence before he added, "Well done, killing Zoe."

She sighed. "I wish it hadn't been necessary, for Galahad's sake."

"They made their own decisions."

"You had to be stopped, though. They weren't wrong about that." She nursed her own glass of alcohol. "But I guess it had to be me."

"Yes, it seems so." He leaned his head against the high back of his chair.

She downed half of her glass in one gulp and coughed. "Fuck, I needed this earlier today."

"How painful is it?"

"Right now?" She looked at her bandaged hand. "It aches. Stings from time to time for a little while. But man, when Tim did it, I saw stars. I thought I was going to pass out or throw up."

With a huff, he turned his attention to the flames. "You let the guard do it?"

"I wanted Mae to do it, but she couldn't."

"No, I wouldn't expect so." He frowned. "I did not even consider that you would do such a thing."

"I tried to melt the ring off. No dice. I didn't have time to try anything else." Turning her hand over, she put it on the arm of the chair. "Could be worse. I could be dead. Or, y'know, chained to you with a glorified on-off switch wired to my brain. That was *extremely* not cool, Mordred."

"I know. I simply thought..." He shut his eyes. "It does not matter what I thought."

"Two reasons. One, I still love you. I'm just exceedingly angry with you. And I don't know how long that'll outweigh the rest of my emotions. And two? You couldn't kill Galahad. You deserve a quiet death somewhere else."

"Galahad. Did you end his suffering?"

"No. Kind of? He's going home to Tir n'Aill. Going to go become a tree, or something. Fae stuff. He leaves in the morning. Do you want to be there?"

Mordred chuckled quietly. "That sounds like a fitting end for him. And... no. I would not be welcome."

Another long stretch of silence.

"I will keep this island safe." Her voice sounded like that of a true queen. Whatever strength she had come to find when she battled through his magic to wake from her dream, and then to stand against him—it was formidable.

And by the Ancients, it made him love her all the more.

"Even if it means..." She trailed off.

Even if it means you say goodbye to me. He shut his eyes. Mordred had expected anger. Fury. He could have dealt with that. He could have responded to that. But this icy, impassive response? It felt more like the closing of a tomb upon his heart. It burned him more than her flames ever could.

Gwen finished her second glass of whiskey. "I should go."

"Wait." He stood before kneeling at her feet. She watched him carefully, the look of wariness in her eyes pouring salt on an already deep wound. He took her injured hand and gently unwound the bandages. It was a clean cut. Someone had had the presence of mind to cauterize the wound. He doubted it would become infected.

But it was wrong to have her missing a part of herself.

"You have no reason to trust me."

"No, I don't." She stared at him. "And if you try any shit this time, I *will* put you in a very deep hole for a very long time."

He smiled and laughed once. "As you wish, my queen. But allow me to give you a gift as we part. Something, perhaps, to remember me by."

"No magic."

"I will leave that to you." He placed her hand in his, palm to palm. Her hand had always looked so very small in his gauntlet, but now it seemed even more so—bruised and raw, the wound angry and seeping.

Using some of the iron from his own armor, he began to sculpt. A new finger, from the knuckle to the tip, to replace the old. Made of polished steel, and far more delicate and gentle than his own claws. There was no jagged talon at the end. No rust. The nail was sharp but understated.

When he finished, he sat back on his heels.

She lifted her hand, studying the piece. Then, with a breath, she flexed the finger experimentally, pouring her magic into it to control it like it was a part of her. Slowly, she made a fist, then straightened her fingers one by one, testing it. When she looked back to him, she smiled. Just a little. Just enough. "I'll take it."

And he would accept that. Taking her hand, he kissed her knuckles before standing and lifting her to her feet.

Walking to the door, she hesitated before leaving, resting

her hand against the doorjamb. She didn't look over her shoulder at him. "Goodbye, Mordred."

"Goodbye, my firefly."

She shut her eyes, flinching in pain, before she left down the hallway.

Sitting in his chair, Mordred shut his eyes, and let himself weep.

* * *

The morning came. Gwen had spent the night alone—well, okay, the dog didn't count—in her old room. It felt like a goodbye to the keep. And it was. She remembered how terrified she'd been when she arrived. Cowering and panicking at everything she saw. And now?

Now, she was queen.

Of the whole island.

The sun had just started to rise as she walked down the stairs to the beach where the skiff waited. Eod came with her. Standing at the shore were Maewenn and Galahad, quietly talking. The cook was shoving baskets of food into the knight's arms, even as she sniffled loudly.

Eod walked up to Galahad, tail wagging sadly.

Today was a day of goodbyes.

Galahad knelt to hug the dog, letting the hound lick his cheek.

"It is all right, friend," Galahad told the animal quietly as Eod whimpered. "I am going home. I will find peace there. All joy for me has left this island."

Gwen had the sudden urge to ask him to change his mind. To rethink the slow death of attrition he'd suffer when separated from Avalon's magic. But the words didn't leave her mouth because they were purely selfish. She wanted him to stay for *her*. Because she wanted her friend.

This was what Galahad wanted. This was what he needed to do.

Walking up to him, she waited for him to stand before throwing her arms around him and hugging him tight. "I'm going to miss you *so much.*"

"I will never be far. We fae do not believe in death like you do. We are always in the world and the life that shines around you." He stroked her hair. "I will only ever be a dream away."

Now, she was the one crying. She wiped at her eyes and sniffled. Everything in her wanted to beg him to stay. To change his mind. But the look on his face—the grief, the sadness, the tiredness—she knew it was time. Anything else would be cruel.

He climbed into the skiff. "Farewell until another day."

"Goodbye, Galahad." Gwen could barely get the words out through her tears.

The skiff lurched. And slid into the mist that formed around it.

Gwen held Mae as they cried.

* * *

Gwen gazed up at the ruins of Camelot. It felt right to call it home, to try to fix it up and everything. But it still felt like she was pretending, somehow—just standing in the shoes of her father when she was a toddler.

"It is yours, now."

"*Gah!*" Gwen jumped almost a foot in the air.

Merlin chuckled. He had a large wooden walking stick with him. It really completed his *I-just-crawled-out-of-a-D&D-campaign* vibe. She opted not to make fun of him about it. "That never gets old."

"Yeah, but you do." She stuck her tongue out at him.

"Very queenly."

"Whatever." She looked up at the castle again. "You sure Arthur wouldn't mind?"

"Not in the slightest."

"He's not haunting the place, is he?"

Merlin chuckled. "No."

"Phew. That's all I need. Uncle Arthur lurking in the hall-ways, judging me." Gwen snickered. "Or Lancelot. Or Percival. Or Galahad. Or... a lot of people." She frowned, her mirth instantly fading.

"You're quickly learning the cost of power."

She glanced down at her steel finger. It was beautiful, she had to admit. She loved it. She just wished she didn't have to have it. "Yeah. But hey. I come with a bonus letter-opener now."

Merlin laughed and patted her on the back. "I hope you never lose your sense of humor."

"Are you staying?"

"Me? Bah! No. This island is only big enough for *one* all-powerful magic-wielding lunatic." He waved his hand dismissively in the air. "You hardly need me now."

"But maybe I want the company."

"You will have no shortage of company. Every single one of the elementals and the villagers will be vying for your favor now. You'll have to fend friends off with a stick." Merlin shook his head. "No, I would just get in the way."

She tucked her hands into her coat. She couldn't really feel the steel finger—but she had an awareness of it. Like it was really shot up with Novocain. It still ached, underneath where it attached. She figured it was going to hurt for a while. "I guess. But I'm still going to miss you."

"I know. And I will miss you too." He put an arm around her shoulder and tugged her into his side in a hug. "You did phenomenally."

"Did I? I... I don't know, was I too harsh on Mordred?"

"No. You did exactly what you had to do to get the elementals to trust you. And you'll need to keep it that way if you want to keep the peace around here."

"I love him, though." Cringing, she sighed. She did really love Mordred. The thought of going forever without him hurt. But the idea of forgiving him and moving on like he hadn't done anything at all felt equally as wrong.

"Like I said. The cost of power." Merlin let her go and began to walk away. "That is what we wizards do! Figure things out. That is all we are, when you think about it—just a series of endless points in time where we *make shit up* and *get things done.*"

The old, dignified man that Doc had become sounded really hysterical when he swore. She chuckled. "I guess." More good-byes. "Bye, Doc."

"Goodbye. You will be brilliant. Not as brilliant as me, mind you. But brilliant." He grinned at her over his shoulder before disappearing into thin air.

She really hoped she didn't go as nuts as he did. Was. Is. Whatever. But she figured that amount of time would do that to anybody.

Looking back up at the ruins of Camelot, she took a breath, and let it out in a rush. "Let's get started then."

EPILOGUE

THREE HUNDRED YEARS LATER

Every now and then, Gwen would sit at her round table and look at the faces of her council and consider how much things had changed over the years. Bert was the only original member of her court who was still there. The others had either retired or died from old age.

Three of the governors of the major cities attended to represent their people. Three elementals. Herself as the seventh, and Bert as the eighth, and the ninth was a volunteer chosen at random from the population and cycled every few years or so.

The matters they discussed were generally pretty mundane.

So-and-so wants this dispute settled. The arrival of visitors from some other dimension has caused a stir. The gates to a thousand strange worlds had reopened as soon as Camelot had been completed, and now a regular flow of new folks had begun.

Some of them stayed.

They had flying fish on the island now—literally fish that just swam through the air instead of water, which was rather enjoyable to watch. Gwen's dogs loved to chase them around, barking and trying to catch them, like they were squirrels.

Eod had passed on, as was the way with pets, many years

ago now. But his lineage remained, and she had raised generations of his great-great-whatever-grand pups. She still missed them all, especially her best boy. But he had lived a long, healthy, happy life, and had chosen when it was his time to go. And that was the most anybody could ask for, she supposed.

Speaking of which, one of her dogs was asleep under the table on her feet, and she couldn't feel her toes.

"And now on to the final matter." One of the elementals, a creature of water named Iban, interrupted her thoughts. "One of the newest of our kind, an air elemental named Eulain, raided the supply depot of a merchant trader at the port. He refuses to give up what he stole. He is claiming that it is his by right."

Gwen sighed and shut her eyes, shaking her head. "And you've told him what'll happen now?"

"I have." Iban's lips thinned into a look of tired consternation. "Eulain's response was that he did 'not believe the myths and stories,' and that he would 'greet this so-called specter of death himself.'"

She shrugged. "Then it is what it is. We've warned him."

Iban pondered the statement for a moment. "Forgive me for asking, my queen. Perhaps it is because I am still new here, but... *is* the myth real?"

"That there is a deranged elemental who will murder anyone who dares breaks the peace of Avalon?" She smiled warmly, her tone not matching her words. It was on purpose. She'd had this conversation a *lot* over the past few centuries. "You could always find out for yourself if you wanted."

"I—no, I simply... I know those who transgress go missing, I simply did not know if it was *you* working to do such a thing, or..." Iban shifted in his seat nervously.

"I suppose I would be responsible for it, ultimately, if I let it continue." Gwen reached over for her goblet of wine, the light from the overhead chandelier of candles glinting off her steel finger. No one dared ask how she lost her finger anymore, and only Tim, Maewenn, and Bert knew. She suspected they enjoyed being on the "in" as much as anything else. Well, that and Tim couldn't talk.

It wasn't like she was trying to hide anything. Honestly, she'd had it for so long she honestly forgot it was there. It was just normal to her.

"But no," she finished. "I'm not responsible for the disappearances. It's just a myth."

"Then I suppose he shall find out for himself whether or not the myth of the impossible elemental is true." Iban reached for his own goblet of wine. "It will be no loss for our people."

"Do we have any other matters to discuss?" She was tired. Mostly of the conversation, but also in general. She was eager to go to bed. It was late. When no one spoke up, she got up from her chair. "I say we call it a night."

Her dog Milo snorted awake and climbed out from his spot under the table with a large yawn and a stretch. "*Sleepy.*"

"Me too, buddy." She scratched his head between his brown, floppy ears. They all knew she could talk to the animals, so nobody gave her an odd look.

"I should get back to the kids." Bert stretched before standing as well. "Or else Mae will have my head. Literally."

Gwen chuckled. "I'm glad she finally let you have your body back after the last time you screwed up. I'd rather not deal with carrying you around again." Bert had said something or done something—Gwen didn't even really remember the details —and Mae had shoved his body in a closet and forced him to be hauled around as only his pumpkin head for a week. The two of them made the oddest, but sweetest couple.

Their children were adopted orphans—children who came to Avalon without their parents. It was perfect for the cook, as she had more than just the denizens and visitors of Camelot to care for. Gwen had honestly never seen Maewenn happier.

The rest of the court all made their farewells and good-nights before filing out of the room. When they were finally gone, she headed out herself down the hallway with Milo walking at her side, tail idly wagging, eager to curl up in bed and sleep.

Now and then, she couldn't help but walk through Camelot and remember what it looked like so long ago. The broken ruins and the fallen beams, grown over with ivy and moss. They had tried to reuse what remained of the original building, using all the salvageable stones or timber they could find. She'd wanted the building to be as much of the original Camelot as possible, including one or two old tapestries that hadn't fully been claimed by time and weather. The tomb beneath the castle was still there, though, thankfully, no one had been added to its ranks in a very long time. The remains of Percival and Lancelot had been buried in the tomb, along with a golden sword for Galahad. Bors and Tristan she *believed* were now married and living happily off in the woods somewhere, though they wanted little to do with her, and she respected that.

Gawain had taken up teaching at a local college. It was adorable. Now and then, he'd send her a book or a letter, but they had never been close.

Gwen opened the door to her chambers and wanted nothing more than to crawl into a warm bed and sleep.

It seemed that wasn't on the cards just yet.

Milo's ears perked up and he growled low in his throat before running into the darkened room. Someone was there. Summoning Caliburn, Gwen grasped the hilt and readied herself for a fight.

Milo ran to the balcony, growling. The door was open. The sky was starry, and the moon was full, making it almost bright enough outside to see as though it were day.

An imposing figure stood there, cloaked in black, the hood pulled up over its head. The silhouette of a nightmare.

When Gwen drew close, she saw Milo sitting on the ground at the man's feet, staring up at him in curiosity. A clawed iron gauntlet reached out to pet the dog's head. Milo grinned, tongue hanging out, and he began to happily pant. "*Dad!*"

How they knew, she'd never understand. Something in the genetics.

She dismissed the sword back into the ether. "You need to learn to knock."

Mordred's quiet chuckle told her that no, he was never going to knock. "I have not met this one yet."

"His name's Milo." She walked out onto the balcony and went to stand beside him. The view from her room was beautiful, overlooking the forests. The sea was just barely visible, shining in the moonlight.

"The elemental named Eulain will die." Mordred turned to her, his face still obscured in darkness.

She placed her hand on his chest. He wasn't wearing his armor, and she wanted to feel the warmth of his skin. "Will he suffer?"

"No. His crimes do not warrant that." Mordred placed his hand over the back of hers, holding it there.

To say that their relationship was... strange, was to put it mildly. But it suited them. And it was comfortable, now, after so many centuries. But there was a pattern that she knew they would repeat every night he came to her.

"Have you forgiven me?" He stepped forward, wrapped his arm around her and pulled her closer to him.

Reaching up, she slid her arms around his neck and pressed herself close to him. "No. Does that change anything?"

"Never." He leaned down to kiss her, his embrace hungry and eager. Their passions had never dulled. When he parted, he stroked her cheek. "I love you, my firefly."

"And I love you, my dark lord." She rested her head against his chest.

"The darkness to your light."

Without which, neither of them could exist. He was the monster that haunted the dreams of children. The fear of a gruesome demise that kept all who would shatter the peace of Avalon in line. They could never be together in the light.

But here, in the shadows, she would always be his.

And he was hers.

And nothing would ever change that.

Fin.

A LETTER FROM KATHRYN

I want to say a huge thank you for choosing to reading *The Iron Crystal* series. It's hard to believe this is the last book in Mordred & Gwen's story! I hope you enjoy reading it as much as I enjoyed writing it.

If you'd like to stay in the loop for all my future series and releases, just sign up at the following link. Your email address will never be shared and you can unsubscribe at any time.

www.secondskybooks.com/kathryn-ann-kingsley

There are several kinds of writers out there in the world—those who are happy to tell their story to a blank page, and those who thrive on hearing about how their readers engage with their tales.

I am definitely the latter.

I love to hear from you and hear what you think of the Iron Crystal and Mordred & Gwen's adventures in Avalon. Please leave me a review or stop by one of my many social media spots!

I absolutely love hearing from my readers – you can get in touch via my social media or my website to interact with both me and other fans.

Stay Spooky,

Kathryn Ann Kingsley

KEEP IN TOUCH WITH KATHRYN

www.kathrynkingsley.com

facebook.com/kathrynannkingsley

x.com/vodriel

instagram.com/kathrynannkingsley

amazon.com/stores/Kathryn-Ann-Kingsley/author/B07NZ8JJRF

PUBLISHING TEAM

Turning a manuscript into a book requires the efforts of many people. The publishing team at Bookouture would like to acknowledge everyone who contributed to this publication.

Audio
Alba Proko
Sinead O'Connor
Melissa Tran

Commercial
Lauren Morrissette
Hannah Richmond
Imogen Allport

Cover design
Daria Klushina

Data and analysis
Mark Alder
Mohamed Bussuri

Editorial
Jack Renninson
Melissa Tran

Copyeditor
Rhian McKay

Proofreader
Catherine Lenderi

Marketing
Alex Crow
Melanie Price
Occy Carr
Cíara Rosney
Martyna Młynarska

Operations and distribution
Marina Valles
Stephanie Straub

Production
Hannah Snetsinger
Mandy Kullar
Jen Shannon

Publicity
Kim Nash
Noelle Holten
Jess Readett
Sarah Hardy

Rights and contracts
Peta Nightingale
Richard King
Saidah Graham